T0037318

CLAW
HEART
MOUNTAIN

CLAW HEART
MOUNTAIN

DAVID OPPEGAARD

CamCat
Books

CamCat Publishing, LLC
Fort Collins, Colorado 80524
camcatpublishing.com

This is a work of fiction. Names, characters, places, and incidents are either products of the author's imagination or are used fictitiously.

© 2023 by David Oppegaard

All rights reserved. Printed in the United States of America. No part of this book may be used or reproduced in any manner whatsoever without written permission except in the case of brief quotations embodied in critical articles and reviews. For information, address CamCat Publishing, 1281 East Magnolia Street, #D1032, Fort Collins, CO 80524.

Hardcover ISBN 9780744307504
Paperback ISBN 9780744307511
Large-Print Paperback ISBN 9780744307528
eBook ISBN 9780744307535
Audiobook ISBN 9780744307559

Library of Congress Control Number: 2022941978

Book and cover design by Maryann Appel

5   3   1   2   4

FOR JOYCE JORGENSON

I

WINDFALL

1

CLAW HEART MOUNTAIN SAT APART FROM EVERYTHING, LIKE A forgotten god hunkered in thought. It looked both eternal and lonely, without a friend in sight, surrounded by rolling hills dotted in sagebrush and cheatgrass, the summer sky a hazy blue above it. Nova watched the mountain through the SUV's windshield, hypnotized by its looming presence. She was driving, while Mackenna sat in the front passenger seat, playing a game on her phone. The three dudes—Landon, Isaac, and Wyatt—were sprawled in the SUV's two-tiered backseat. Landon and Wyatt were asleep, while Isaac listened to music on his earbuds.

The SUV was quiet except for the soft whir of the air-conditioning fans. Nova didn't like listening to music or talk radio when she drove; she preferred to focus on driving, which she took seriously. The SUV, some kind of luxury Mercedes and probably super expensive, belonged to Mackenna's wealthy family. At eighteen, Nova didn't have much driving experience. She was worried she'd wreck the vehicle in a random accident, get everybody mad at her, and ruin her driving record before it had really started.

A petite five-two, Nova felt slightly ridiculous piloting such a massive beast of a vehicle, like a toad telling a dragon what to do. Still, they'd made it this far. They'd left Greenwood Village, a suburb in south Denver, later than planned, because predictably, Mackenna had shown up late. Mackenna had driven for the first two hours, through the traffic of Denver and into the mountains, before asking Nova to take over. Nova protested, hoping Landon, Mackenna's boyfriend, or one of the other guys would take the wheel, but it turned out all three of the dudes had eaten marijuana gummies before they'd even left Greenwood Village. She should have known. This was their big end-of-summer road trip before returning to college, so naturally they'd be stoned from the get-go.

They'd all gone to the same prep academy in the Denver suburbs. Nova, a year younger than the others, had just enrolled as a freshman at Colorado College in Colorado Springs, where the others would be sophomores. Nova had told her parents she'd be spending the next three nights with Mackenna's entire family at a cabin in Vail. This was partially true—they were going to stay at *one* of the Wolcotts' cabins—but it was her family's cabin on Claw Heart Mountain, across the state border in Wyoming, and Mackenna's parents would not join them.

Nova didn't like lying to her sweet, trusting parents (and this trip was by far the largest lie Nova had ever told them) but she knew they would have said no. It was the end of a long summer for Nova—a summer that had started with getting dumped by her boyfriend—and she'd grown tired of hanging around her house and her lame suburban neighborhood, going for walks and eating her dad's overcooked barbecue. The memory of endless time on lockdown during the COVID-19 pandemic still fresh (sometimes it felt like being stuck at home, bored, had been her entire teenage life), by mid-August Nova had finally reached the point where she feared she'd wither away and die if she didn't go *somewhere*.

So, basically, Nova had lied to her parents to save her own life. Kind of.

Nova glanced at Mackenna, who was still absorbed in her phone. Mackenna was a tall, tan, volleyball-smashing Nordic beauty with a mane of curly blond hair that cascaded down her shoulders. Nova, with her pale skin, brown pixie-cut hair, dark eyebrows, hazel eyes, stubby nose, and short chin, thought she resembled a woodland elf more than anything an average person would consider "sexy."

Which was fine with her. The attention Mackenna attracted, both in high school and the real world, from all kinds of people, seemed like a huge pain in the ass. Nova would much rather float under the sexiness radar, free to live her life without everyone drooling over her all the time.

Mackenna looked up from her phone. "What?"

Nova looked away and focused on the road. "Nothing."

They weren't far across the border into Wyoming, maybe thirty miles, but Claw Heart Mountain already seemed different from the mountains in Colorado. Its outline appeared indefinite, its edges somehow blurry. Which didn't really make sense, because like the mountains in Colorado, Claw Heart must have been a part of the Rocky Mountains, which stretched all the way from New Mexico into Canada.

Mackenna leaned forward against her seat belt and peered through the windshield. She drummed her hands on the SUV's dashboard.

"Huh. Claw Heart looks even more badass than I remember."

"How long has it been since you've been here?"

Mackenna tilted her head, thinking. "Last summer, I guess."

"You haven't been to your own cabin for an entire year?"

"We used to come here more often, but that was before we got the second cabin in Vail. Now Dad mostly uses this one for hanging out with his business buddies and entertaining clients. Claw Heart Mountain's good for hunting. Dad pays a neighbor to look after it for most of the year."

"So why aren't we just going to Vail?"

Mackenna wrinkled her nose. "It's being fumigated. Mom saw a cockroach when she was there last weekend for her book-club retreat."

"Vail cabin problems, huh?"

Mackenna sat back and sighed. "I know, right?"

Nova glanced in the rearview mirror. The dudes were all oblivious—eyes closed, ears stuffed with earbuds, minds still buzzed. Nova felt like a mom driving her kids to summer camp. For the seventh or eighth time that day, she wondered why she was even friends with these people. Or friends with Mackenna, anyway, since Nova hardly knew the dudes at all. Landon, with his good looks and blond, fake bedhead hair, was hot but sort of dumb, the kind of guy she'd normally ignore and be ignored by, the average Great White Bro. Isaac was smart but mean, a handsome Jewish kid with piercing brown eyes. Wyatt was probably the nicest of them, a genuinely sweet Black guy with a big smile. He'd moved to Colorado from Minneapolis three years earlier and didn't seem worried about being popular, which, of course, made him super popular.

Nova swerved to avoid a dead critter in the road. It had exploded all over the place and was unrecognizable. Nova felt her heart go out to the creature, whatever it had been, and straightened in the driver's seat, determined to avoid any further roadkill. The highway sloped sharply upward as they reached the base of the mountain and climbed the first length of a switchback highway, which appeared to zigzag all the way up the mountain.

Isaac removed his earbuds and leaned forward from the backseat. Nova could smell his cologne, a subtle musk that made her think of a dim coatroom at a cocktail party.

Isaac pointed at the windshield. "What the hell is that?"

Nova frowned and examined the road. It took her a moment to see what Isaac was pointing at because it was light blue, almost the same color as the sky. It was a brick-shaped armored van, lying upside down on the road, wheels in the air. The van's small side windows had shattered, and its roof was crunched.

"Holy shit," Mackenna said, lowering her phone. "Looks like an accident."

Nova stopped twenty yards from the overturned van. She put the SUV in park, rolled down her window, and stuck her head out to look at the armored van and then up the mountain. A path of broken trees and torn earth went straight up, maybe a hundred yards, to the next switchback tract of highway. A haze of dirt hung in the air, still filtering down from above. Nova sat back and turned to Isaac and Mackenna. Landon and Wyatt were still sleeping in the backseat, oblivious.

"They fell," Nova said.

Mackenna blinked. "What?"

"They fell down the mountain."

"Whoa," Isaac said, sitting back and rolling down his window. The smell of gasoline drifted into the SUV and Nova pulled to the side of the road in front of the overturned vehicle. She thought back to her excruciatingly dull driver's ed classes and activated the SUV's flashers.

She wondered if they had a road kit. They could light some road flares and set up a warning lane. They needed to call 911. They had to check for survivors.

Nova put the SUV in park. She noticed her hands were trembling and rubbed them together, as if the conductive heat would offset the trembling. She unbuckled her seat belt and opened her door.

"What are you doing?" Mackenna asked.

"We have to help. We might need to give them first aid."

"But this is so . . . dangerous. This road is super narrow. What if a semitruck comes along and smashes us too?"

"We'll be fast."

"We will?"

Nova nodded, feeling a surge of adrenaline. This was finally it. A real-life important adult-type situation. An adventure. Nova got out of the SUV and slid around on the loose rock that had been sprayed across the highway. She peered up the mountainside, checking to see if anything else was poised to come crashing down to the highway. She noticed a disturbance among the trees. Something enormous was moving through the shadows—something almost as tall as the trees themselves—but it appeared to be headed farther up the mountain, not down, and within a few seconds its shape disappeared into the trees altogether, leaving Nova wondering if she'd really seen anything at all.

Shaking off the unsettling vision, Nova ran up to the front of the overturned van. The side of the van read STEEL CAGE AR-MORED SERVICES. Gasoline was pooling around the van, its surface a hypnotic sheen of purple and blues. The smell was so strong it made her dizzy.

Nova got down on her hands and knees and crawled closer, trying to get a better look inside the van. Both front seats were empty, as was the rest of the van's cab. A steel partition wall, still intact, blocked off the rear cargo area of the van.

Nova scrambled to her feet and brushed the road grit from her pants. Isaac and Mackenna had exited the SUV along with Landon and Wyatt, who both looked dazed and confused after their edible nap.

Nova went around to the back of the van. Its rear doors had buckled and one thick steel door was wedged open about two feet. Nova pulled on the door to increase the gap, but it wouldn't budge. She shouted hello into the opening. No response. She turned on her cell phone's LED flashlight and shined it into the darkness beyond.

2

NOVA HAD EXPECTED TO FIND THE ARMORED VAN'S DRIVER HURT, maybe even dead, but no one was in the back. Instead, she found the shattered fragments of a wooden pallet and a large green-and-white cube wrapped in clear, industrial-strength packaging film. Through the film, Nova could make out stacks of paper bound into packets.

It was a cube of money.

So.

Much.

Money.

"Nova? What is it?"

When Mackenna approached, Nova instinctively shielded the van's opening as best she could with her body, but Mackenna was taller and peered over the top of her head.

"Holy fuck." Mackenna gasped and gripped Nova's shoulders.

"It might be fake," Nova said, half hoping this was true.

This was too much. This was too much of a thing. She could already feel the energy caused by the sight of the money cube radiating from Mackenna's fingertips clawing into her shoulders. It was a wild, hungry energy. A crazy energy.

"It's not fake," Mackenna said, starting to bop up and down. "I know cash when I see it. That's real money, Nova. Fucking real money!"

Nova stepped through the two-foot gap between the van's jammed door and its frame, shining her phone's light in front of her. Jagged shards of wood, the smashed remains of the pallet, were covering the cargo hold like confetti. Nova leaned down and picked up a piece. It looked like a huge toothpick, or a knife. She looked at Mackenna.

"Where'd the driver go?"

Mackenna shrugged. "Maybe they walked away to get help."

"I doubt it. Would you leave all this money behind?"

"Hell no."

"I wouldn't either. I'd wait for help to come along."

Mackenna turned. The highway was still quiet behind them. "It seems so deserted out here," Mackenna said, putting her hair back in a ponytail. "I still don't see anybody coming in either direction. Maybe they didn't want to wait for somebody to come along. Maybe they couldn't wait."

Nova heard Isaac's voice coming from outside the van, asking what was going on. His head popped into the doorway a second later. He looked at Nova crouched with the wooden shard in her hand and the cube of money behind her.

"Is that . . .?"

Nova shrugged. She poked into the plastic with the shard, gouging a hole into its clear surface.

Maybe the money was fake. Maybe this was some kind of elaborate prank.

Once she'd made an opening in the packaging wrap, Nova pulled out a single bundle of cash, which was held together by a white paper band with yellow edging that had **$10,000** printed on it. She ran her thumb against the edge of the bundle, examining the bills.

"Are those all hundred-dollar bills?" Isaac asked.

"They feel real," Nova admitted, holding the bills up to her eye and focusing the light of her cell phone on them. "They look real."

Mackenna slipped her hand through the cargo-hold doorway. She moved fast, like a snake striking its prey. She had those athletic fast-twitch skills.

"Here. Let me see."

Nova looked at her friend, hesitating. Since Nova had first peeked into the back of the armored van, a cold, uneasy feeling had steadily been growing in her heart. Mackenna saw the hesitation in Nova's eyes and darted forward, snatching the packet of money from Nova's hand.

"Hey!"

Mackenna thumbed through the money, while Isaac stepped back from the doorway and shouted to the other dudes to come quick. Nova stood up and exited the upside-down cargo hold, returning to the world of wind and heat and fading sunlight. Even though they had barely started up the mountain, she could already see far across the plain below. Mackenna was right. No other vehicles were in sight for miles. Nova had never seen such a deserted stretch of highway. She peered up the mountainside and checked for traffic coming from higher up. Nothing moved. All she could hear was the wind rustling the trees.

Landon and Wyatt came around to the back of the van. They looked at Mackenna, who was grinning and slapping the bundle of cash against her palm, her eyes gleaming with manic joy.

"It's our lucky day, fuckers."

———————

The guys each grabbed a bundle of cash and thumbed through it themselves. It was surreal. Everyone except Nova was now holding ten thousand dollars in cash by the side of the road, in broad daylight. The van still smelled like gas, but at least it hadn't blown up. Yet. She wondered what it would be like to watch the cube burn. Millions of dollars igniting in a hot blaze.

You'd be able to see smoke rising from the valley below, maybe all the way to the last town they'd passed through twenty miles ago.

What was that town called again? Some kind of insect?

Oh yeah.

Scorpion. Scorpion Creek.

"This isn't our money," Nova said, patting the side of the armored van. "We can't just take it."

Mackenna snorted and looked around, shielding her eyes with the flat of her hand. "Well, I don't see anybody around, do you? Haven't you ever heard of finders keepers?"

"This is a lot of money," Landon said. "This is so much money."

Isaac smirked. "Thanks, Captain Obvious. Nobody else here noticed that."

"We'll never need to work again," Wyatt said, his eyes foggy at this idea. "Even after splitting it five ways. We could pay our student loans. We could all buy our own mansion with a swimming pool."

"Shit," Landon said, "my family already has a swimming pool. I'm going to buy my own private plane and travel around the world."

"You mean, *we'll* travel around the world," Mackenna said, putting her arms around Landon's neck and kissing him. "We'll be a millionaire power couple. How fun will that be?"

Isaac poked his head into the back of the van again. "Nova's right, though," he said, his voice muffled. "This isn't our money. If we take it, somebody will come looking for it, sooner or later. The armored-van company probably has its own detectives."

"How do you know that?" Mackenna said. "You don't know."

Isaac stared back at the group.

"Have you ever heard the expression 'Nothing in life is free'? This random van stuffed with cash is probably included in that."

"Shit, why are you fighting this, dude?" Landon asked, scratching the side of his head. "Is it because you're Jewish?"

Wyatt laughed. "Oh fuck. Landon's racist. I knew it."

"I just meant, are you worried about the stereotype," Landon said, looking sheepish. "About how Jews love money so much. Like, are you worried about reinforcing it?"

Wyatt laughed again and slapped Isaac on the back.

Isaac rolled his eyes. "No, dipshit. I'm not worried about reinforcing Jewish stereotypes. Also, fun fact: Everyone loves money. Our stereotype is more about how good we are at handling it, fuckface."

"Oh. Right."

Mackenna clapped her hands. "Hey, I know! How about we stand around with our thumbs up our butts until another car comes along and sees us? How about we do that, huh?"

They looked at each other. Wyatt cleared his throat and Nova knew what he was going to say before he said it. She'd known this suggestion would be inevitable since the moment she'd first argued the money wasn't theirs. It was how groups of people had been making huge mistakes since the beginning of time.

"Okay," Wyatt said, raising his arm in the air. "Let's take a vote."

3

BANNOCK ADDED MORE WOOD TO THE FIREPLACE IN HIS STUDY. Even though it was a warm summer afternoon in Utah, he liked the firelight and the company it provided as the wood was slowly consumed. He thought watching a fire burn was a good lesson on the impermanence of all things, how even the brightest flames went out, sooner or later. You didn't have to do anything. You just had to wait for time to do its work.

An electronic ringing came from the walnut desk in Bannock's study. He frowned, displeased with the interruption. He got up from his chair by the fire and walked over to his desk. He pulled out the center drawer and dug in a pile of prepaid cell phones until he located the one that was chirping at him. He answered the call, his gaze settling on the fire crackling across the room.

"Hello."

"We need your help. A delivery has been waylaid on its way back from the cleaners."

"By whom?"

"We don't know. The GPS beacon stopped moving in Wyoming thirty minutes ago, and we can't get the transport crew on the phone. They were going through Claw Heart Mountain, twenty miles west of a town called Scorpion Creek."

Bannock grunted. He'd heard of Claw Heart but had never been there. It was supposed to be good hunting. Full of a variety of game. Rich assholes went there to spend the day getting drunk and shooting guns. Occasionally they got drunk enough to shoot each other and you'd read about it in the news. Personally, Bannock loved fishing and hunting in the mountains. He loved being alone. He loved finding the tracks of some animal, big or small, and following them for as far as he could. He'd once followed bear tracks all the way up a mountain in northern Idaho for two days, until he came to the bear's den, where she was preparing to wait out the winter with her two cubs. He'd slaughtered them all with his rifle—the mamma black bear as she charged him and then the two cubs as they huddled together, bleating in their terror and confusion. He'd field dressed one of the cubs right outside the cave, and the skinned bear cub had born an uncanny resemblance to a small human being. Bannock had cooked the bear slowly beneath the stars, feeling like a god walking the earth.

A lot of people didn't like bear meat, but Bannock liked every kind of meat.

Especially if he killed it himself.

"We've already sent a driver. His name is Gideon. He'll arrive in twenty minutes. You should make it to Claw Heart in under five hours."

Bannock scratched his shoulder, still gazing into the fire across the room. He was a lean, weathered Caucasian man in his mid-fifties, but his skin was a burnt-ochre red from a lifetime of exposure to vast quantities of sunlight all over the world.

"I work alone. You know this." Not only did he work alone but he also lived alone, fifteen miles southeast of Salt Lake City.

"We understand. But this was a significant delivery. You will need assistance moving it, once you find it. And it is unclear who intercepted it. You might need the support."

Bannock considered refusing the job and returning to his crackling fire. He'd been planning on reading Hemingway's *For Whom the Bell Tolls*. This would be the sixth time he'd read it. He enjoyed how it captured the brutality of war and the necessity of dynamite.

"We'll pay you two million."

The firewood shifted in the fireplace, collapsing inward and sending a few harmless sparks sailing into the air. Bannock imagined the outline of Claw Heart Mountain. Well, it wouldn't hurt to take a look. Perhaps the mountain had more wilderness still bottled inside than he thought. Perhaps he would enjoy himself.

"Okay," Bannock said. He terminated the call and disassembled the burner phone, snapping it into pieces. He returned to the fireplace and tossed the phone fragments into the fire. The plastic burned with an unnatural blue light, and acrid black smoke rolled up from the fireplace and curled into the air.

Bannock didn't mind the smoke. He'd smelled a lot worse things burning in his life.

Switching into go-mode, Bannock doused the fire in his study with water and retrieved a black duffel bag from the wall safe in his bedroom. The contents of the bag were heavy and clanked against each other as Bannock set it down and unzipped it. The duffel contained a sheathed combat knife, a hatchet, a scalpel, nylon rope, duct tape, a handsaw, a flathead screwdriver, needle-nose pliers, a circular saw, two extension cords, a ball-peen hammer, a mini-flashlight, a box of disposable latex gloves, a box of disposable face masks, a six-pack of plastic face shields, a pack of hand towels, a medical kit, and a bag of plastic zip cuffs. Also included in the bag was Bannock's favorite weapon: a takedown recurve bow-and-arrow set in a canvas carrying case of its own, the bow currently disassembled.

Bannock returned to his wall safe and retrieved two handguns: an untraceable SIG Sauer P226 that had been in his private collection for decades and a reliable Berretta M9, also untraceable. Both guns were already loaded. Bannock added the weapons to his work bag, along with some extra boxes of ammunition and a small backpack containing three days' worth of clothes and toiletries. He didn't expect this assignment to take three days, but it didn't hurt to be prepared, especially if his clothing happened to get stained with blood.

Bannock zipped up the bag and carried it out to the front hall of his house. He peered through a window and scanned the street. It'd been six minutes since he'd ended the call with his employer and destroyed the burner phone. His ride was due in fourteen minutes. The street outside his small bungalow was quiet and saturated with sunlight. Bannock liked living in Utah. He liked the dry heat and the blowing wind—

Bannock went still. He'd seen a flash of unusual movement on the rooftop of the ranch-style house across the street. Something unusual popping up along the roofline and dropping out of sight almost as quickly.

It had almost been . . . tubular shaped. Black, yet glinting in the sunlight. Perhaps metal.

Bannock crouched so he was clear of the windows and unzipped his work bag. He pulled on a pair of disposable latex gloves. He ignored the two handguns and selected the combat knife—a twelve-inch fixed blade—and, still sheathed, stuck it into his waistband. He dropped to the floor, army crawling across his living room and down the main hallway of his bungalow. He stood as he entered his kitchen and went to the back door. He pressed his ear against the door and listened. When he didn't hear anything, he unlocked the door and flung it open, stepping back and withdrawing from the line of fire.

No gunshots. No assholes in commando gear burst through the doorway, spraying his kitchen with bullets or tossing flash grenades. Bannock waited thirty seconds before stepping into his backyard. The summer heat washed over him and the sunlight was near blinding.

Still no gunfire, though, which meant his visitor was likely working solo and hoping the element of surprise would be enough. He wouldn't be the first challenger to underestimate Bannock. They came to him every two or three years, popping up whenever somebody from his past chanced on a piece of lucky intel and sought revenge for some ancient grievance Bannock could barely recall. These would-be assassins were part of the tiresome cycle of Bannock's trade, freelancers hired to take out other freelancers. They were all pawns, like Bannock himself, sent forth into battle by the dirty money that ran the world.

Bannock crossed his backyard in a straight line, using his house to shield himself from the street. He unbolted the door in the rear fence, slipped into the alley, and closed the door behind him. He walked down the alley until he reached the end of his block and turned left. He tried to move naturally, like a standard civilian out for an afternoon stroll. He encountered no fellow pedestrians, though two vehicles did drive past. He crossed the street that ran along the front of his house without breaking stride. When he came to another alley, he turned left again. The ranch house was five houses down.

A dog barked at Bannock and he gritted his teeth, wishing he had time to properly deal with it. He didn't like dogs much. He'd seen what they could do to a human body, especially with starvation and beatings as encouragement. He reached the alley location behind the ranch house and peered through the iron bars of its backyard fence. The yard had two lemon trees and a set of wicker lawn furniture arranged on a concrete patio near the house. The neighboring yards appeared deserted. A man in gray clothing was draped across the gray slate roof. He was peering through the scope of a sniper rifle, his back turned to Bannock and the alleyway.

Bannock sighed and shook his head.

Would the idiocy never end?

The door to the backyard fence was slightly ajar. Its simple lock was covered in scratches, as if a frenzied gorilla had attacked it. Bannock pushed the door open farther and passed through the iron doorway. He crossed the backyard slowly, scanning the lawn for trip wire and avoiding sticks or anything else that might crunch underfoot. The sniper remained motionless on the roof. Good snipers could remain still for hours, governing their breath and waiting for the one critical second they needed. This immobility also made them vulnerable to rear assaults if they, like most assassins, worked alone.

Bannock noted a tactical assault ladder resting against the house. Slim, shiny, and black, it must have cost a thousand bucks. Light and strong, it would take his weight easily without making the kind of noise you encountered with an aluminum ladder. Bannock stepped up to the base of the ladder and examined it for clever little traps. He saw none. He took out the tactical knife, removed it from its sheath, and tossed the sheath into the grass. His breath did not change. His pulse did not rise. He noted a plane approaching, headed north by northwest for Salt Lake City International Airport.

Bannock grinned. He knew the bloodwinds were with him now. He waited for the plane to grow closer. He climbed the tactical ladder with the knife in his right hand, keeping his head up. He reached the top of the ladder and took a deep breath, feeling the familiar buzz of imminent violence pass through his body. The sniper still had not moved, though Bannock could discern his back rising and falling with measured breath.

The plane, now roaring like an enraged dragon, was nearly overhead. Bannock climbed onto the slate roof, which was searingly hot beneath the summer sun. He walked up the roof at a slant, angling his body like a veteran roofer while he grasped the knife loosely in his right hand. Luck had it that his shadow fell behind him, not before him, and so neither sight nor sound gave his presence away.

Bannock considered forcing the sniper to divulge who'd sent him, who it was this time, but such knowledge would only complicate Bannock's life, giving him a new set of chores to accomplish. And Bannock was sick of chores, especially the retribution-based kind that didn't pay well. Instead of pausing to interrogate his target, Bannock stepped on the sniper's lower back with one heavy boot and stabbed him in the right kidney. The sniper grunted and struggled to turn over. Bannock waggled the knife's hilt, digging around some more in the man's soft interior, before withdrawing the knife slowly. Bannock took a deep breath, his boot still pressed on his target, before stabbing the sniper a second time, this time plunging the knife through the sniper's spinal cord and sawing through its nervous tissue as if he were cutting a thick rope.

The sniper moaned and sailed away toward the dark shores of death, blood pooling on the gray slate beneath him. Satisfied with his work, Bannock wiped his knife clean on the dead man's shirt and tossed it onto the lawn. He picked up the sniper's rifle and examined it with professional interest. He noticed a car coming down the street and watched it approach through the rifle's scope. It was a silver Honda Accord. Recent model. Well maintained. The car's only apparent occupant was a white male, dressed in a shirt and tie, wearing sunglasses.

The Honda drove right up to the front of Bannock's house and parked. The driver remained in the car a moment, checking his phone, before stepping out and looking around. Bannock rested the sniper rifle's butt against his hip. He climbed to the apex of the roof and whistled down to the driver. The driver flinched and looked up from the street, shielding his eyes despite his sunglasses.

"You Gideon?"

"Yes, sir. You must be Bannock."

Bannock nodded. "Give me a minute. I had unexpected company."

4

THE VOTE ABOUT THE MONEY THEY'D FOUND WENT AS EXPECTED; greed won. Mackenna, Landon, and Wyatt voted to keep the cash while Nova and Isaac voted to leave it alone and call the cops instead. Nova suspected Isaac was putting on a show, supposedly doing the right thing while knowing all along they'd lose the vote. Once the vote was over, Isaac seemed as excited to be filthy rich as everyone else. It was like seeing and holding the money had cast a spell on everyone. A greed hex.

"Great, it's settled," Mackenna said. "We'll keep the cash."

"Unless we find the owner," Nova said, looking around at the group. "Right?"

"Sure," Mackenna said. "Whatever."

"How should we move it to the SUV?" Landon asked. "We can't carry that whole cube, right? And it won't fit through the doorway."

"We need bags," Wyatt said. "Lots of bags."

Everyone spent a few seconds thinking.

"We have our luggage," Isaac said.

Mackenna grinned. "I brought three bags and all you guys made fun of me for overpacking. Who overpacked now, fuckers?"

Everyone ran back to the SUV except Nova, who lagged behind in protest. Mackenna popped open the back of the SUV and started tossing out bags, working like an airline baggage handler buzzed on speed.

Landon grabbed his leather duffel bag, unzipped it, and immediately dumped it out right there on the highway. He had a wide, goofy smile on his face, like a kid who'd just opened the best present ever on Christmas morning.

"Jesus," Nova said to him. "Don't dump your shit on the highway, dummy."

"Why? You worried about littering too?"

"No," Nova said. "About leaving a trail."

Landon blinked, his blond windblown bangs curling into his eyes, giving him the look of a handsome surfer in a teen rom-com. "Oh yeah. Right."

Landon scooped up his shit—mostly clothes with some toiletries and an iPad—and carried it around to the side of their SUV, where he opened the passenger door and chucked it all inside. The others followed his example in a happy frenzy of chucking and emptying, eager to dump out all the stuff they'd packed for the weekend as if it was nothing but twigs and dead leaves.

When Nova hesitated to dump out her own luggage, a brown leather weekend bag, Mackenna grabbed it off the ground and dumped it for her. "We need to hurry," Mackenna said, shoving the empty piece of luggage into Nova's arms. "Somebody could drive by any minute."

They returned to the armored van and Landon went into the cargo hold this time. Wyatt and Isaac turned on their cell phone flashlights and set the phones inside the van so Landon could see better. Landon started yanking at the hole Nova had cut into the packaging film, cutting at the tough material with his keys, and gradually opened it far enough that he could grab entire handfuls of cash packets. He started filling the first empty bag with it, working with a frenzy and energy Nova had never really seen before—in anyone—and soon the first bag was stuffed with cash and zipped shut.

"Next!" Landon shouted. Wyatt tossed in a second bag and grabbed the first, grunting with the weight as he carried it back to the SUV.

"This is so hot," Mackenna said, watching Landon work. "I'm going to dump my cash on our bed as soon as we get to the cabin. I want to have sex on it like in the movies."

Nova's face scrunched up as she thought of all the germs that must be on that money. It'd be like touching all the people that had handled the cash before. As if they were touching your privates themselves.

"Here," Landon said, handing out the second filled bag. He was drenched in sweat now. Isaac grabbed it and carried it to the SUV, staggering slightly under its weight. Mackenna tossed in her biggest suitcase, a pink hard-shell, and it landed with a clatter. She had a matching set in three different sizes. They looked expensive all by themselves. "They'll hold a lot of money," she said, beaming at Nova. "Maybe an entire mansion's worth."

Nova looked at the ground. She'd packed light for the trip. Only one small canvas satchel (where she kept her wallet, cell phone, and other stuff) and the weekend bag.

"Don't worry," Mackenna said, grabbing her hand and giving it a painful squeeze, sharing an electric current of her manic energy with Nova. "We'll share the money five ways, like we said. We can buy all the luggage we want."

Their luck held and they filled every bag they had before another vehicle came along. The back of the SUV was stuffed with cash-filled luggage and the cube was only two-thirds depleted. Mackenna and Landon wanted to take it all, armload by armload, but for once common sense won out.

"We're pushing our luck, even for an empty highway," Isaac said. "Sooner or later, somebody is going to come along."

"Isaac's right," Wyatt said, bouncing on his feet. "We've got enough. Let's go."

Mackenna and Landon looked at each other with bright and shiny eyes, and Nova could see another stupid argument brewing. "Besides," Nova said, trying to derail the stupid. "If some of the money is still here, maybe they'll think the cube burst open on the mountainside and the rest of the money just blew away. They won't think anybody else came along and stole some. They won't even bother searching for us."

Mackenna frowned and kicked the road, glancing into the back of the armored van. Nova could sense Mackenna battling with her urge to buy one more mansion or summer house.

"Nova's right, babe," Landon said, putting his arm around his girlfriend's shoulder. "It'll be the perfect cover."

Nova nodded. Maybe Landon wasn't such a handsome dum-dum after all.

Mackenna sighed, ducked into the back of the van, and came out carrying one last stack of banded bills. "All right. Let's get out of here."

Mackenna threw out a half-full bag of gluten-free granola from the pocket in her driver's-side door and replaced it with two more packets of money. She put the SUV in drive and accelerated away from the crashed van. Her phone connecting to the SUV's audio system via Bluetooth, she started playing some annoying, upbeat pop music while drumming on the steering wheel and singing along, her voice surprisingly good.

Nova rolled down her window and stuck her head out, first peering up the mountainside and then down, looking for signs of the van's driver or any passengers. A broken body lying prone somewhere in the trees. A splash of color, indicating machine-made clothes, or a shining patch of hair blowing in the wind. The driver had to have gone somewhere. The armored van hadn't been driving itself.

They went around a turn and headed up another length of the switchback highway. The dudes were planning what to do with their new wealth. Wyatt was going to go to every World Cup for the rest of his life. Landon wanted to tour all the trance clubs in Europe and buy a luxury yacht. Isaac wanted to go into space on one of those private space missions. Nova wondered why they were all so excited, anyway, since they'd already been rich when they'd woken up that morning. Most students attending Colorado College, where the annual tuition was nearly sixty thousand dollars, were either upper middle class or plain filthy rich. Nova was the poorest member of their group and her father was a dentist, with his own busy practice, while her mother was one of the most successful divorce attorneys in Arapahoe County.

Well. Maybe it was freedom Mackenna and the dudes were after. Now, with this sudden windfall, they wouldn't have to ask their parents for money ever again.

But would that really be freedom? Or would all this money be like another kind of prison? One where you woke up with no real purpose every day, because you didn't really need to do anything when your existence was already paid for?

Mackenna turned down the music.

"Hey. Nova."

Mackenna reached over and squeezed Nova's knee and Nova pulled her head back into the SUV. She hadn't seen any bodies out her window, but that didn't mean they weren't there, lurking in the trees and bushes, waiting to be discovered. Perhaps in need of help.

"Hey, girl. Why aren't you happy?"

Nova closed her eyes. Her stomach was starting to feel queasy as they climbed higher up the mountain. It was a big mountain.

"I don't know."

"Don't you want to be stinking rich?"

"I guess. I don't know. There's probably a reason people call it 'stinking' rich, right? And why would you want to be stinking anything?"

Mackenna frowned and kept silent, probably trying to figure out a clever response. Even with her window open, Nova could smell the money in the back of the SUV. There was so much of it, each bill with its own history behind it. Nova had done a paper on US currency the year before for her Intro to Economics class. People always thought of US dollar bills as paper, but each bill was almost totally cloth. Cotton and linen, with synthetic red and blue fibers sprinkled into the mix.

They went around another stomach-lurching turn in the switchback highway. Nova noticed movement on the side of the road and put her hand on Mackenna's shoulder.

"Hey. Slow down. Look."

An enormous creature emerged from the trees. Mackenna gasped and slammed on the brakes, causing everyone to pitch forward against their seatbelts while all the money-stuffed bags shifted in the back. The SUV came to a halt and the creature moved toward them.

5

THE CREATURE'S APPEARANCE SEEMED DISTORTED, ALTERED IN
such a terrible way they could not tell what it was. It was an animal, that was certain. Huge, brown, and furry. It had antlers,
but they were all messed up, one side of the rack broken down to
antler nubs and the other side hanging at a ninety-degree angle,
barely still attached to the head. Nova thought it was either an elk
or a moose.

A long gash ran from its chest across the left side of its body,
as if its hide had been peeled back for dissection, and blood ran off
the animal's body in steady rivulets. You could see exposed pink
muscle tissue, white fatty tissue, and dark spots that could be its
organs.

"Oh my God," Mackenna said. "Oh my God."

"Yeah," Isaac said from the backseat. "Wow."

It was an elk, Nova decided. Something about how its antlers
seemed spiky and sleek, even the broken nubby ends.

The elk stumbled forward and stopped directly in front of their hood. It looked inside the SUV and stared at them with its dark, liquid eyes. It opened its mouth, shook out its fur-matted throat, and let out a high-pitch shriek. Nova clenched her seat's armrests in a death grip and jammed her feet into the floor. She wanted to scream back at the animal, but all the air had left her lungs.

The elk lowered its head and stared at them. Nova thought it was looking right at her. "Oh my God," Mackenna said, repeating herself.

"It's hurt," Landon said. "I bet it got hit by the money van."

Nova took a deep breath, trying to calm down. "We should help it," she said, her voice sounding far away, her ears still ringing from the elk's screech. "It needs medical attention."

Wyatt laughed, his laughter too loud and tight. "That's a wild animal out there. You know how dangerous it is right now? Wounded like that? It will fuck you up, dude."

Nobody responded. Nova rubbed her ears, trying to get the ringing to stop.

"It doesn't understand what happened to it," Nova said, hypnotized by the way the elk was still staring at them. "It's in shock."

"Maybe it thinks we hit it," Isaac said. "Maybe it thinks we're the money van."

Nova forced herself to break eye contact with the elk. She stuck her head out of her window and peered over the highway's shoulder. She could see where the van had rolled down the mountainside, leaving a path of torn-up ground and broken shrubs, but she still couldn't make out any human bodies, alive or dead. The driver had to be out there somewhere. Between here and the smashed cargo van.

Waiting to be found.

"Oh shit," Mackenna said, grabbing Nova's shoulder. "Look."

The elk circled around the SUV's hood and came up to Nova's side of the vehicle. Every step it took must have been agony. Mackenna squeezed Nova's shoulder.

"Roll up your window."

Nova touched the window switch but didn't press it. She watched the elk instead, hypnotized by its presence. It lowered its head to peer at her through the window, its broken antlers dangling to one side. She could smell its animal musk and the copper smell of blood. Flies were already buzzing around its open wound. A few buzzed in through her open window, exploring the SUV's interior. Nova stared into the elk's eyes. She'd stopped breathing. She could hear her heart thumping in her chest and—even though it was crazy—thought she could hear the elk's heart thumping too. The elk's heart thumped slower and louder than her own, so huge in its elk chest.

"We're sorry," Nova said, her throat tight. "We're sorry for what happened to you."

The elk kept staring at her. Through her and into her soul. It knew they were connected to the armored van somehow.

It could smell their human scent.

It could smell the money.

The elk drew its head back and let out a second, even louder shriek. It started walking again, slowly moving down the shoulder of the highway, but only made it a few steps before it collapsed to the ground and lay still. Nova exhaled, finally remembering to breathe again.

"Goddamn," Wyatt said. "I think it just died."

———

Everyone was subdued for the rest of the drive. They climbed up the mountain without additional trouble, passing the access road to the mountain's only ski resort, and came down the opposite side, entering a small town set in a wooded valley nestled against the peak of Claw Heart Mountain. Cloud Vista was a scenic little town, with log cabin-type buildings on Main Street and a public park filled with sculptures and picnic tables. The mountain peak looming above the town was grayish blue, devoid of trees, and shaped like a worn-down arrowhead. The town reminded Nova of pictures she'd seen of the Swiss Alps, and she felt herself growing calmer. Maybe they could still have a good weekend. Maybe finding the money wouldn't ruin everything.

They passed through Cloud Vista. About five minutes outside town, they turned onto Hollow Drive and started to wind their way around the mountain. Trees crowded the road, arcing over it and blotting out the sky. They passed the occasional driveway entrance, each with its own mailbox. Set back from the road, the houses at the end of each driveway were hard to see through the trees, though they all looked big and nice and relatively new. They'd seen some traffic in town, mostly old pickup trucks and rusted cars, but nobody passed them going the opposite way on Hollow Drive.

"Where is everyone?" Isaac asked.

Mackenna glanced at him in the rearview mirror. "This is sort of like the fall-and-winter-people part of the mountain. The hunters and the skiers. Almost nobody on Hollow Drive lives here year-round and they're usually elsewhere in the summer. The year-round people live back in town, where it's cheaper."

"So, this is like rich-people street?"

"Basically."

They drove past a gray Victorian-style house that was more visible than the others, closer to the road and with fewer trees hiding it. It looked ramshackle and old school. A mud-splattered pickup truck was parked in front and two people were playing catch in the front yard—a bearded middle-aged man and a big redheaded guy around Nova's age, maybe a little older—while a middle-aged woman lay in a hammock strung up between two trees, reading a book. Mackenna lowered her driver's-side window and waved at the family, a genuine smile on her face.

"Those are the Morgans. They're our neighbors. They take care of everybody's house on Hollow Drive when they're gone. They're, like, professional caretakers."

The Morgans all waved back. The young man had copper-red hair and copper-red freckles. Cute.

Mackenna grinned at Nova and winked.

"That's Colton. He's a sweetie."

"Ooh, Colton," Isaac said. "What a rugged mountain man."

"I bet he has a dirt bike," Landon said. "Maybe a couple dirt bikes."

"Probably some guns too," Wyatt chimed in. "Definitely a rifle with a scope."

"Maybe he'll let us borrow it," Landon said. "We could shoot some cans or something. That'd be fun."

"Oh shit," Isaac said, laughing. "Landon with a gun. No thanks."

They came to the next driveway on Hollow Drive. Mackenna rolled up to the mailbox and reached through her window to open it. She pulled out an armful of fliers and junk mail, which she dropped on the floor at Nova's feet.

"Boom. Kindling paper."

"Your family gets mail here?" Nova said.

"Not really. Just junk mail. I don't think my parents even give out this mailing address. Usually everything is addressed to Current Resident."

They continued down the driveway. Mackenna's "cabin" was as large and hidden from the road as the other homes on Hollow Drive, but it wasn't as obnoxiously rich as Nova had feared. The two-story structure was modern and sleek. Made primarily of limestone, dark brown wood, and glass, the rectangular building blended in among the pine trees encircling it. The section above the carport was all windows, like a party room, and a patio ran along outside it. The patio featured a green-tinted glass railing and housed an eight-person table with chairs. You could tell the house was designed for parties, like a time-share in Breckenridge or Vail. Nova bet it had a firepit around back, maybe even a hot tub and pool.

Mackenna drove up to the house and parked in the carport. "Well," she said as she shut off the SUV's engine and unbuckled her seat belt. "We're here."

6

DEPUTY SERRANO STOOD AT THE ACCIDENT SITE AND PEERED into the distance, searching the horizon for the county sheriff. You could see a long way from Claw Heart Mountain on a clear summer evening, even make out the smudge of Scorpion Creek twenty miles distant. The switchback highway was currently clear of traffic, but this only made the deputy uneasy, the strong, hot wind reminding her of how small and vulnerable she was in the grand scheme of things.

Serrano had been headed to Cloud Vista as part of her usual Friday-evening county patrol and discovered the overturned van herself. According to dispatch, nobody had called in the crash or dialed 911. It was a fresh accident and would, undoubtedly, keep Serrano busy with paperwork for the foreseeable future. She hadn't counted the money she'd found in the back of the armored van, but it was easily millions of dollars, enough cash that she'd immediately feared the sort of trouble such cargo could attract.

The deputy had already searched the surrounding area for injured parties and found only a pool of dried blood in the front cab. She'd turned on the flashing red and blue emergency lights of her county-issued Ford Interceptor SUV and cordoned off the crash site with a stack of traffic cones.

She scanned the mountainside with binoculars and noted the torn-up nature of the hillside vegetation. She figured the van had gone off the road further up the mountain and tumbled down to its current position.

Given the distance and probable speed involved, it was a miracle the armored van was as intact as it was, even if it was a structurally reinforced vehicle.

At last Deputy Serrano made out the flashing lights of the sheriff's truck in the distance, headed toward the mountain. She took out her camera and started taking pictures of the accident site, making sure to get plenty of shots of the dried blood and the money in back. She thought it was interesting that the cash was wrapped in thick plastic, which had been punctured in only one location while retaining its integrity everywhere else. Given the shape of the plastic cube and assuming it had been complete before the accident, she guessed maybe two-thirds of the cash was missing.

Serrano also took several pictures of the broken mountain terrain above the overturned van. She expected to see loose dollars scattered above among the flattened trees and shrubs, but the terrain appeared clean. Which meant either the van's occupant (or occupants) had taken off with as much of the cash as they could carry, or somebody else had come along after the accident and departed with as much as *they* could carry. Was this the work of drug dealers ripping off other drug dealers? If so, why hadn't they taken all the money? Was it some kind of oblique message intended for a specialized audience?

Sheriff Carson arrived at the accident site and pulled ahead of the armored van. Now they would have flashing lights on both ends of the accident site to warn passing motorists. It wasn't dark yet—they had another two hours of light—but the highway was already in the growing shadow of Claw Heart Mountain. Sometimes drivers would barrel down the mountain as if they were challenging death—the unemployed, the underemployed, the wealthy, the drunken, the meth cranked, the brokenhearted, the mentally unstable, the dishonorably discharged, the wild local teenagers mistaking high speeds for freedom. Deputy Serrano had seen every demographic smashed up on a Wyoming highway during her eight years as a sheriff's deputy, and they all tended to bleed the same red.

Sheriff Carson exited his vehicle and surveyed the overturned van. He crouched to peer into the cab and clucked his tongue.

"They made their way out somehow, huh?"

Deputy Serrano didn't say anything. She liked to keep quiet and let the sheriff think for himself and see if they came up with the same ideas. It was a game she played to keep life interesting. Marty was Deputy Serrano's boss with twelve other Scorpion County deputies under him, but he didn't rub your face in his power or shout to hear himself make noise. Which was nice. Serrano had worked in a grocery store in high school and her boss had been a real *puta* about everything, even if you did a good job. It seemed like power, no matter how miniscule, often turned people into total assholes.

Sheriff Carson walked around to the back of the van and peered inside. He let out a low whistle that carried on the wind.

"Son of a bitch. Would you look at that."

Serrano nodded. She had looked at that. Sheriff Carson turned his broad shoulders sideways, sucked in his gut, and slipped into the back of the van. Serrano remained outside and listened to the click of his flashlight and his footsteps crunching on the van's metal roof. She'd already been inside, alone with all that money, and knew what a crazy feeling it gave you. It was enough money that you could scoop it up in your arms and never work again. Never worry about anything, except going to jail or worse, being tracked down by whatever ultra-dangerous organization you'd stolen it from.

Rustling sounds came from inside the van, followed by more crunching footsteps. Sheriff Carson appeared in the cargo hold doorway. He was bent over, dragging something heavy. He lunged backward and extracted the entire plastic sack of cash.

"Look at me. I'm Santa Claus."

Serrano grinned.

"You're stronger than I thought, Sheriff."

Sheriff Carson snorted and dropped the cash between them on the highway. It looked even more unreal in the light of day. Like fake movie money.

But there it was. Pulling at you and giving you dangerous ideas. Serrano locked eyes with Sheriff Carson, wondering what he was going to say next. This could go several different ways, Serrano realized. This could be one of those moments that changed your life forever. What would the sheriff say, and how would she respond?

"We need to get this back to the station ASAP," Sheriff Carson said. "Let's put this in your trunk before we call the tow truck. So far only you and I know about it and I aim to keep it that way. I'll call the DEA to come pick it up, but it's late on a Friday and I doubt they'll send anyone until tomorrow morning. You took pictures?"

Serrano nodded, relieved she wouldn't have to consider blowing the whistle on a dishonest superior. She believed in the rule of law, in good and evil, but she didn't like tattletales much.

"Yes, sir."

"Good. Help me carry this monster, would you?"

Sheriff Carson grabbed one end of the plastic money sack and Deputy Serrano grabbed the other. It was heavier than Serrano expected, probably over a hundred pounds, and she had to work to keep up her end. They dropped the cash in the trunk of the deputy's cruiser, which immediately sank closer to the ground beneath its weight. Serrano closed the trunk, and they returned to the van and examined its exterior from all angles.

"Steel Cage Armored Services. You ever hear of them?"

"No," Deputy Serrano said. "Probably a dummy company. I ran the plates and got nothing. They look like California plates, but the vehicle might not even be from California. The VIN number has been removed too. It might as well have come from outer space."

Serrano noticed a small black sphere protruding above the van's rear doors. It was a fisheye security camera, intended to monitor everything happening behind the van. It would be connected to a recording device, likely wired into the driver's console. Armored transports of all kinds loved their cameras, even illegal armored transports. Everybody wanted to keep a close eye on transport crews in case they got sticky fingers.

Serrano pointed out the camera to Sheriff Carson, who smiled and stretched his elbows behind his torso, causing his back to crack.

"Nice work, Deputy. Let's see what we can pull off that."

THEY BROUGHT THE LUGGAGE FROM THE SUV INTO MACKENNA'S two-story "cabin" and dumped out all the cash in the living room, creating an improbable green mountain in the center of the room. The cash seemed to be all hundred-dollar bills, banded into ten-thousand-dollar bundles. Nothing smaller. Nothing larger. Some of the bills were crisp, almost brand new, while others were greasy and creased with age.

Mackenna turned on the lights and closed the blinds, though it wasn't fully dark yet. The living room, which was set apart from the entrance hall by a short hallway, was decorated with antique muskets, rifles, swords, and one enormous buffalo head, all mounted on the walls and illuminated by mellow display lights. The room's leather couch and matching armchairs were big and sturdy, with deep, overstuffed cushions. A stone fireplace served as the focal point and the floor was covered in thick cream-colored carpeting that reminded Nova of polar-bear fur. The chalet décor must have felt cozy in the winter, but it seemed stifling and unnatural on a hot summer evening.

"How should we divide it?" Landor asked, grinning as he thumbed the edge of a cash bundle and made it purr.

"Easy," Mackenna said, cracking her knuckles. "Everybody stack your own minicube. We'll keep stacking until the main pile is running low and then we'll make sure all the cubes are the same size. Everybody stack four rows of six packets each. Then stack a second level with the same amount of bundles, just facing a different way. For stability."

"Like Jenga," Wyatt said, smiling wide and scooping up an armful of bundled cash. "I always liked Jenga."

"Fuck," Isaac said, running his hands through his dark hair. "This is so crazy. We're going to play million-dollar Jenga."

"I told you guys we'd have a fun weekend," Mackenna said, twirling on the white carpet and glowing with happiness. "Hey, who wants a beer?"

Everyone raised their hand, including Nova, who didn't like beer much but didn't want to seem any lamer than she already did for voting no to the money. She was keenly aware that she hadn't been Mackenna's first, or even fifth choice of girlfriends to come along on the trip. All Mackenna's true besties were still abroad for the summer, touring exotic places like Italy or Japan with their families.

The only reason Mackenna was in Colorado in August at all was because Mackenna's mom had forgotten to send Mackenna's application to the fancy California volleyball camp she usually attended. Nova, who'd been doing nothing all summer, had simply been available and female. Nova and Mackenna were no more than casual, hello-in-the-cafeteria friends.

Mackenna left the room while everyone else began their own personal cube. When Mackenna returned, she ordered the house's

AI to play music while she passed out the cans of beer. Grinning, everyone cracked open their beer.

Wyatt stood up. "All right, everybody. I want to say thanks to Mackenna for hosting us."

Everybody cheered and raised their beer.

"And, shit," Wyatt said, breaking into a cheesy grin. "Here's to the best day of our entire goddamn lives!"

Everyone cheered again, louder, and drank their beer. Even if she didn't care for the taste much, Nova had to admit it felt good to drink beer with a mountain of cash sitting in front of you. It made you optimistic.

"Dad likes to keep the fridge stocked with booze," Mackenna said, sitting cross-legged on the floor beside Nova's chair. "In case he stops by with clients."

"That's cool," Nova said, setting her beer on a side table. She continued to build her cash cube, trying not to think much at all. Maybe this was one of those times when you didn't worry and just tried to enjoy your good luck. Really, what kind of person didn't like becoming an instant millionaire?

"We barely see my dad anymore," Mackenna said, drinking her beer. "He's working, like, all the time."

"Huh," Nova said. "That sucks."

"Yeah, I guess so. But I'm used to it, right? Even back at Pioneer Prep, I felt like I lived on my own, my parents both worked so much. They're always going to concerts and parties and fundraisers and stuff like that. They say it's business. Networking."

Nova looked at Mackenna, who was staring into the distance with a glazed look in her eyes, clutching her beer and dangling it between her knees. Her happy glow had faded and Nova noticed crinkles around her eyes. Nova could see an image of Mackenna at forty years old, or maybe a little older, all dressed up in a fancy formal evening gown, staring into a mirror with sad, empty eyes.

"But you have Landon, right?" Nova said, adding another level to her cash cube, making sure the stacks were flush and stable. "You guys are in love."

Mackenna laughed. "Love. Right. As long as I suck his dick, Landon totally loves me."

Nova blushed and looked across the room. Landon showed no sign of listening to what his girlfriend had said. The background music was loud, and he was busy building his own cube.

"Landon is a hot rich guy," Mackenna said, drinking more beer. "Hot rich guys in college are like dogs when you take them to the dog park. They love to run around and sniff as many other dog butts as they can. When he finds a new dog butt he likes, he'll dump me and move on."

"That can't be true," Nova said, though she thought it probably was. "You guys have been dating for over a year, right?"

Mackenna shrugged. "Yeah."

"You must have a strong connection, then. College relationships usually last, what, three months?"

Mackenna looked across the room at Landon. He must have felt her staring, because he looked up and grinned back, holding ten grand in each hand.

He really was cute, Nova had to admit. His blond hair was somehow messy and controlled at the same time, as if by some kind of magic trick. If Mackenna and Landon ever had kids, they would be *Children of the Corn* blond and probably the cutest American-Scandinavian kids who ever lived.

"We get along," Mackenna said, finishing her beer in one long gulp. "And who cares, you know? We're all rich now. We can screw anybody we want."

Mackenna set her empty can aside and stretched toward the main pile of money, showing off her flexible yoga form. She scooped a stack of packets into her arms and dragged the money back to where she was sitting on the floor. She hunched over, nestled her face into the money, and took a deep breath.

It took twenty minutes to finish dividing up the cash. When the main pile was gone, Mackenna measured the dimension of each cube with a tape measure and adjusted each accordingly, adding or subtracting ten-thousand-dollar packets, until everyone had the same amount: 2.12 million dollars each. Satisfied, everyone grabbed their luggage and started stuffing it with their divvied cash. Two million one hundred and twenty thousand dollars took up a lot of space. Nova had to get a plastic bag from the kitchen to handle the extra cash bundles. She also got a second plastic bag for her stuff, still dumped out on the floor of Mackenna's SUV.

Nova took her bags, both plastic and leather, and went upstairs to the second floor, where she picked a smaller bedroom with a view of the front yard and the woods beyond it. She dumped her bags on the room's queen-size bed. She stared at the bags for a second and decided they looked too exposed and vulnerable just sitting there. She pulled back the bed's comforter and tucked both bags under the blanket, creating a child-sized lump. "Sleep tight," Nova whispered to the lump. "Don't let the bedbugs bite."

When Nova went back downstairs, she noticed Mackenna outside on the front steps, chatting with the redheaded neighbor. Intrigued, Nova stuffed her extra plastic bag into her back pocket and went outside to join them. The sun had gone down and it was getting cooler. They were definitely in the mountains. Soon it would be chilly enough for a jacket.

"Hey, it's Nova!" Mackenna said, her face lighting up like she'd spotted her favorite celebrity. "Nova, this is Colton Morgan."

"Hey," Colton said, nodding.

"Hey," Nova said.

Up close, Colton was bigger and his copper-red hair and freckles stood out more, even in the fading light. His nose was slightly crooked, like he'd once broken it, and he had broad shoulders and thick arms. He was taller than Mackenna, probably six-two, and he was big enough to make Nova feel even shrimpier than she did around most people. He also looked older, like twenty or twenty-one.

"Nova's a poet," Mackenna announced, putting her arm around Nova's shoulders and giving her a squeeze. "She won a writing contest at school last year."

"That's tight," Colton said, nodding. "I play guitar and I've been trying to write some songs. It's harder than I thought it would be."

"Have you tried using a rhyming dictionary?" Nova said, slipping out from under Mackenna's heavy arm. "They can help when you're stuck."

"Whatever," Mackenna said, adjusting her ponytail. "Have you seen some of the idiots who write songs and make millions off them? It can't be that hard."

"A lot of pop stars have songwriters who work for them," Nova said. "The famous ones sometimes have entire teams of writers."

Colton nodded and shifted his weight from one foot to another. "Yeah, but I could never do that. A good song has to come from the heart. From your heart to your head to your guitar."

Nova rubbed the back of her scalp, where her pixie was cropped shortest. "I like that," she said. "Heart to head to guitar. Like a good-song flowchart."

Colton kicked an invisible rock. Mackenna made googly eyes at Nova, her carefully teased eyebrows jumping up and down.

"Nova's single, Colton. FYI."

"Jesus, Mackenna!"

"What? I'm just putting it out there. You know, into the universe."

Colton grinned, his freckled face going red. Nova felt a strong urge to push Mackenna into a lake.

"And Colton, you're also single right now, aren't you?"

"Mackenna, please," Nova said. "Knock it off."

Even in the dying light, Colton had gone full tomato red. "Yeah, I'm single," he admitted, sounding like he was confessing to a crime. Yes, Nova, admitted to herself, Colton definitely was cute. Maybe even more than cute.

"Excellent," Mackenna said, really enjoying herself. "Now we're all caught up on everybody's dating status."

Colton kicked another invisible stone and glanced up. "Not quite. What about you, Mackenna? You never mentioned yours."

Nova rolled her eyes. Of course. Of course he was into Mackenna. Every boy in the universe was thirsty for Mackenna. It was inevitable, like the pull of gravity.

"My boyfriend is inside the cabin, unpacking," Mackenna said, studying her nails. "His name's Landon. I think you'd get along."

"Sweet," Colton said, seeming both unfazed and unsurprised by this news. "Anyway, I came over to tell you guys there's a party tonight at the Overlook. You should all join us."

"Awesome," Mackenna said, smiling. "We're definitely in the mood to party."

"Nice," Colton said. "It starts around eleven. See ya."

"Bye-eeee," Mackenna said, flapping her hand at Colton as he turned and headed across the front lawn. Instead of going down Mackenna's driveway and returning to his house via the highway, he entered the woods, heading down a narrow trail Nova hadn't noticed before.

"All the houses on Hollow Drive are connected by trails through the woods," Mackenna explained, noticing the puzzled expression on Nova's face. "They're like our personal pathways so we don't have to walk on the highway when we want to visit each other."

"What's the Overlook?"

"A local party spot. Everybody knows about it, but the cops leave it alone because you have to hike to get to it, which cuts down on drunk driving. We'll just hike from here. There's all kinds of paths on this mountain."

The plastic bag crinkled in Nova's back pocket. She took the bag out and smoothed it back into bag shape.

"I was going to get my stuff from the SUV."

"Good call," Mackenna said, looking at the Mercedes. "I forgot about our regular crap. I'll get some more bags."

Nova headed toward the Mercedes while Mackenna went back into the cabin. The SUV was unlocked and a total mess of clothes and toiletries. Nova picked through the chaos in the backseat, grateful their trip had just begun and all the underwear was still clean. She found her clothes and toiletries at the bottom of a pile and dug them out, trying to remember exactly what she'd packed so she didn't miss anything.

Not that it really mattered now. She was a millionaire. She could buy all the clothes she wanted.

Which wasn't insane at all.

Nova kept digging until she found her olive-green canvas satchel, which she liked to wear strapped across her chest. She gathered everything in her arms, backed out of the van, closed the sliding side door, and headed back into the cabin. She went upstairs to her bedroom and dumped her stuff on the bed beside the cash lump.

"You sleeping well, Lumpy?"

Nova pulled back the comforter, half-expecting the lump to be nothing but a couple of pillows now, magically re-transformed, like Cinderella's coach turning back into a pumpkin at midnight. But her bag and the extra plastic bag were still there, stuffed with cash. Nova stared at the money for a minute, transfixed, until she noticed motion in the corner of her eye. She went to the bedroom windows and peered across the front lawn.

It was deep into mountain twilight now, but the pine trees on the edge of the lawn still glowed bluish green, holding on to the last bit of summer light. Among the dense trees, Nova thought she could make out the contour of something unusual in the shadows. The shape was undefined, a patch of vague, deeper darkness among the trees, too big to be a person.

A trick of the light.

Probably.

Wyatt shouted Nova's name from downstairs, calling her to dinner. Nova continued to stare at the shape, willing it to move, to reveal its true identity, but it remained absolutely still, though she couldn't shake the feeling that it was watching her with an alert, human-like consciousness.

Wyatt hollered for her again. Nova looked away from the window and shouted she'd be right down. When she turned back to the window, the shape had been reabsorbed into the darkness among the trees.

Nova exhaled.

A trick of the light. That was all.

8

CLAW HEART MOUNTAIN WAS MORE FORMIDABLE THAN BANNOCK expected. From what little he'd heard about it, Bannock had anticipated a dumpy little plains mountain, nothing remarkable, but Claw Heart had a decent size to it—its summit elevation must have been somewhere above nine thousand feet. The descending sun cast a rosy light on the mountain's bluish-green mass as they approached it from the west, lending it a hazy watercolor aura, like a mountain in a Turner painting.

As they reached the base of the mountain, Bannock felt his spirits begin to rise. His driver, Gideon, had not spoken since they'd left the suburbs of Salt Lake City, even when they'd stopped for gas an hour earlier.

"The GPS signal went dark on the other side of the mountain," Gideon said, breaking their shared silence. His voice was flat, devoid of any discernible accent or emotion. A thin, pale young man dressed in a cheap gray suit and black wing tips, Gideon reminded Bannock of an old-fashioned Bible salesman. The strange, unblinking kind that made you wince when you saw them standing on your doorstep.

"The drivers?"

"Two Russians. Clean records. Loyal. Been with the Organization for fifteen years."

"What were they driving? Box truck?"

Gideon shook his head. "Armored van."

Bannock nodded, picturing an armored van chugging up the same mountain road they were currently climbing. It would be a hell of a struggle for such a heavy vehicle.

"It must have been hauling a significant amount."

"Fifteen million."

"Yes. I'd call that significant."

They kept climbing. They passed a paved road labeled Hollow Drive. Five minutes later, they passed through a town named Cloud Vista that was trying too hard to look picturesque and play mountain cowboy, though the bare, arrowhead-shaped peak rising above it was impressive in a timeworn way even the encroachment of humans couldn't lessen. Gideon drove through town slowly. Bannock noted a diner directly off the highway and filed this information away for later, in case they passed through town again.

As he scanned the passing buildings, an image of the rooftop sniper slipped into Bannock's thoughts. He'd left his carved-up body on the roof along with the sniper rifle for the locals to sort out. Bannock wouldn't be returning to Utah anytime soon and was untraceable through his Cottonwood Heights residence. It would be time to find a new residence when this current job was over. Somewhere more easily defended and harder to find. Maybe abroad, somewhere warm, where the American dollar still went a long way.

They put the town behind them, heading down the eastern side of the mountain, passing a sign for a ski resort called the Sunshine Lodge as the road transformed into a narrow switchback. Gideon drove smoothly but Bannock's stomach, which had gotten more sensitive as he aged, still lurched with every curve. Bannock kept his eyes straight ahead, resisting the urge to look past Gideon at the expansive vista that had opened before them. He noticed a large carcass on the side of the road and felt a sense of relief—it would give him a reason to stretch his legs and calm his churning stomach.

"Stop the car."

Gideon slowed the car and pulled over. The mountain highway had a thin gravel shoulder cut into the right edge of the switchback. When Bannock opened his door, it brushed against the mountain itself. He got out of the car and shut the door behind him. He crossed the highway, which appeared deserted in both directions and felt as lonely as any road in the world. He stood over the carcass and considered its broken body.

It was a bull elk. A lovely beast. Magnificent, really. Its antlers fully grown at the end of the summer, nearly four feet each, their velvet growth coat shed. Why was it up here on Claw Heart Mountain? Had it been coming down the mountain, or going up? It was mid-August. Mating season for elk. It should have been searching for herds of cow elk to rut with, not wandering around lost on a mountain highway, waiting to get hit.

The elk had obviously been struck by a vehicle going fast. Something big, like their missing armored van. But it hadn't been struck in this spot. A trail of blood ran thirty feet farther up the road. A tough beast, indeed, to rise again with such wounds, even for a short time. Bannock couldn't help admiring it. He reached down, grabbed one of the tines dangling from the elk's broken antlers, and snapped it off. Bannock sniffed the tine and put it in his mouth, biting down. He could taste the elk's fear, pain, and confusion. He could taste the final moments of its life.

Bannock put the tine in his jacket pocket and followed the elk's blood trail up the highway to its termination point. He squatted and examined the ground. Broken glass, fragments of metal, some additional blood and fluids. Judging from the trampled vegetation, the elk must have been thrown one direction, into the switchback wall, while the vehicle that had struck it had clearly gone the other way, rolling down the mountainside. Even in the fading light—it was past nine now—Bannock could make out the path of broken vegetation leading down to a lower section of the switchback highway.

However, no demolished vehicle was resting on the highway below, armored van or otherwise, though a county sheriff's SUV was parked in the general area. The cruiser's blue and red lights flashed silently, without additional signs of activity. The damaged van had already been towed. The officer or officers in the parked SUV were likely finishing up their paperwork and getting ready to leave as well.

Even two dead men—if the drivers *were* dead—and fifteen million dollars couldn't be granted infinite police time and resources. Everything had undoubtedly been hauled back to the nearest police department for the night.

Bannock walked back to the car and slid into the passenger seat. "They hit an elk," Bannock said, buckling his seat belt. "Their van rolled down the mountain and crashed on the stretch of highway below us. That's when the signal was lost."

Gideon looked through his side window, imagining the scene. "Bad luck, then. No disloyalty. No enemy ambush."

Bannock shrugged. "Maybe. Maybe not."

Gideon rubbed the side of his smooth face. "What should we do now?"

"There's a police cruiser down there right now, finishing up with the scene. The van's already been towed. I assume the Russians have been taken either to the local jail or morgue. Likely the morgue, considering how far they fell."

Gideon thought a moment. "Not Cloud Vista. Too small for a morgue. Scorpion Creek, maybe. Twenty miles east."

Bannock nodded, thinking about how this development would complicate extracting the money. Gideon put the car in drive and they continued down the mountain. Bannock pictured the accident site in his mind and saw the elk suddenly bursting onto the highway, giving the armored van's driver little time to react. Maybe the elk hadn't been wandering aimlessly down the road, but instead had been flushed out, pursued by a predator looking for lunch. The elk had been good-sized and filled with fighting spirit. Whatever had chased it into traffic would have been big and nasty.

They passed the sheriff county's cruiser, continuing down the mountain and onto the plains. Gideon took his cell phone out of his suit pocket. He hadn't been able to get cell service on the mountain and Bannock could tell it had been making him uneasy. The men Gideon worked for didn't like it when their underlings didn't answer their phones. They kept their dogs on a tight leash.

"So, the local cops have the money now," Gideon said, dropping his phone into his pocket and returning his full attention to driving.

Bannock crossed his arms, picturing the array of weapons in the Honda's trunk rattling around in his work bag. He thought of himself as an artist who painted with a broad palette.

"Don't worry," Bannock said. "They won't have it for long."

9

ISAAC AND LANDON HAD COOKED A MOUNTAIN OF SPAGHETTI marinara for dinner. The group sat at the diningroom table and dug into their food with gusto. Nova noticed everyone ate their pasta elegantly, twirling it carefully around their forks, with a limited amount of slurping and marinara splatter. Say what you wanted about rich kids, but they usually had decent table manners. Mackenna had even opened a bottle of red wine she'd brought up from the cabin's cellar (because naturally every rugged mountain cabin had a wine cellar). She'd set a wineglass in front of every plate, but Wyatt and Landon had declined the wine, preferring to pour beer into their wineglasses like true fancy gentlemen.

Mackenna had dimmed the overhead diningroom lights for "mood lighting" and switched the background music from pop to classical. Light and airy classical music, like Mozart and Chopin.

"This is kind of weird," Isaac admitted, setting his fork and spoon on his plate.

"Yeah," Wyatt said. "I feel like I'm having dinner with my parents."

Nova snorted. "Yeah. Mackenna's giving off some serious mom vibes."

"Hey. Somebody has to take charge around here."

"I like classical music," Landon said, twirling spaghetti onto his fork. "It makes me feel smart and sophisticated."

"It makes me feel like falling asleep," Isaac said, yawning. "This is the kind of music they play in clinic waiting rooms."

Wyatt swirled the beer in his wineglass and held it up for inspection. He took a sip and smacked his lips, making little popping bubble noises.

"A fine vintage. Pale ale, I believe."

Landon grabbed his own beer-filled wineglass and sipped from it, extending his pinkie as if he were drinking tea at an English garden party.

"Yes, sir. I do believe it is a fine vintage indeed."

Mackenna slapped Landon's shoulder and he spilled some beer on the white tablecloth. Landon's eyes widened in mock outrage and everyone laughed. Mackenna sat back in her chair and crossed her legs beneath her. "You guys laugh, but everyone at this table is a multimillionaire now. You'll need to know your wines and champagnes."

Nova rolled her eyes and rolled more pasta onto her fork. "You think they'll have a lot of champagne at the bonfire tonight?"

"Oh yeah," Isaac said. "I'm sure the mountain folk will have all kinds of reds and whites. Maybe even a rosé."

"Are we really going to this hillbilly party?" Wyatt asked, burping and pounding his chest. "I mean, have they ever met a Black person before? I don't want some mountain blowout turning into a drunken lynching."

"Jesus, dude," Landon said, tossing back the rest of his beer.

"What? It's an honest question."

"You'll be fine, Wyatt," Mackenna said, reaching across the table and squeezing his hand. "Everyone is totally cool around here. Cloud Vista is a tourist town. They're used to visitors from all over the world."

"Yeah, to go skiing. That's a white-people sport."

Nova grinned. She loved it when people messed with Mackenna. She was always so worried about being an "ally" to everybody and "overcoming her white privilege" that she was the world's easiest guilt target.

"Don't be ridiculous, Wyatt—"

The cabin's doorbell chimed, cutting Mackenna off. Everyone looked at the diningroom doorway, which led to the living room, which led to the front hall. The mood in the room immediately grew tight. Mackenna shook her head, as if rebooting her thoughts, and slowly stood up, pushing her chair back from the table. "It's probably Colton again," Mackenna said, sounding uncertain. "Maybe he's double-checking to make sure we come to the party."

Nobody said anything. When Mackenna went to answer the door, Nova stood up and followed her into the living room. Nova knelt on a couch and peeked through the blinds. An SUV was parked outside, its headlights bright and focused on the cabin.

Cops.

Nova dropped the blinds back into place, worried that she'd been seen peeking. The three dudes entered the living room behind her. Nova waved them back toward the kitchen, but they looked at her with blank confusion, which made her feel even more agitated.

"It's the police," Nova hissed. "Go back."

Understanding dawned in their eyes—first Wyatt, then Isaac, then Landon—and Wyatt herded everyone back into the dining room. Nova stayed on the couch, out of sight from the front hall but within listening distance through the hall doorway.

She heard Mackenna whisper, "Oh shit!" as she undoubtedly saw who was waiting on her doorstep.

Nova heard the bolt lock turning and the door opening with a whoosh.

"Good evening, ma'am."

"Good evening."

"I'm Deputy Serrano. I'm with the Scorpion County Sheriff's Department. Are your parents home?"

It was a female cop with a slight accent. Maybe Mexican American? Was Serrano a Mexican last name?

"No," Mackenna said. "But I'm nineteen and this is my family's cabin."

Nobody spoke for a moment. Nova pictured the police officer looking Mackenna over, trying to decide if she was telling the truth.

"Your name?"

"Mackenna Wolcott."

Another pause. Nova imagined the deputy writing Mackenna's name in a little notebook, like the police did on TV.

"Ms. Wolcott, your neighbors told me you arrived on the mountain today with some friends. Is that correct?"

"Yes."

"What time would you say you arrived?"

"I don't know. Like four o'clock, maybe? I wasn't paying close attention."

"Did you see any accidents on your way up the mountain?"

"Like car accidents, you mean?"

"Yes."

A brief pause, as if Mackenna was really thinking about it.

"No. I don't think so."

"You didn't see an overturned vehicle on Highway 72, near the bottom of the mountain? A sky-blue armored van with California license plates?"

"Um, no. I would have definitely remembered something like that."

It was a smooth lie. If Nova hadn't known better, she would have thought her friend was telling the truth.

"All right," Deputy Serrano said, her voice neutral and weary. "We're letting everyone in the area know there was an accident earlier today on Highway 72. The vehicle's occupants haven't been located. They could possibly be armed and dangerous, so please exercise extra caution for the next few days. Lock your doors and windows, even during the daytime. Don't go out alone. Call 911 if you happen to see any suspicious persons."

"Okay. Wow. I will, Officer. I promise."

"Have a good evening."

"Thanks. You too."

The door whooshed shut again and the bolt lock turned. Mackenna came into the living room and looked at Nova with wide eyes. The dudes joined them, a look of panic on their faces. Outside, the police car turned around in the yard and drove away from the cabin, its engine rumbling.

"We need to hide the money," Mackenna said, her voice unsteady. "We need to hide it, like, right now."

Everyone put on their coats and brought their share of cash down to the living room. Nova had talked Mackenna into lending her one of her big rolling shell suitcases so she could condense all her money into one piece of luggage and ditch the plastic bag. Now the armored-van money was divided five ways into three rolling suitcases and two fat duffel bags. The presence of the overstuffed luggage dominated the room, pulling at everyone as if it emitted its own gravity field.

"Do you really think we need to do this?" Landon asked, zipping up his parka. "Maybe you're being paranoid, Mack."

Mackenna shook her head. She'd put on a pink wool beanie but her wavy blond hair still spilled down to her shoulders. Nova, who hadn't had long hair since middle school, was starting to miss it after spending an entire day around Mackenna. You could only do so much with a pixie cut, which was both its greatest strength and weakness.

"What if that cop comes back?" Mackenna said. "What if she comes back tonight with a search warrant for the house?"

"Why would she?" Isaac asked. "Nobody saw us take the money."

Nova crossed her arms. "Are you completely sure about that? One hundred percent, totally sure?"

"Um, I guess not . . ."

"What about camera drones?" Nova said, feeling herself getting worked up again. "What about random people hiking on the mountain?"

"The cop said they still haven't found the van's driver," Wyatt said, his voice low and uneasy. "What if the driver was watching us?"

"He would have said something," Landon said, nudging one of the bags with his toe, his hands crammed into his jacket pockets. "Right? I mean, why would you let anybody take your money like that? Plus, he would have been hurt. He would have shouted for help."

Nobody said anything. Nova imagined some poor guy with a broken leg, or a broken arm, or a bloody head. She pictured him lying among the trees somewhere farther up the mountain, watching their group take load after load of cash to their SUV. Maybe he had a punctured lung and couldn't shout. Maybe he had a concussion and couldn't understand what he was seeing. Maybe he had amnesia.

Wyatt leaned over and put his hands on his knees. "I think I might be having a panic attack."

"Don't even start, bro," Isaac said, shaking his head. "If you have an attack, I'm definitely going to have an attack."

"Nobody's having any attacks," Mackenna said, grabbing one of the rolling luggage pieces by the handle. "We just need to hide this shit for a couple of days until everything calms down. This is just a precaution."

Nova looked at her phone. It was ten thirty. She felt exhausted and they hadn't even started hiking yet. "And you really still want to go to the party?"

Mackenna blinked in surprise, like the thought of not going had never even occurred to her. "Heck yeah. After today, we deserve to relax. We deserve to celebrate."

Landon cupped his hands around his mouth and whooped. Isaac and Wyatt smiled and whooped back. Everyone grabbed a piece of luggage and together they headed out into the night, bundled up like kids stepping into a snowstorm.

10

THE SCORPION CREEK POLICE STATION WAS ON THE WEST EDGE of town. It was right off the highway, wedged between a strip mall and a snowmobile dealership. Every building other than the police station was dark. Every twenty or thirty minutes a vehicle passed on the highway, going one way or the other. The only vehicles parked in the station's lot were one oversized truck and two sheriff deputy's cruisers.

Bannock and Gideon were parked next door to the police station in the snowmobile dealership parking lot, their car partially obscured by a mass of snowmobiles parked on the dealership's front lawn. They'd been on stakeout for two hours, monitoring the lack of action outside the station. If its interior lights hadn't been on, you might have thought the station was locked up for the night.

The whole scene was small-town quiet, which was either peaceful or unsettling, depending on your state of mind.

"What's the population of Scorpion Creek?" Bannock asked, tapping the elk's tine against the car's dashboard.

Gideon fiddled with his cell phone. "Three thousand, two hundred and thirty-nine."

"Too small for its own com center."

"Indeed," Gideon said, his head bobbing in the ghostly light of his phone. "County dispatch is run through . . . Rawlins."

"That's a ways off."

"Wyoming is a big, sparsely populated state."

Bannock yawned. "What are the station's normal hours?"

"Eight a.m. to ten p.m. on weekdays. Sheriff is named Carson. He looks like he's lifted some weights but never been to war."

"Have you ever been to war, Gideon?"

Gideon smirked. "No, sir. I have not. I prefer to make money."

Bannock glanced at the digital clock on the Honda's dashboard. It was 10:42.

"They should have closed by now."

Gideon nodded. As if summoned by their discussion, a skinny male sheriff's deputy emerged from the station's entrance and got into one of the parked SUVs. The deputy didn't look nervous or alert. Just tired and ready to enjoy the rest of his Friday night. If there was fifteen million dollars locked in the police station, he didn't know about it. Which meant either the money wasn't here, or Sheriff Carson was playing his cards close to the vest. Maybe the old boy had discovered the accident himself.

The deputy drove away. Nobody else exited the building and the station's interior lights remained on. Bannock could sense more people inside the building. It was like a hum in the air.

Perhaps they were counting the money. It would take them all night.

"I'll be back in a few minutes," Bannock said, opening his door. Gideon looked up from his phone. The younger man looked remarkably pale, his already intrinsic paleness doubled by the cell phone's white light. He reminded Bannock of a cephalopod, creeping across the impenetrable darkness of an ocean trench floor.

"Do you need any help?"

Bannock stared at Gideon and slipped the antler tine back into his jacket pocket, wondering if Gideon was the kind of man who enjoyed molesting small children and causing them pain. He was getting that clammy, scrabbling kind of feeling from him. It was something to file away in the back of his mind, a trait that could either be troublesome or useful, depending on the situation.

"Just pop the trunk," Bannock ordered.

Bannock grabbed his duffel bag from the Honda's trunk and walked behind the snowmobile dealership, where he attained a full view of the rear of the police station. He saw a metal door, a security camera, and a smashed-up sky-blue armored van that looked like it had fallen from the sky and landed right there in the station's back parking lot. Painted on the side of the van was the name STEEL CAGE ARMORED SERVICES.

So, their guesswork had been right. The evidence from the accident site had been hauled back to Scorpion Creek, at least for the night. The sheriff would have contacted the DEA about finding fifteen million dollars in laundered money (if he'd contacted anyone at all) but it would have already been late on a Friday evening and, as Gideon had said, Wyoming was a big, sparsely populated state and reinforcements hadn't arrived yet.

Bannock set his bag on an industrial air-conditioning unit and unzipped it. He stuck his combat knife into his belt and opened the carrying case for his recurve takedown bow. The case could be slung over his shoulder by a strap and contained twelve thirty-inch carbon arrows, a plastic tube-shaped quiver, a bow stringer, an archery glove, a leather arm guard, and an extra bow string. When fully assembled and strung, the bow had a right-hand draw weight of fifty-five pounds and could send an arrow through just about anything made of flesh. Bannock had been hunting with it for twenty years, gradually replacing its limbs when better materials and designs came along but sticking with the same polished yew riser, which had brought him much luck over the years.

Bannock assembled the bow, strung it, and notched an arrow. He strapped the tube-shaped quiver across his chest, the tube's opening within easy reaching distance. He left his bag on the air-conditioning unit and began walking toward the police station next door. He glanced to his left and observed the pale outline of Gideon watching him from the car. Bannock walked smoothly, minding his breath, and came around the side of the police station, holding the recurve bow casually at his side. He noted a second security camera monitoring the building's entrance. He peered inside the station's large, highway-facing windows and saw what appeared to be a bullpen area with several desks and office chairs. A lone sheriff's deputy sat behind a desk about twenty feet inside the building, his body turned sidelong to the entrance as he worked on his computer. The rest of the bullpen appeared empty.

Bannock tried the station's front door. He was betting it was unlocked—wagering on the confidence and complacency of an isolated small-town police station—and he was correct. He passed through a short airlock entryway and opened a second door. The deputy turned to look at Bannock as he entered the station. The deputy was young, maybe twenty-five, his face pitted with acne scars and his eyes glazed from staring at a computer monitor.

"Can I help you?"

Bannock brought the bow up from his side into firing position and drew the bowstring back until it was at full tension. The deputy's eyes widened and he stood up, his hand falling to his side-arm, which was still buttoned securely into its holster, per carrying procedure. Bannock took a deep breath, unhurried, and sighted his target. The deputy fumbled with the snap on his holster, sputtering something that sounded like "Stop." Bannock exhaled and released the bowstring, sending the notched arrow flying through the air, its fletching rippling with lethal intent.

The arrow struck the deputy in the chest as he struggled to draw his weapon. He fell back on the floor with a loud gasp, as if he'd been punched in the stomach, and the light faded from his eyes as he stared at Bannock, a shocked expression on his face. Bannock drew another arrow and notched it as he continued through the bullpen, scanning the empty desks for additional movement. He walked down a middle hallway that led to another hallway—the station was laid out like a capital I.

Bannock discovered the evidence locker on his immediate left, but it was locked, protected by a formidable blast door with a keypad lock. Bannock went the opposite direction down the back hallway until he reached a doorway with the nameplate SHERIFF CARSON beside it. The door to the office was open. Bannock could hear the soft plastic clacking of keyboard typing inside and smelled a mixture of stale coffee and microwaved burrito. He drew the string of his bow to full tension and stepped into the office doorway.

As he expected, the good sheriff was sitting behind his desk, likely typing up a report that pertained to finding an overturned armored van with fifteen million dollars inside.

Bannock, going with statistics, shot Carson in the right shoulder first so he couldn't draw his weapon. Then Bannock reloaded and shot Carson in the left shoulder, making it a pair. The sheriff was a nice wide target, shaped like a rectangular pincushion. He bellowed something unintelligible and stood up behind his desk, his arms hanging useless at his sides. He came around the desk and lowered his big head, trying to bullrush Bannock.

Bannock stepped back and stuck his leg out as the big man charged. The sheriff, blinded by pain and rage, tripped over Bannock's leg and fell hard into the hallway, unable to brace his fall as he dropped face-first. Bannock set his bow against the wall and unsheathed his knife. He stepped into the hallway and kicked the sheriff in the side as the big man tried to roll over, knocking the wind out of him.

"Hello, Sheriff." Bannock knelt down and grabbed the sheriff by his hair. He pulled the sheriff's head back until his throat was nicely exposed and held the knife's blade against it. The sheriff ceased his struggling and went still.

"I'm going to need to retrieve something from the evidence locker. Do you think you can help me with that?"

The sheriff swallowed, his Adam's apple brushing against the knife's blade. Bannock could tell he wanted to say something big and brave, but there it was . . . that knife at his throat.

11

THEY TOOK ONE OF THE WOODED TRAILS CONNECTING THE homes on Hollow Drive. Mackenna led the way with a flashlight while Wyatt brought up the rear with a second flashlight he kept aimed at the ground. The trail was composed of old wood chips and crushed rocks, and its soft, lumpy surface made it difficult to roll their luggage. Nova envied Wyatt and Landon, who had duffel bags and didn't need to roll anything. She thought about asking them to swap with her for a while, but her usual sense of stubborn pride rose, scorning help from anyone, even though her arms had begun to ache like they might break and fall off.

Nova, who'd spent a lifetime as a shorty, was tired of boys asking if they could carry things for her, if she needed help reaching something or opening a jar, or if she could see the stage at a concert. Her first and only boyfriend, Tennyson, had been only five-foot-ten, which was a regular height for a dude, sure, but he practically towered over her when they hugged or danced. The longer they dated, the more Nova suspected Tennyson got off on being so much taller than she was, as if he had a sexist power thing going on in the back of his mind, bubbling like an ingrained dude cauldron. He also liked to be right all the time and was hypercompetitive about everything from grades to Scrabble to social media. Arguing with him often felt like going to war.

On the other hand, Tennyson had been cute, with a great smile, and when he actually tried, he could make you feel like you were the only girl in the world. That he loved you so much he could hardly even stand it.

Also, he was named Tennyson, after Alfred, Lord Tennyson, one of the greatest Romantic poets in history. And she couldn't deny that he was a good kisser, gentle with his hands and not too pushy. After six months of making him wait, Nova had finally given in and had sex with him in his bedroom, while his parents were at the movies and his little brother was visiting a friend. They'd listened to chill music, burned a vanilla scented candle, and used a condom for protection. It had been a little painful for Nova, but it had been nice too, and they'd cuddled afterward and taken a nap together.

Tennyson broke up with her three days later.

Over text.

This was three months ago, back in May. Tennyson had said he was worried they were getting too serious and he wanted to be free to date other people during his summer internship in London. He'd only texted Nova once since, sending her a picture of Buckingham Palace with three exclamation points beneath it. The whole breakup made Nova feel sad and stupid at the same time. Worst of all, she'd have to see Tennyson again in two weeks, because they were both going to be freshmen at Colorado College, along with two dozen other kids from Pioneer Academy. She still didn't know if she wanted to kill him or get back together.

Isaac, who was walking ahead of Nova, tripped over something and staggered forward, dragging his rolling suitcase off its wheels. "Fuck me," he swore, struggling to get his suitcase back on track. "How far are we going, anyway?"

"It's not much farther," Mackenna said, glancing back at the line of hikers. "Maybe ten minutes."

Nova grinned, happy that she wasn't the first one to complain. Hearing somebody else bitch made her arm sockets ache a little less.

"Hey," Wyatt called out, still at the back of their line. "Are there, like, bears on this mountain?"

"Sure," Mackenna said. "It's a mountain, isn't it?"

"Grizzlies or black bears?" Nova asked.

"Both, I think."

"Oh good," Wyatt said, adjusting his duffel bag's shoulder strap. "Grizzlies."

"They won't bother us," Nova said, switching her suitcase dragging arm once again. "It's August and they're getting fat for winter. They're a lot more dangerous in the spring, when they're fresh out of hibernation and starving."

"Unless we surprise them," Landon said. "We need to make a lot of noise so they can hear us coming."

"Great idea," Isaac said, snorting and kicking up a spray of wood chips. "Let's make a lot of noise while we're burying stolen money."

"We didn't steal anything," Mackenna said, pushing back a branch. "We found it on the side of the road. Like collecting litter."

"Hmm," Nova said, switching arms again with her rolling suitcase. "I don't think that'll hold up in court."

"Whatever," Mackenna said, anger flaring into her voice. "It's done now."

They came to a fork in the trail.

Mackenna chose the path to the right without slowing down. They'd passed three houses on the trail so far, all higher up on the mountainside, their lights glowing and warm, inviting in the darkness. It had been a while since the last house, though, and the new trail slowly led them downward as they started to loop around the mountain, edging above a dark valley that could have contained anything.

Nova was impressed by how unworried Mackenna was at the head of their group, pushing on without stopping, rolling her enormous suitcase as if it was empty. She seemed at home on the trail, unfazed by the darkness or the occasional rustling in the surrounding trees. It was a clear night and the stars were shining bright in the sky, way more stars than you could see back in Denver, and a crescent sliver of a moon gave the woods a diffused silver glow. The temperature had fallen, and it suddenly felt like October instead of August. The air smelled like woodsmoke.

They came to a massive boulder sitting beside the trail. It looked like an avalanche waiting to happen.

"Ah," Mackenna said. "Here it is. Now we go off trail."

"What?" Isaac sounded alarmed.

Mackenna ignored him and tossed her luggage down the mountainside. It crashed and rolled through the weeds. Mackenna followed, shining her flashlight on the ground. Everyone stood at the edge of the trail and peered down into the dark trees. "Come on," Mackenna shouted from the darkness. "Throw your bags down too. Aim for my flashlight."

"You sure, babe?" Landon said, frowning as he leaned forward.

"Yes."

Landon looked at the others, shrugged, and tossed down his duffel bag. It landed with a heavy thud somewhere below. Wyatt threw his duffel bag next, then Isaac, then it was Nova's turn. She rolled her suitcase to edge of the trail and peered down.

"You want help?" Landon asked, stepping up. "You want me to chuck it for you?"

Nova scowled.

"I can throw it myself, dude. I just don't want to squash your girlfriend."

"Okay," Landon said, raising his hands in the air. "Whatever."

Nova picked up the suitcase by its handle and swung it by her side, ignoring the aching flare in her shoulder. She counted one, two, three and let the suitcase go, sending it sailing into the dark. It made a satisfying amount of crunching noise as it crashed through branches and rolled down the mountainside.

It felt good, Nova thought, throwing so much money away.

"You all go," Wyatt said, coming up to the edge of the path with the second flashlight. "I'll keep the light on the ground so you can see."

Nova smirked and wiped her sweaty hands on her jeans. "You want us to get eaten by bears first, huh?"

Wyatt flashed Nova his famous, heart-melting smile. "I have no clue what you're talking about, *chica*. No clue."

Nova and the others scrambled down the dark hillside and joined Mackenna on a flat, rocky shelf covered in clumps of scrub brush. She'd already recovered their tossed bags and piled them beside a hole in the ground. Everyone gathered around the hole, which was about three feet in circumference, while Mackenna pointed her flashlight into it.

"There's a little room down there. I used to play in it with my sister when we were little. We called it the Cave of Wonders."

Landon laughed. "Like from *Aladdin*?"

"Yeah. I so wanted to be Princess Jasmine. She had her own fucking tiger, you know?"

Wyatt got down on his knees and examined the hole with his own flashlight. "Is it safe down there?"

"That looks like a good snake pit to me," Nova said. "Actually, I'll be surprised if it's *not* a snake pit."

"There's only one way to find out," Isaac said, kicking a loose stone into the opening. "Why don't you do the honors, Nova?"

"No thanks," Nova said, folding her arms. "I'd prefer to stay alive."

"We played down there for years," Mackenna said, tucking a loose strand of hair behind her ear. "We never saw any snakes."

"You never know though," Wyatt said, leaning forward and sticking his head into the opening. "Snakes migrate, don't they?"

Nobody said anything. Nobody knew if snakes migrated or not.

"What do you see?" Landon asked, leaning over Wyatt's prone body like he could somehow help him by looking over his shoulder.

Wyatt grunted and elbow-crawled back from the opening. "Nothing. It looks empty."

"No snakes?" Nova asked, imaging an entire pit of writhing cobras with huge fangs, waiting for their next unsuspecting victim.

"Naw. Just some branches and pinecones. Shit like that."

Wyatt looked up at Nova and offered her the flashlight. "You want to see for yourself?"

"Okay."

Nova took the flashlight and got down on her knees beside the opening. She looked at Mackenna. "Hold my ankles, okay? I don't want to fall in."

"Sure, girl. No problem."

Mackenna knelt behind Nova and grabbed her ankles while Nova leaned over the opening. She lowered her arms and head into the opening and swept the flashlight back and forth. The Cave of Wonders was smaller than she'd expected, but big enough to feel like a hobbit home for a child. Maybe a four-foot drop to the floor, short enough you could slip inside and climb out again. No beer bottles, graffiti, or other signs of recent human visitation. Only rocks, branches, and pinecones, just like Wyatt had said. Actually, the burrow felt cozy and warmer than the night air above her, like a good hiding spot from the world. Nova had once had a little cave like it when she was a kid, in the woods behind their house, before the land had been sold and the entire woodlot was leveled for more houses.

It had been a nice, safe place, that cave. She could hide there after school and write in her journal and nobody would bother her. It had been her fortress of solitude. Her refuge.

Nova crawled back from the opening and Mackenna let go of her ankles.

"Well?" Mackenna asked. "You satisfied?"

Nova nodded and stood back up, slapping the dirt from her knees. "Yeah. Thanks for holding my ankles."

Mackenna smiled. "No problem."

"So, are we really going to do this?" Isaac said, crossing his arms. "Are we really going to drop over ten million dollars into a hole in the ground and leave it?"

"It's only for a few days," Mackenna said. "We can come back and get the bags before we leave on Monday."

"We can always turn the money in," Nova said, blowing warm air into her hands. "It's not too late. We could drop the bags somewhere and make an anonymous phone call to the police. They'd never know it was us."

Landon laughed. "Right. Turn it in after hauling it all over the place? No thanks. I'd rather keep it and be rich."

Nova looked at Wyatt and Isaac, hoping for some support. "Don't you feel guilty? Like it's not supposed to be ours?"

Wyatt shrugged. "We deserve it as much as anybody. Maybe I'll donate some to the Red Cross."

"Yeah," Mackenna said, her voice brightening. "Let's all donate, like, ten thousand dollars to a charity. Would that make you feel better, Nova? If we all donated some of it? We could give money to Planned Parenthood or something."

Nova stared at the bags. Five people times ten thousand dollars. Fifty thousand dollars was a drop in the bucket. Fifty thousand dollars was hardly anything.

"What about—"

"My family actually needs the money," Isaac said, interrupting Nova. "We're in debt. Like, major debt."

Everyone looked at him as the night wind rustled the trees. Nova could still smell woodsmoke on the air.

"But your dad is a hedge-fund manager, isn't he?" Landon said, lifting his duffel bag into the air and dropping it again, making it thump. "They make serious bank."

"I know," Isaac said, nodding. "He does. He also has a gambling problem. Well, it's more like a drinking and gambling problem. He gets drunk and gambles on stocks, sports, cards, horse racing. He's a gambling fiend. They finally had to fire him last month. My mom says she's going to divorce him. We have to sell our house."

"Shit," Wyatt said. "I'm sorry, man. I had no idea."

Isaac's openness surprised Nova. She wondered if the darkness was helping him talk. Similar to talking during a sleepover after the lights had been turned off and somebody's mom told everyone to go to sleep.

Nova had always liked talking like that when she was younger, even with girls she hardly knew. Laughing and talking about your crushes and feeling so happy and cozy you wiggled your butt inside a sleeping bag and hugged your pillow. She'd enjoyed talking with the lights out more than watching movies or playing dress-up, or the board games or all the snacks. People were more honest in the dark.

"You shouldn't give your dad the money," Mackenna said, grabbing the handle of her suitcase. "He'll just gamble it away. You should, like, figure out a way to hide it from him until he gets help. You know, like Gamblers Anonymous."

"Yeah, I guess."

"Don't worry, dude," Landon said, putting his arm around Isaac's shoulder. "My family isn't rich either. Our credit cards are, like, totally maxed. My mom's obsessed with looking rich and buying the same crap our neighbors buy. It's fucking ridiculous, man. We get like five packages from Amazon every day. She makes sure we all have the newest iPhone the day they come out. Even when we don't *want* the newest iPhone."

Mackenna made a hissing sound and looked at Nova, her flashlight waving at the ground. "It's true. Cassie is a little too into shopping online."

"All right," Nova said, shrugging. "So what? None of this stuff is so bad. You guys will be okay. It's not like you're Ukrainian refugees."

Mackenna sighed and crossed her arms. "We already voted, Nova."

"Yeah, we did. But that was before the cops showed up."

Nobody said anything.

"Screw it," Mackenna said, setting her flashlight down on the ground and lifting her suitcase into the air. "I'll go first."

Nobody moved to stop her. Mackenna swung her hard-shell suitcase over the opening and dropped it. It landed with a thud inside the hole. Mackenna dusted off her hands and picked the flashlight back up.

She stepped away from the opening and gestured toward it with the flashlight's beam. "C'mon. We still have a campfire party to go to."

Landon dropped in his duffel bag next.

Then Isaac and Wyatt did the same. Nova rolled the hard-shell suitcase she'd borrowed from Mackenna to the opening and peered into the darkness. This time nobody asked if she needed help. She rolled the suitcase into the hole and it landed on top of the others. Nova stepped back and Wyatt shined his flashlight into the opening. You could see the dark edge of Nova's suitcase sticking out against the beige colored rock. Just a little, but it was there.

Mackenna came forward with an armful of pine branches. She draped them across the opening and arranged the branches so you couldn't see it. "There," she said, holding her flashlight to her chin so it made her face glow against the night. "Now we're safe."

12

DEPUTY SERRANO DROVE DOWN CLAW HEART MOUNTAIN, HEADED back toward the Scorpion Creek police station. It was past eleven at night and she was exhausted. She'd spent the last three hours going door to door around Cloud Vista and the surrounding area, asking if anyone had seen the armored-van accident or had any details about strangers appearing in the area. She'd encountered the entire gamut of responses, from chatty old ladies to the mildly curious to the drunk and sullen. All that legwork, and Serrano had accomplished nothing other than starting a town-wide gossip chain.

The yearlong residents of Cloud Vista lived on a mountain because they liked the isolation and quiet. They didn't like strangers coming around and asking questions. They had big dogs. They had loaded guns mounted above doorways. They had silent children with big, staring eyes that watched you with unnerving intensity. The Old West was still alive and well in Cloud Vista despite the central heating, pickup trucks, and internet. Serrano had heard more than one rumor about local justice being dished out when someone stepped out of line. Bodies buried on the mountain in unmarked graves, dropped into one of the dozens of old mining shafts that perforated Claw Heart. Rival families settling feuds with fists and knives. Abused children running away into the woods, never to be seen again. Beaten women disappearing their husbands. Nothing ever proven. Evidence evaporating into thin air. A veil of silence.

Which made any investigation difficult, of course. The missing armored-van crew wasn't as baffling as the untouched money. Serrano could see a few enterprising locals knocking off an armored vehicle, but why would they go to so much trouble and not take all of it?

One of the defining characteristics about money was that nobody ever seemed to get enough of it, especially when it was just sitting there for the taking. Serrano was eager to see the van's security footage, which they'd sent via deputy to the state crime lab in Cheyenne for analysis. Sheriff Carson had called in a favor with a lab tech there, who'd promised to retrieve the footage and get it to them by tomorrow afternoon.

Deputy Serrano passed the elk carcass on the side of the mountain highway. It was even uglier and more disturbing in the wash of headlights with several turkey vultures perched on it, tearing it apart strip by strip. She'd already notified Game and Fish about this particularly nasty item of roadkill, but they obviously hadn't gotten to it yet.

Sometimes with roadkill such as elk or moose, you might catch somebody trying to saw off its head and antlers for personal use, either to sell or mount on the wall in their own home. But this elk was so mangled, including its antlers, that so far it appeared untouched by human scavengers.

Serrano descended the final stretch of switchback highway and drove onto the plain toward Scorpion Creek. She felt her shoulders loosen as Claw Heart Mountain dropped behind her and she realized how tense she'd been since finding the armored van earlier that day. Her cell phone buzzed and she put the call through to the car's stereo.

"Hey baby. How's the crime fighting going?" Her husband, Miguel, sounded tired. He worked as a grocery-store butcher in Scorpion Creek. They had two energetic little boys who loved to run both of them ragged.

"It's going," Deputy Serrano said. "I can promise you that."

"You going to be home soon?"

"Soon-ish. Probably midnight? I'm heading back from Claw Heart and need to swing by the station and check in with the boss man. See if there's anything new and exciting before I hang up my cape for the night."

"You work so hard, lady."

Serrano smiled and squeezed the steering wheel with both hands. "You know it, *mi amor*. How are the boys?"

"Finally in bed. I had to wrestle them away from their Play-Station."

"I bet you did, my big, strong butcher man."

"See you soon. I'll try to stay awake."

Serrano laughed. "Right. Good luck with that."

They both knew Miguel would be asleep on his recliner when she got home, a half-finished beer on a side table and their cat Mooshy curled in his lap, both of them snoring. Serrano would have to wake him up and lead him upstairs to bed, the cat trailing at their heels, happy to complete this final ritual of their day.

Just thinking of home, Serrano drove a little faster.

———

Normally, they locked up the police station at ten at night and didn't open it again until eight the next morning. Tonight, however, Sheriff Carson and a deputy would be on duty all night to watch over the money and the armored van.

Deputy Serrano parked beside Sheriff Carson's truck in the front parking lot. As soon as she exited her vehicle, an uneasy feeling settled in her gut. The lights were on, but she couldn't see either Deputy Heller or Sheriff Carson inside the station.

Serrano pressed the speaker button on her uniform's shoulder mic. "Sheriff Carson, you there?"

No answer.

"Deputy Heller, you there?"

Still no answer. Serrano unsnapped her holster and drew her gun, proceeding with caution toward the station's entryway. She pushed the exterior door open, which should have been locked but wasn't, and opened the interior door as well, moving forward now as if compelled in a dream.

Deputy Heller was lying on the floor in the middle of the station bullpen. His arms were thrown out, like he'd fallen backward with force, and his eyes were open with surprise. His weapon was still in its holster, though the holster was unbuttoned, and he had what looked like the shaft of a fiberglass arrow sticking out of his chest. A clean shot, right to the heart.

"Sweet Mary," Deputy Serrano whispered, a great trembling filling her body. She scanned the rest of the bullpen, saw no additional threats or victims. She knelt and checked the deputy for a pulse. Nothing. Serrano stood and proceeded through the bullpen deeper into the station. The trembling in her body grew worse as she went down the station's central hallway. She could smell the copper of fresh blood and other foul bodily aromas. She turned left at the end of the hallway and saw the back hallway was smeared with a trail of blood that connected the sheriff's office to the evidence locker. The heavy metal door to the evidence locker stood wide open.

Deputy Serrano fought a powerful urge to run away as she peered inside the doorway, her weapon still raised. Inside the room was a second body, tied to a chair with nylon rope. Sheriff Carson was obviously dead as well. He had an arrow sticking out of each shoulder, as if he'd reached for his gun and been dissuaded. His clothes had been cut away and his body had been carved up with great skill. Among other things, both his eyes were missing, their sockets carved hollow with a skillfulness Serrano's husband would have admired.

On the metal evidence shelves behind Sheriff Carson was an empty space.

The money was gone.

13

THEY SCRAMBLED UP THE HILLSIDE BACK TO THE MAIN TRAIL.
Mackenna promised the Overlook was around the bend, only ten
more minutes. Nova's cell phone wasn't getting any reception, but
it did tell her it was 12:42 a.m. Past midnight, and here they were
tromping around a dark mountain, their path illuminated only by
two wavering flashlights. Nova's mother would have stroked out if
she'd known these basic details, not to mention the stolen money
they'd just buried in the ground like a bunch of teenage pirates.
Nova dreaded the call she'd need to make tomorrow to check in
and prove she was still alive. Her mother would grill her and she'd
have to lie her ass off, something she'd never been good at. Lying
always made Nova feel like she'd swallowed a balloon, and the
more she lied the bigger the balloon grew, making her feel bloated
and queasy.

"There," Mackenna said, pointing up ahead at a red flickering
glow in the distance. "See? Not too far."

"Sweet," Landon said. "I love bonfires."

The dudes had lit a joint and were passing it between themselves, blowing hazy plumes into the cold night air. Mackenna and Nova had both declined, but Nova was now reconsidering her decision. Cannabis normally made her sleepy and hungry, but maybe it would be nice to take the edge off and stop worrying so much. Maybe she just needed to relax.

People huddled around the fire in puffy coats and stocking caps. Mackenna led their group into the clearing and a boy stood up, tall and broad. It was Colton Morgan, now wearing a green fleece vest and a trucker hat, his freckles like sparks against his pale skin. Nova felt her heart squeeze at seeing him again, which was ridiculous, because first, they didn't even know each other; second, she'd be gone in a few days; and third, he was into Mackenna anyway.

"Hey," Colton said, grinning. "You guys made it."

Several logs were placed around the pit for seating, along with a half dozen tree stumps, while a pile of stacked deadwood as tall as Nova sat at the edge of the firelight.

"I was worried you got lost," Colton said, handing Mackenna a can of beer. "We were about to send out a search party."

Mackenna cracked open the beer and took a big swig. "Nope. We didn't get lost. We just like to be fashionably late."

Colton laughed, as if this was the funniest thing he'd heard all day, before introducing the people sitting around the fire. Nova had expected a larger group, a party kind of crowd, but she counted only six others beside Colton. Three chicks and three dudes. All white. All around eighteen or nineteen. All emitting strong mountain-townie vibes.

One of the dudes had a vape pen and two of the chicks were smoking cigarettes. Two cases of beer sat on the ground, their cardboard ends ripped open, empty beer cans strewn about. Nova wondered whose older sibling or friend had been willing to buy alcohol for them.

Colton handed out beer to the rest of the new arrivals and everyone sat around the fire, with the townies on one side and their group of suburban kids on the other. It felt very ceremonial and classic, like a scene from the Middle Ages.

Two groups of strangers, meeting on a dark night to share a fire and libations. Nova opened her beer and a little explosion of foam shot out, covering the back of her hand. She shook her hand to dry it and sipped the foam from the rim of the can. She still wasn't too excited about the taste of beer, but she was thirsty from all the hiking.

Colton raised his beer in the air.

"Hey," he said, winking at Nova. "Welcome to the Overlook."

Everyone drank, watching the fire in silence. You could see a bed of white-hot coals at the base, each coal glowing like a miniature sun. Nova leaned closer and closed her eyes, enjoying the warmth. She listened as the wind rustled the trees and the wood crackled in the fire. She felt relaxed for the first time since leaving her house that morning.

"Did the cops visit you guys too?"

Nova opened her eyes. She did her best to keep her face blank and expressionless. Smoke swirled around her, making the night hazy.

"Yeah," Mackenna said, sounding fake casual. "A lady cop stopped by and asked us if we'd seen a car crash when we were driving up the mountain. I told her no. We would have remembered something like that, right?"

The locals nodded from across the fire. Colton took a sip of beer and belched. "Weird how they couldn't find the driver, right? You think they'd be smashed all over the place if they crashed going down the mountain."

"My cousin Andy died going down that switchback," one of the local girls said, blowing a plume of cigarette smoke from the side of her mouth. "It was January and the road was coated with black ice. He lost control for a second and that was all it took. Boom. Down the mountain. They had to chisel him out of the highway."

"Fuck," Landon said, taking a long toke on his joint. "That's gruesome."

The girl nodded. The other locals didn't look particularly horrified. They'd all heard the story before, probably a hundred times.

"People disappear around here," one of the local dudes said. "Happens all the time."

"Shit, not this again," Colton said, sighing and crumpling his can of beer in his hand. "You and your lame ghost stories, Max."

Max didn't say anything. He stared into the flames and their flickering light reflected in his eyes. He didn't seem drunk or stoned. Just locked into the fire.

"What story?" Nova asked. "What do you mean?"

"Yeah," Wyatt said. "Tell us, dude. I love ghost stories."

Max looked across the fire, directly at Nova. She returned his gaze, not flinching. She felt the night fold in around them, as if there was only this fire now, with these twelve people sitting around it.

"Back in eighteen fifty," Max began, "a small wagon train of settlers headed for California decided to cross Claw Heart Mountain instead of taking the South Pass farther north. This was back in the gold rush days, right? The settlers were hoping they'd strike it rich on the mountain and show up in California already loaded with gold."

Nova shifted on her seat, turning over the phrase "strike it rich" in her mind. She pictured their cache of suitcases, hidden not that far away.

"Claw Heart was still wild back then, with only one old fur-merchant trail running over it. No forts or towns. Just pine trees, bears, and streams packed with cutthroat trout. The settlers made their way up the old merchant trail and reached the valley where Cloud Vista is now. They panned for gold. After a couple of months, they found a decent vein. The settlers built a few log cabins, spent the winter on the mountain, and cleaned the deposit out by the following summer."

Nova glanced at Mackenna. She was all cuddled up against Landon, drinking her beer and smiling like she knew a secret, maybe a dirty one. The firelight made her blond hair glow beneath her ski cap, each strand catching the light. Even bundled up against the cold, she looked beautiful, her cheeks rosy with health.

"Everybody was happy with the find, except this one old Indian fighter named Reginald Sutton. Sutton had been hired by the settlers to protect them, but he mostly drank and practiced throwing his knife into trees. He was an angry, greedy asshole. The night before they headed down the mountain, Sutton decided to kill all the settlers and keep the gold for himself."

Max poked at the fire with a stick. A white-hot log collapsed into the bonfire's embers, causing Nova to flinch on her tree stump.

"It was a cloudy night. You couldn't see anything once your fire went out. Sutton crept into each cabin in camp and slit everyone's throat while they slept. Men, women, children. He even carved up the babies before they could even start to cry."

Wyatt whistled softly, and one of the townie girls gave a nervous laugh. Nova shivered, imagining Sutton creeping through the night with his knife. She pictured him with a crooked spine and a face covered in old scars. He might be hanging out at the Overlook with them right now, standing just beyond the reach of the firelight. He could be waiting to drag somebody into the trees.

"In the last cabin in camp was an old Spanish witch," Max continued. "The witch had come on the journey because she wanted to see the Pacific Ocean before she died. When Sutton stabbed her in the heart, robbing her of her final wish, the witch cursed him with her dying breath, which makes any curse even stronger."

Max looked around the fire, his dark eyes daring anyone to challenge this claim.

No one did.

"At first, nothing happened. Sutton loaded all the gold and some supplies into one wagon. He left the valley where they'd made camp and headed down the mountain. A few hours later, Sutton felt a pain in his stomach. At first, he tried to ignore it, but the pain grew so bad he couldn't sit on the wagon anymore. He jumped down and lay on the ground. It felt like his insides were eating themselves. The pain was so bad he passed out, right there on the trail, with his horses still hitched."

"Dude was fucked up, huh?" one of the townie boys said, which made a couple of the girls laugh and rustle in their chairs. Max ignored them.

"When Sutton woke up, he could tell something had changed. He didn't feel right. He felt warm, even though it was a cold mountain night. His clothes lay in shreds on the ground. When he looked down, he saw his body was covered in fur and his fingers had turned into claws. He found a pool of water and looked at his reflection in the moonlight. He wasn't human anymore. He'd turned into some kind of . . . beast."

Max leaned back from the fire and took a swig of beer. Everyone, including the townies, was staring into the bonfire as if it was a movie screen, transfixed by what they saw there. Nova wanted to have this power as a poet. To cast a spell with her words. To make everyone grow so quiet you could hear embers popping in a fire.

"Sutton was hungry now," Max continued. "Hungrier than he'd ever been in his life. He ate all the rations in his wagon, but he was still hungry. He killed a deer and ate the whole carcass, but he was still hungry. No matter how much he ate, Sutton was always hungry, always in pain. The best he could manage to do was gorge himself, burrow deep into the mountain, and hibernate."

Max swallowed and locked eyes with Nova. She could see tiny, reflected dots of firelight in his pupils.

"The witch had also cursed Sutton with immortality, so he would have to suffer forever. He became a wraith. *The* Wraith. He became the Hunger in the Mountain."

Max fell silent, his tale ended. Released from the story's dream-web, everyone started talking and laughing again, their faces flushed in the firelight. Unwilling to have the ghost story quickly dismissed by doubters, Nova got up and walked away from the bonfire. Above the Overlook, the stars were out in all their glory, dazzling and abundant. Nova checked her cell phone, a glowing square in the darkness. She had a few bars now. She felt a strong urge to call her mother and tell her everything about the trip, confess to stealing the money, but it was too late at night and she could already feel the words sticking in her throat.

Nova slipped her phone into her pocket. She looked up at the stars, so bright and multitudinous, until somebody called her name, releasing her from her reverie. Nova stumbled back to the crackling fire, glad for the heat and the light.

She was glad she was not alone.

14

BANNOCK SAT ON A BACKYARD PATIO IN THE BLUE LIGHT OF predawn, facing east as he drank coffee and waited for sunrise. He'd only slept three hours, but that was enough. He could feel the recent killings humming in his blood, stirring up the old wartime energies. He'd enjoyed attacking the police station in Scorpion Creek the same way an athlete enjoys returning to the field after coming out of retirement. The charged moment before the game begins, the roar of blood in your ears, the pounding of your heart, and that first beautiful moment when your opponent becomes aware of your intentions and desperately tries to counter them, only to fail and fall upon the field of battle.

Bannock had missed the killing. He'd buried a part of himself during his self-imposed semiretirement in Utah. Perhaps the worthiest part of himself. The part closest to the gods and the ancient ways. The part developed and honed in the mud and the cold of his ancestor's brutal lives, thousands upon thousands of years of killing and survival. The part so many men of this time had forgotten and ignored in favor of comfort and safety. Bannock's true nature had lain dormant, sleeping while he dwelled in his cozy home. But it was all coming back to him now.

A bat fluttered past Bannock on the patio, likely heading home for the day. The air smelled like cow shit and sagebrush wet with morning dew. Bannock and Gideon were visiting a ranch two hours northwest of Claw Heart Mountain. They'd chosen the ranch at random, looking for an isolated location to hide out while waiting for further instructions from the Organization. They'd discovered a few surprising things during their visit to the Scorpion Creek police department that required further digestion. They'd found only a third of the shipment of cash they'd been sent to retrieve. The rest was mysteriously missing—no matter how much Bannock had carved into the local sheriff, the gentleman had been unable to provide Bannock with additional information.

Also curious was the armored van's missing crew. Bannock had assumed the two men would either be in the morgue or the county hospital, but the sheriff had informed Bannock that they'd been absent from the scene. Which led to all sorts of intriguing suppositions, such as:

- The crew had been ambushed by a rival operation, who left the dead elk on the side of the road as a red herring. For whatever reason, the rival operation's crew had only taken two-thirds of the cash delivery. Perhaps as an additional red herring, or due to unforeseen operational complications. Though it was hard to imagine what would induce anyone to abandon five million dollars ripe for the taking.
- The crew had set up the entire accident themselves. The dead elk, the armored van rolling down the mountainside,

the mysteriously abandoned money. All of it had been planned. They'd been satisfied with ten million between them and left the remainder as a smokescreen, perhaps hoping that not taking it all would somehow placate the Organization and induce them to call off any ensuing retrieval operations. If this was the case, they were even bigger fools than the usual fools who tried to steal from the Organization.

- The crew had truly been involved in an accident on Claw Heart Mountain. Afterward, they'd abandoned the armored van for some reason, perhaps due to shock, disorientation, or fear of the authorities arriving on-site. They'd removed ten million from the van's cargo hold, leaving the rest behind due to time or transport constraints. They could still be awaiting help from the Organization to extract.

- The crew had truly been involved in an accident on Claw Heart Mountain. They'd either been killed or incapacitated. A third party, likely random, unrelated civilians, had come along soon after and discovered the money in the cargo van's hold. Seeing a once-in-a-lifetime opportunity, they'd taken both the money and the crew, loading everything up as fast as they could to avoid being discovered on the highway. They'd been forced to leave the remaining cash due to time and/or transport constraints. If the van's crew hadn't been dead at the accident scene, they would be now, likely buried in a shallow grave somewhere hundreds of miles from Claw Heart Mountain.

Bannock hadn't settled on one particular theory yet. He liked to keep an open mind to provide operational flexibility. He'd seen a lot of unlikely things in his life, and none of the possible theories seemed that outlandish to him. Money, particularly a great deal of it, had a way of generating chaos in the lives of those who came across it. It was an elemental force, like the wind or rain, and needed to be considered accordingly.

A glass sliding door opened and Gideon stepped onto the patio. Bannock's driver looked relatively fresh despite the long hours of travel they'd put in the day before. His cheap gray suit looked unrumpled and crisp, his powder-blue eyes clear and alert. His pale skin glowed in the growing light, as if he were a specter come to haunt Bannock for all the considerable wickedness he'd done in his life. He was carrying a pot of coffee in one hand and a cup in the other. He sat beside Bannock at the patio table so he could also look out at the grassy fields delineated by barbed-wire fencing.

"It's not much of a view, but there's a lot of it," Gideon said. "Refill?"

Bannock nodded and Gideon refilled his mug. Gideon's own mug was already filled, nearly to the brim. Gideon set the coffeepot down on the plastic patio table and lifted his mug to his mouth slowly, not wanting to spill on his suit, and took a cautious sip. Bannock waited, allowing the man to speak when he was ready. He could already sense another long day spread out before them. No use in rushing toward it when it would come either way.

"The Organization will pay you one-third of the discussed fee," Gideon said, looking at Bannock through the steam rising above his mug. "They feel it is proportional to the retrieval of one-third of their money."

Bannock didn't say anything.

"However, if you are able to retrieve the remaining amount, they are willing to pay the full fee, along with an additional one-million-dollar bonus."

Bannock did the math. The bonus would increase his original fee by 50 percent, netting him three million dollars for a few days' labor. The Organization must have been truly worried the remaining cash was in the wind. They had no idea what had happened on Claw Heart Mountain. Not a fucking clue.

"The Organization believes the van's crew may be hiding out on the mountain, biding their time until things cool off. They're currently monitoring local police channels and will pass on any useful information."

Bannock drank his coffee. It was generic and stale, the kind of coffee old ranchers drank. The kind of preground coffee you bought once a month in bulk, when you drove a hundred miles to a proper city.

"We'll have to go back to the mountain," Bannock said. "Today."

Gideon nodded.

"It'll be dangerous after Scorpion Creek," Bannock said. "The local cops will be on alert. The DEA will probably be swarming around too."

"We erased the police station's security footage and wiped the scene. Nobody knows what we look like."

Bannock pictured Claw Heart Mountain, which still loomed in his mind. It was a big mountain. Bigger than he'd expected. It had also given off an unusual energy, something he couldn't quite discern. Something he'd never felt before.

"We'll need another vehicle."

Gideon smiled and blew on his coffee. "Our hosts have a pickup truck in the barn. We'll fit right in."

"Sure," Bannock said, rapping the table with his knuckle. "You and that suit you're wearing will blend in perfectly."

Gideon looked down at himself. "I suppose you're right," he allowed. "I could borrow some more casual items from the husband's wardrobe."

Bannock visualized their day. The two-hour drive back to the mountain. Stopping at that small town. Cloud Vista. Trying to poke around while evading suspicion. Hunting two dangerous men who may or may not have stolen ten million dollars. He felt his blood warm simply thinking about it, his nerves sparking to attention.

"What about our hosts?" Gideon asked. "What should we do about them?"

Bannock sat back in his chair and looked out across the plains. The sun was finally rising above the horizon in the east. It would be another hot, dry summer day in Wyoming. Earlier that morning he'd broken into the house, killed the couple's border collie, and subdued the couple before they managed to turn on the bedroom light. The old couple was secured at the moment, mummified by duct tape and squirming in their bed like larvae. Likely terrified out of their minds and praying to their maker.

"We'll throw them in the trunk of your car and drive separately," Bannock said, draining the rest of his coffee. "Whoever visits the house next will think they're on vacation. We'll drive the car into a lake somewhere between here and the mountain."

"All right." Gideon got up and cleared the table. "I'll wipe everything down inside the house and change."

Bannock nodded. He stood up and stretched. His back was feeling stiff from all the recent action. He was no longer a young man, that was for certain.

But the day was young, and this sunrise sure was beautiful.

SUNSHINE

15

NOVA STOOD NAKED IN FRONT OF HER BEDROOM WINDOW, bathing in the morning sunlight. Golden light filled her mind, warming it, softening her edges. She arched her back and reached for the ceiling, finishing a sun salutation yoga flow that usually gave her a nice stretch and got her blood flowing.

Today, however, Nova was hungover and the yoga was rougher than normal. Her head felt groggy and achy, while her nose was stuffed up. Her memory of the night before was clouded, starting with the second half of the bonfire and their drunken march back to the house. She had a bad feeling she'd said something stupid and embarrassing. Something she should have never said in a million years.

She stared out the window, wondering what it would feel like if somebody appeared among the trees and saw her naked, but the only things in sight were trees and birds, which didn't care much about a shrimpy eighteen-year-old girl.

Nova dug through the plastic bag filled with her clothes and pulled out her orange one-piece swimsuit. She'd only seen it briefly the night before, but she'd been right about Mackenna's cabin having a pool in the backyard. Nova loved swimming and thought that if anything was going to cure her hangover, a morning swim would.

An air-conditioning vent kicked on in the ceiling, sending a stream of cold air into Nova's bedroom. Nova put on her swimsuit and slipped into her flip-flops. She went across the hall to the bathroom to brush her teeth, trying to get the morning hangover stank off her tongue. She grabbed a towel from the shelf—not a proper, made-for-poolside beach towel, which would have bothered Nova's mother, but Nova's mother wasn't in Wyoming, and this wasn't her towel. Nova stepped back out into the upstairs hallway and listened. Mackenna's cabin was quiet, everyone else still asleep after the late-night partying and the drunken hike back. Really, they'd been so loud and clumsy, it was a small miracle nobody had tripped and broken their neck.

God. There was her mother again, creeping into Nova's brain with her worried-mom thoughts. Her mother's anxiety was so bad it gave Nova anxiety just thinking about it. Why couldn't her mom be a little more like her dad, a workaholic who barely noticed her existence? Already, the woman had left her two voice mails and seven texts "checking in" to see how the trip was going. Nova had texted back that everything was great, that her mom needed to chill, but that had only led to another text begging for fun details and some cabin pics.

Nova felt an urge to text her mother money-themed emojis in response, cash gifs with people rolling around in cash, but she texted a kissy face and a bunch of hearts instead, her go-to smoke-screen text when she wanted to appease her mother without communicating any information.

Nova exited the bathroom and walked down the upstairs hall-way, her flip-flops thwacking on the carpet. She noticed Isaac's bedroom door was cracked open and crept up to it, curious to know if somebody else was awake. She peeked through the open-ing and saw two figures lying in a queen-size bed, the bedsheets tangled and kicked to the foot of the bed. Isaac and Wyatt were curled up together, Wyatt's dark brown skin glowing in contrast to Isaac's pale white. Both dudes were only wearing their boxers. They looked deeply asleep. Content.

This was unexpected.

Nova hadn't realized either dude was gay, or bi, or whatever they were, much less that they were into each other. True, she only really knew them as two older boys from their shared time back at Pioneer Academy—Wyatt as the super popular dude and Isaac as the smart, grumpy nerd. Still, Nova was surprised by their hookup and more than a little jealous. As shitty as Tennyson had handled their own breakup, she still missed him, missed being in a relationship. It felt so good, knowing somebody you weren't re-lated to was thinking about you every day, cared about your life so much you could text them and know they'd text you back right away if they could. Tennyson was like a ghost who still haunted her heart, whether she wanted him to or not.

Nova pulled back from the doorway and headed for the stairs, clutching the plush bathroom towel against her chest. She'd left her cell phone in her bedroom on purpose, just to get away from any more texts from her mother, and she felt oddly light without it. She went into the kitchen, grabbed a Diet Coke from the fridge, and opened a glass sliding door that let out into the backyard.

Even though it was still morning, the August heat was already building. The dark red cedarwood patio that circled the pool was sprinkled with deck chairs and little round tables. A tiki bar sat off in one corner, shaded by a little thatch roof. It was easy to imagine Mackenna's father making cocktails behind the tiki bar while eighties music blared in the background. Clients would mingle around the patio, wearing ugly Hawaiian shirts and leather sandals. They'd talk about golf, the stock market, and their favorite high-end prostitutes, all while smoking Cuban cigars and laughing.

The swimming pool was lined with tiles colored different shades of aquamarine, making it look like the bottom of the pool was a rippling ocean wave, glittering in the sun. It was a truly beautiful pool, half in shadow and half in light as the sun rose above the mountain. Even the scattering of green aspen leaves floating on the pool's surface was pretty, like leaves in a Monet painting.

Nova dropped her towel on a cushioned chaise lounge and walked up to the edge of the deep end. She stuck her toes over the lip of the pool and wiggled them, something she always did for good luck. Then she took a deep breath and dove into the pool. The water was colder than she expected, chilled from a night exposed to mountain air, and the chill rebooted her mind, chasing away all thoughts but cold. Nova kept swimming with her eyes closed, thrashing hard to warm up, until she felt the shallow end beneath her feet and raised her head above the water.

Mackenna's cabin loomed above her on one side and the forest on the other, the tree line set back about twenty feet from the patio. Nova thought of all the money waiting for them tucked away in the mountain, a real-life buried treasure, and her skin rippled with goose bumps. She didn't need to worry so much like her mom. She could be brave and unpredictable. She could date anyone she wanted. Heck, now she could have her own cabin and pool. Nova dove back under the water and continued swimming, lap after lap, warming up until she didn't notice the cold anymore and her hangover was shed like a dead skin.

16

AFTER EVERYBODY WOKE UP, THEY ALL PILED INTO MACKENNA'S SUV and headed into town to one of Cloud Vista's two restaurants, a diner called Al's Griddle.

Al's Griddle was in an old-timey wooden building, like all Cloud Vista's downtown buildings. A sign announced BREAKFAST ALL DAY, and several wide bay windows showed off the red booths inside. The parking lot was cluttered with old pickup trucks, shiny motorcycles, and cars that looked like they hadn't been washed in months.

"Wow," Mackenna said. "This is so fricking hick. I love it."

Isaac groaned. "Don't say that when we go inside, okay? Actually, it's probably best you don't talk at all. I don't want to get thrown out before we eat."

Mackenna looked in the rearview mirror and stuck her tongue out at Isaac. She maneuvered the SUV into one of the few open parking spots.

As she unbuckled her seat belt, she looked down at the driver's-side door and yelped.

"What is it?" Nova asked, because someone had to.

Mackenna darted down and came back up with two fistfuls of bundled cash. "The extra money I put in the door pocket yesterday. I totally forgot about it."

Nova reached out and set her hand on the money, lowering it to Mackenna's lap as she looked around the parking lot. They'd parked facing away from the diner, so at least they had a little privacy from prying eyes.

"Jesus, Mackenna. Put that away. Somebody will see."

Mackenna grinned and tucked the cash back into her door's pocket. She pulled out a single hundred-dollar bill and fanned her face with it, her blue eyes sparkling. "Breakfast is on me this morning, y'all," Mackenna said in a bad Southern drawl. "Have whatever your sweet little hearts desire."

Nova unbuckled her seat belt and dug around the random clothes lying in the passenger footwell. She handed Mackenna a T-shirt and nodded toward the door pocket. "Cover that up."

"My, my, aren't you a prickly little pear."

"Mackenna."

"Fine," Mackenna said, taking the T-shirt and stuffing it into the door. "Such manners, honey. I do declare."

Nova rolled her eyes, fighting back a grin. She had to admit that Mackenna wasn't *always* trying to be cool but let herself be a goofball sometimes. Nova did appreciate that about her.

Late-morning sunlight washed over everything, harsh and bright, as they got out of the SUV. Somewhere a chainsaw revved and bit into wood, sending its screech across town. Nova could see people sitting at booths inside the diner, shaded and air-conditioned, looking out at their group as if they were watching animals at the zoo. Nova waved, but nobody waved back.

"Creepy," Isaac said, falling in beside Nova. "Small towns always creep me out."

"Because you're gay?"

"What?"

Nova shrugged. "I saw you and Wyatt cuddling this morning." Isaac stopped and glared at Nova. The others kept walking.

"You looked cute and comfortable together," Nova said, touching her earlobe. "I was jealous. Really."

"Whatever," Isaac said, exhaling. "It's just a thing."

"Okay."

"A drunken-vacation thing."

"Hey," Nova said, grinning at Isaac, who had ditched his usual cool, jaded façade, instead showing signs of panic. "You don't have to explain yourself to me, Isaac."

"Why, are you one of the million girls in the world who have a crush on Wyatt? Is that why you care?"

Nova squinted one eye, as if she was actually considering this. "Wyatt? Nope. I don't think so."

"Good. I hear you've already had your heart stomped on enough lately by Mr. Fucked-Off-to-London. You might as well crush on a unicorn."

Nova's grin faded. Isaac smiled, victorious, and marched ahead of her. Everyone else had already gone into the diner. Nova felt her post-swim early-morning optimism drain away. She didn't belong here with these people. Even her attempt at a gentle tease had practically launched a war. Everything she'd said or done over the last twenty-four hours seemed to annoy everyone. She was the classic nerdy first year, tagging along with the cool sophomores.

Nova waited for Isaac to get ahead of her before she followed behind, dragging her feet on the parking-lot asphalt.

Al's Griddle was loud with conversation and a sizzling kitchen grill. Greasy smoke hung in the air, filling the diner with the smell of frying potatoes, onions, and bacon. They wedged their group of five into a four-person booth, with Nova pushed up against a window beside Mackenna. Nova had a view of the parking lot, with all its rusting trucks and gleaming motorcycles. Wyatt sat across from her with Isaac by his side. The two dudes kept a gap between them, acting as if nothing romantic had happened the night before.

Nova studied her oversized laminated menu, reading every option like a novel she was particularly interested in. She could feel the eyes of the other patrons on their group, checking them out. She wondered if they could somehow sense the stolen money on them, that the hundred-dollar bill Mackenna had peeled off in the SUV was only the beginning.

Which was crazy, of course.

Unless someone had seen them, somehow.

"I'm so hungry," Mackenna said, setting her menu down and raking a hand through her long blond hair. "I could probably eat one of everything."

A waitress came over with two coffee carafes. She was mom aged, with a friendly face and big hair. Her name tag said PAM.

"Hi folks. Welcome to Al's Griddle."

"Hello Pam," Landon said, smiling as he looked up from his menu. "Good morning."

"Who wants coffee?"

Everyone raised their hand.

Pam grinned. "Well, all right, then."

Pam poured coffee all around without spilling a drop. She set the carafes down and took their order, jotting everything down on a little notepad. Pam seemed busy but content, someone totally in her element. After she left with their orders, everyone fussed with their coffee, adding cream and sugar and stirring it up with their spoons. Nova blew on her coffee and felt the steam rise into her face. It was warm in the diner, despite the air conditioning, but the steam still felt good. Like it was loosening something up behind her eyes.

Mackenna pulled out her cell phone and studied it. "It's Colton. He says he wants to show us something."

Landon leaned into Mackenna. "Is it his dick?"

Mackenna elbowed her boyfriend in the ribs, almost knocking him out of the booth.

"Don't be gross. He says we should meet him at the lodge after we eat."

"The lodge?" Wyatt asked. "Where's that?"

"The Sunshine Lodge," Mackenna said, typing into her phone. "We passed the entrance to its access road yesterday on our way up the mountain. It's a ski lodge, so it's closed from April to November. Colton and his dad work there. They, like, maintain it while the owners visit Europe every summer."

"Nice," Wyatt said. "I like ski lodges."

Pam returned with a huge tray loaded with plates and set it down on a folding stand. She handed everything out and went back to the kitchen, returning a minute later with a second tray. It was a lot of food. Nova alone had ordered eggs benedict, a short stack of buttermilk pancakes, a side of hash browns, and a side of bacon, while all three of the dudes had ordered even more food than she had. Only Mackenna had ordered no more than she would eat: a veggie omelet with wheat toast.

"Wow, you all ordered enough for a small army," Pam said, picking up the second tray and collapsing the stand.

"We are a small army," Isaac said, cutting into his French toast and looking across the table at Nova. "These are our field rations before we head into battle."

Pam smiled. "Well, good. You're growing kids. You should be eating well."

Pam took her tray and folding stand away and they dug into their food. The table got quiet as they concentrated on eating and became cocooned by the murmur of conversation around them. Everything Nova had ordered was good and she could feel the coffee and carbs kicking in, providing her with a new wave of energy. She took out her cell phone and snapped a pic of everyone eating with the table loaded with food and sent it to her mom: *Best breakfast ever!!! XOXO*. About three seconds later, her mother texted back: *Wow looks good!!* with an amazed smiley face and a bunch of hearts.

Nova put away her phone and bit into a piece of bacon. As she chewed, a truck with Wyoming plates entered the diner's parking lot and parked right in front of Nova's window. Like most cars in the lot, it was splattered with dead grasshoppers across its grill. Two men got out.

The driver was pale, pudgy, and dressed in jeans and a forest camouflage shirt that looked too big for him. The passenger was lean and tanned a deep red as if he'd been in the sun all his life. He wore a black windbreaker, which seemed weird for such a hot day. As he walked toward the diner with an easy grace, Nova was reminded of a tiger stalking its prey, conserving his energy until he really needed it.

The two men entered the diner, removed their sunglasses, and surveyed the room.

Nova felt a strange buzz as the red-tanned man's gaze swept across their booth and their eyes met.

The man paused, as if filing Nova's face in his memory, before speaking to the hostess and following her to a booth on the other side of the room.

"So, what do you think, Nova?"

Nova shook her head, chasing away a shiver rising up the middle of her back. Mackenna was looking at her, expecting an answer to something.

"You want to go to the ski lodge and see whatever Colton wants to show us?"

Nova blinked. "Sure. Why not?"

17

DEPUTY SERRANO WOKE IN A TANGLE OF DAMP, TWISTED BED-sheets. The spot on the bed where her husband usually slept was empty, and sunlight shone along the edges of their bedroom curtains. She felt hungover, though she hadn't had anything to drink the night before. The alarm clock said it was already past eleven, much later than she normally slept, even after a late shift. What was going on? Where was—

Serrano sat up, remembering.

Marty Carson was dead.

Jeff Heller was dead.

Serrano swung her legs out of bed and set her feet on the floor. She leaned forward and put her head between her knees, focusing on her breathing. An unwelcome image of Sheriff Carson appeared in her mind, an arrow sticking out of each shoulder. Enormous gashes in his legs and across his chest. A rope of pink intestine spilling out of his stomach, not unlike a rope of sausage. His eyes carved out and missing. His empty eye sockets staring into something terrible and dark.

Deputy Serrano took a deep breath and blocked out the image. She exhaled. Took another breath. Waited for time to pass. The bed she was sitting on and the floor beneath her feet both felt like they might give way at any moment. It was like she'd woken up in a terrible alternate reality. She rubbed her eyes, which felt raw, and looked around her bedroom through a blurred filter. She stood up on shaky legs, walked over to the safe sitting on her dresser, and punched in the code to unlock it.

The safe was empty.

"Shit."

So, it was all real. Sheriff Carson and Deputy Heller were dead. The state police, DEA, and FBI had all swooped in to investigate the crime scene, which only a few hours earlier had simply been a sleepy police station. Serrano had spent three hours answering their endless questions before they'd taken her badge and gun away and sent her home on indefinite paid leave while they investigated the homicide of two officers and the theft of approximately five million dollars. Everyone had been studying her with mistrustful eyes. Acting like she should feel lucky that she was being allowed to go home at all rather than being arrested right there on the spot.

Which Serrano understood. They were all just doing their jobs, and she was the first witness on the scene, the first to call in the homicides and the only living witness who had seen the money. Still. It was infuriating, not being allowed to work right when one of the biggest crimes in Wyoming's history had happened in her own hometown.

Deputy Serrano realized her house was quiet. Way too quiet. It was a Saturday. The boys were normally up and crashing around by now, their energy filling the house as they shouted and fought and wrestled from room to room. Serrano put on her robe, opened her bedroom door, and shuffled out into the hallway. She listened.

"Hello? Miguel?"

Nobody answered.

"Manny? Alex?"

A small orange cat appeared at the end of the hallway. It stared at Serrano with green eyes flecked with gold.

"Hey Mooshy. Where is everybody?"

The tabby cat opened its mouth and let out a silent meow. Deputy Serrano walked along the hall and poked her head into the bedroom her two sons shared. The floor was covered in the usual heaps of clothes and toys and the beds were unmade. No boys, though, and the room felt empty without their bubbling presence. Serrano continued down the hallway into the living room. Three pairs of shoes were missing from the shoe mat, one big pair and two little pairs. Her husband's car keys were missing from their hook.

Serrano went into the kitchen, where she found a note in her husband's chunky handwriting.

Hey babe,

Thought you could use a quiet house today. I dropped the boys off at Grandma's for the weekend before going to work. Call my cell if you need anything.

Love you!
Miguel

Deputy Serrano left the note on the counter, shuffled back through the living room, passed through the central hallway, and went into the bathroom. She hung up her robe and turned on the shower. Steam filled the bathroom. Serrano stepped into the shower stall without checking the water's temperature. She didn't mind how it scalded her skin. She lathered up with body wash and scrubbed and scrubbed. She tilted her head toward the shower-head, seeking its heat like a flower seeking sunlight, and she began to weep into the water's constant pressure. She'd showered when she'd come home from the police station earlier that morning, but she still didn't feel clean. She could still smell death in her nostrils and taste the copper tang of blood. She wept and scrubbed and wept some more. She stood in the shower until the water turned lukewarm and then she turned the water off.

Serrano stepped outside the shower stall and dried off with a towel that was still damp from her earlier shower. The bathroom was warm and full of steam. Serrano couldn't see herself in the mirror, but it was probably for the best. She thought about how all her life she'd thought of herself as a tough realist, the daughter of Mexican immigrants, people who'd been forced to leave their country and work themselves to the bone just to survive, but she'd always thought life was basically fair. You did a good job and you were eventually rewarded. You lived a good life, good things happened to you. Sure, accidents happened sometimes, or people were stricken by God with terrible diseases, but it had all seemed to be part of a greater plan Serrano was happy to abide by. God's plan.

But what had happened to Marty Carson . . .

No.

It did not seem like it could be a part of any plan at all. No sensible plan would call for such suffering from an upright man. A man simply doing his job.

Serrano finished drying off and got dressed. She went into their bedroom closet, where a second safe was located, and retrieved her civilian gun, a compact Glock 19. She loaded the

Glock's magazine with fifteen bullets, inserted the magazine, and thumbed the slide back. She couldn't be an official police officer today, but there was no law against a civilian enjoying her time off and taking a look around. The deputy felt an urge to return to Claw Heart Mountain, sensing she'd perhaps missed something the day before. Something simple yet important.

Besides, Serrano had nothing better to do. She sure as hell wasn't going to sit around her house and cry all day.

18

THE SUNSHINE LODGE AND SKI RESORT WASN'T ANYTHING TOO fancy. Colton Morgan met them in front of a staircase that led from the parking lot up to the lodge, a big grin plastered on his freckled face. The lot was empty except for what must have been Colton's truck, parked right beneath the stairs. As they climbed the stairs, Colton explained the resort had only twelve ski runs—two easy, three intermediate, four expert, and three expert only (aka double black diamonds)—and one terrain park. Claw Heart Mountain was several hours from Yellowstone National Park and, with a summit elevation of 9,845 feet, was a total shorty compared to a lot of mountains; but a mountain was still a mountain, and skiers had been steadily coming to the resort since it opened in 1952.

Or so Colton claimed. Nova wasn't too sure about the popularity of the resort these days. It didn't look much like the fancy ski resorts she knew. The main lodge seemed shaggy, its wooden exterior faded in the August sunlight and its windows caked with dust. It had a triangular roof that made it look like a church, two massive stone chimneys, and a wooden deck that wrapped around its second floor.

"Maybe it looks better in the winter," Mackenna whispered to Nova as Colton gave them his tour-guide lecture, which he'd obviously given many times before.

"Shit, I hope so."

Both girls giggled. It was always funny to whisper while somebody else was giving a big speech about something. Besides the massive lodge, Colton continued, there was a dining hall, a spa, a medical building, and a maintenance building. The lodge had its own bar in the basement for overnight guests only.

"Oooh," Mackenna said, leaning toward Nova. "A sexy basement VIP bar."

"Yeah. Maybe we'll go down there and get lucky tonight."

Both girls giggled again and Colton smiled bashfully, embarrassed by his own enthusiasm for the Sunshine Lodge. Nova had to admit it was sweet how much Colton cared about the dumpy ski resort and how he'd been showing off ever since they'd arrived the day before. He was like a big, friendly puppy dog, looking for attention from the new visitors with all their new-visitor smells.

Colton led them along the sidewalk and up the hill toward the main lodge. Nova bumped Mackenna with her hip. "He's doing all this for you, you know," Nova said, not whispering, exactly, but speaking lower than the general conversation. "He's trying to impress you."

Mackenna rolled her eyes. "Shut up, Nova. Colton and I have known each other since, like, we were five."

"Did you ever kiss him or anything?"

Mackenna grinned. "Maybe."

"Ha. I knew it."

Mackenna ran a hand through her hair, which glowed like blond fire in the sunlight. "I've kissed a lot of guys, Nova. And you saw what it's like in Cloud Vista. There's not a lot of options when you're hanging around with your family."

Nova snorted. She had to admit Mackenna had a good point. She might have made out with Colton a time or two if she'd been in Mackenna's place. Hanging around a mountain all day, listening to the wind blowing through the trees and the cicadas buzzing nonstop. She thought of that famous poem by William Wordsworth, the one about wandering lonely as a cloud.

"Anyway," Mackenna said, "I'm with Landon now and Colton knows it. I think you're the one he's trying to impress."

Nova shaded her eyes with her hand, looking up at Colton as he joked with the dudes. "Yeah right. Compared to you, I must look like a mouse to him."

Mackenna laughed and slapped Nova's shoulder. "Are you kidding? You're cute AF. Big guys like him love petite brunette chicks. And your pixie haircut? So punk rock, especially around here. He's probably so intimidated by you, he doesn't know what to say."

"Right," Nova said, but she smiled and blushed with pleasure. Mackenna had never really given her a compliment about her looks before. Nova had wondered if Mackenna liked having her around just because she made Mackenna look taller, blonder, and bustier by comparison.

Colton led them past the lodge toward a chairlift. Nova had been so engrossed in talking with Mackenna she hadn't noticed the chairlift was operational, humming with electricity and creaking with movement as its bench seats slowly went around. Each bench was wide enough for two people in bulky winter coats and their skis. They were open, like park benches, so you could hop on and off, relying only on a curved tilt to keep people from falling off.

Colton stopped in the embarkation area for the chairlift and raised his arms in the air. "Ta-da!"

Nova looked at the others, who seemed as confused as she was.

"A chairlift?" Isaac said, staring at Colton through his sunglasses. "That's what you wanted to show us?"

"Not exactly. More like where it's going to take us."

Colton gestured higher up the mountain, where a blotch of brown sat perched on a rocky shelf, encircled by pine trees. "The Lookout Bar," Colton said. "The view is amazing, and today it's all ours. I have a skeleton key for all the buildings."

"Awesome," Mackenna said, clapping her hands. "The view up there really is super pretty. You can see, like, all the way to Scorpion Creek."

Colton pointed to a green plastic cooler Nova hadn't noticed sitting in the grass. "My mom made us lunch. She went crazy on the sandwiches."

"Is there beer?" Landon asked.

"No," Colton said, his smile faltering. "My mom isn't that cool."

"I've got weed," Wyatt said, raising his hand in the air.

Landon grinned. "Good enough for me."

Mackenna slugged Landon in the shoulder. "Not everything needs to be about getting stoned, you know."

"I know," Landon said, still grinning like a dope as he rubbed his shoulder. "It just makes everything better."

They paired up to ride the chairlift. Wyatt and Isaac went first, then Mackenna and Landon, then Nova and Colton, the plastic cooler wedged between them. The chairlift was old and noisy, but it gathered them smoothly enough, taking their weight as they settled into the bench and rose into the air. Nova's stomach shifted at the sudden weightless feeling, but it was also exhilarating, something she hadn't known she needed. It could be exhausting, being tied down to the earth all the time, allowing gravity to keep you imprisoned with its pull.

Colton didn't say anything as they rose higher. Nova realized he was giving her space to appreciate the view and take it all in. He'd seen it hundreds of times before, maybe thousands, but he knew this was her first time seeing Claw Heart Mountain from the air. Nova scanned the tiny trees and the mountain's rocky outcroppings, looking for ridgelines, houses, and other telltale markers. She wondered if she could see the spot where they'd hidden the money from here, or if it was farther around the mountain.

That was another thing she felt less connected to up here.

The money.

"It's beautiful," Nova said. "You live in a beautiful place, Colton."

"I know," Colton said, nodding as the wind tousled his copper hair. "Sometimes I actually dream about the mountain."

"Really? Like what about it?"

Colton closed his eyes. Their bench rocked gently and Nova leaned even deeper into the bench's curved pocket.

"Sometimes I dream I'm hiking through a valley in the mountain. Somewhere hidden and off-trail, where nobody ever goes. Maybe somewhere nobody has ever gone. I'm by myself, but I'm not lost. I think I know where I'm going and I'm not worried. I'm just exploring."

Colton opened his eyes. They were high up now. Forty feet, at least. If somebody jumped off the lift here, they'd break their legs. Maybe die. Nova had read online about a depressed snowboarder in Boulder who'd killed himself that way. Just detached from his snowboard, chucked his helmet, and leaned forward until he plummeted headfirst into a boulder fifty feet below.

"I keep hiking," Colton continued. "I notice birds watching me. All kinds of birds. Crows. Sparrows. Vultures. Mountain jays.

Robins. They're perched in the trees and on boulders and lined up all along the valley wall, on both sides, like an audience. I ignore them and keep going. I come to a cave at the end of the valley. It's dark and loud."

Nova licked her lips. The hot wind was drying them out. "Loud? What do you mean?"

Colton looked at her. "There's, like, a howling noise. Like the wind, but not. Like something half wind and half alive." He leaned back and tilted his face toward the sun. "Sometimes the dream ends right there, but sometimes it keeps going. Sometimes the birds start screeching behind me, like they're cheering me on, and I enter the cave. The cave is dark and the howling is even louder. I keep going until I look back and see the opening to the cave is only this small rectangle of daylight, so far away. When I look up, I can tell I'm inside the mountain now. Like, standing inside its inner-most chamber."

Their destination appeared up ahead. The brown blotch Nova had seen earlier had turned into a cute wooden chalet. In another minute, Isaac and Wyatt's chairlift bench would arrive at the top of the ridge and drop them off first.

"The howling inside the cave grows so loud it makes me cover my ears," Colton said. "It's so, so loud. When I can't take it any-more, I start howling too, like I might as well join it."

Colton exhaled.

"And then, just like that, it stops. The howling stops and the mountain is totally quiet. Even the wind disappears."

Nova swallowed, trying to imagine that kind of silence. It would feel so huge. As if it was trying to crush you under its silent weight.

"The silence makes me feel sad," Colton admitted, as if he knew what she was thinking. "I feel so lost and sad that I wake up."

The mountain was rushing toward them now.

Nova reached across the plastic cooler and put her hand on Colton's shoulder.

"So, you never get out of the cave?"

Colton shook his head.

"No. I don't."

19

THE OTHERS WERE WAITING FOR THEM, CLUSTERED ON THE hillside beneath the Lookout Bar. They cheered as Nova and Colton hit the ground running, lugging the cooler between them until they cleared the moving bench and were able to drop it on the ground. Nova basked in the cheering, unable to repress a smile.

"Nice work, Nova," Landon said, coming up and picking up the cooler by himself, his muscles popping out of his white tank top. "You can haul."

"Thanks, Landon."

Nova turned around. The view from above all the ski runs was amazing, as promised, and the air was clear enough she could make out a gray smudge in the distance that must have been a town, connected to the mountain by a thin strand of highway. Everything else in sight was hills, carrying on in all directions, like waves on a greenish-white sea. Nova imagined standing in the same spot the day before. You could have seen Mackenna's SUV approaching the mountain for a long time, though it would have been the size of an ant. A little tiny ant, slowly crawling across the landscape with no idea what it was going to find.

Feeling a poem floating in the back of her mind, Nova patted the front pocket of her capris, instinctively checking for the little spiral notepad she liked to carry with her. She took it out with the purple mini-pen she kept clipped to it and flipped to an empty page.

She sat in the grass while the others talked around her, feeling the world recede while she made a sketch of the landscape. Nova wasn't great at drawing, but she tried to catch the gist of a scene in a way taking a cell phone pic never managed to. A digital picture was too accurate, too clear. It blocked the floating, free-associating part of her brain, where the best lines and images seemed to come from.

A picture left nothing to the imagination, when all she wanted was imagination.

Once the sketch was done, Nova wrote a little poem beneath it, then closed the notepad, satisfied to have written something during the trip. She sat back and stretched her legs out, rolling her capris up to her knees. She curled her toes inside her lace-up Keds, wondering if she should take them off and let her feet get some air. Her feet always seemed to be too hot in the summer and too cold in the winter. Her mother said Nova got her poor circulation from her side of the family.

"Hey."

Wyatt sat beside her in the grass. He did it so casually Nova was caught off guard. Maybe everything came so free and easy when you were as cute and cool as Wyatt. Like the whole world was just waiting to see what you would do next.

"I saw you writing. New poem?"

Nova closed one eye and squinted at Wyatt. "Maybe."

"That's tight. I guess if you were going to get inspiration from anywhere, high up on a mountain would be a good place, right?"

"Yeah. It's beautiful up here."

Nova glanced over her shoulder, half expecting Isaac to be looming nearby and glowering, but everyone else had wandered away toward the bar, which really did look like a mini version of the shaggy lodge below, including lots of big windows and a deck. Every building in the resort had probably been built at the same time, by the same builders using the same materials. A sign on the roof proclaimed LOOKOUT BAR. Landon had set the cooler down on the deck beside a picnic table and everyone was leaning against the deck railing, taking in the view. Everyone looked relaxed, even happy in the sunshine.

"Can I ask you something?"

Nova turned to look at Wyatt. "Sure."

Wyatt hunched forward and hugged his knees. "Do you believe in heaven?"

Nova nodded. "Sure. I guess."

"My whole family believes in it," Wyatt said, picking a piece of grass and sticking it in the corner of his mouth. "They're all super Christian and stuff. Southern Baptist."

"That's cool."

Wyatt laughed.

"I don't know about cool. It's intense, though. Lots of 'Praise Jesus.'"

Nova didn't say anything. Her family was Methodist. She didn't know much about Baptists, though the name made her think of tent revivals, loud choirs, and people standing up and speaking in tongues.

"Yesterday, when we found the money, I thought it was God giving us his blessing," Wyatt said, twirling the strand of grass in his mouth. "Now, I'm not so sure."

"You're not?"

Wyatt shook his head. "I keep feeling this uneasiness, you know? Deep in the pit of my stomach. I'm starting to wonder if maybe God wasn't blessing us but instead was, like, testing us, you know? Like the money was a test and we failed."

Nova leaned back and peered into the blue sky. She tried to picture God up there somewhere, taking the time to test a couple of puny teenagers. Going to the trouble of making an armored van loaded with money appear out of nowhere.

"I don't know, Wyatt. That seems crazy elaborate. Even for God."

"But you voted no yesterday. You told us it was wrong and we shouldn't take it."

Nova shrugged. "I was scared. There are a lot of things I don't do because I'm scared."

Wyatt went quiet, thinking. He plucked the strand of grass from his mouth and threw it in the air, where it caught a breeze and went spinning away. Nova looked out across the crackling hills and into the distance. A truck was headed toward the mountain from Scorpion Creek, its shape shimmering like a mirage, and Nova couldn't help wondering who else was visiting the mountain now.

———

Nova and Wyatt walked to the Lookout Bar and climbed the stairs to its deck. The view was even more impressive from the deck's raised perspective. So much blue sky—it felt like they were floating above the mountain itself. Below them the chairlift continued to operate, endlessly lifting benches up the mountain and spinning them back down again. On the deck, Colton popped open the plastic cooler and threw back its lid. Nova could hear ice crunching as he dug around inside the cooler and pulled out a can of sparkling water.

"I hope everyone's hungry. My mom made a ton of sandwiches and potato salad."

"Maybe in a little while," Mackenna said, holding her stomach and puffing her cheeks out. "We just ate at the diner."

"Oh," Colton said, his face deflating. "Right."

"I'll have a sparkling water, though."

Everybody else also requested water. Nova took a pomegranate, her favorite.

The sun's warmth saturated everything. Mackenna brought out a tube of sunscreen from her purse and sent it around, forcing everyone to lather up, especially Colton, with his redheaded complexion. Soon the smell of coconut hung all around them, mixing with the smell of sun-warmed pine sap and cedarwood.

"We could suntan up here," Mackenna said, stretching her elbows back and pushing her chest forward.

"I think we have lounge chairs in the back," Colton said. "I'll go check."

"I'll help," Nova said, setting her sparkling water on the table. Colton smiled at her and they started walking around the deck. The view shifted slightly with every step they took, revealing more of the mountain as they turned the first corner. As impressive as the view of the hills was to the east, the side profile of the mountain was even more beautiful. The way the trees bristled along the mountain's edge made it look like the air was blurring in the space between tree and sky.

Or maybe that was the August heat, blurring the lines between everything.

"What the hell?"

They'd just turned another corner of the wraparound deck. The bar's back door was ajar, the wood around its lock shattered.

A trail of blood ran from the door to the rear deck stairway. Colton and Nova stared at the smeared blood. "Something's inside," Colton said, his voice flat. "It broke the door."

"Maybe it's an animal," Nova said. "Maybe it's wounded and looking for shelter."

"Yeah. I doubt an animal kicked in the lock."

"Doesn't the resort have, you know, an alarm system?"

"It does," Colton said, rubbing the back of his neck, "but it kept going off at random last summer and Mr. Harris finally turned it off. He hasn't fixed or replaced it yet. He's kind of cheap about stuff like that."

Colton pushed the door open farther, stepping inside the building. Nova hovered behind him, caught between the safety of the sunlit outdoors and the mystery of the darkness inside. After a few seconds of internal debate, she followed Colton. The bar smelled like dust and mildew. They were standing in a hallway with doors along both sides. One door was marked EMPLOY-EES ONLY and the other two were restrooms. Colton flipped a switch and panels of yellow light came on in the ceiling, illuminating a trail of blood on the floor, which Nova had stepped in by accident.

"Colton," Nova whispered, tugging on his shirt. "Colton."

"You can go wait with the others," Colton said, glancing back over his shoulder. "My dad and I are the caretakers. I have to check it out. Mr. Harris trusts us."

Colton continued down the hallway. Nova gritted her teeth and followed at his heels, waiting for something bad to happen. They came out of the hallway and entered the bar's main room, which was filled with tables and benches. The trail of blood hooked past a shuttered counter and extended to another door. "The kitchen," Colton said, talking to himself as much as Nova. He pushed the door open and disappeared inside the next room.

Nova took a deep breath, her entire body humming with adrenaline, and followed him inside the bar's kitchen. He flicked on another light, revealing dusty metal counters, a big grill, two enormous refrigerators, an industrial sink, and an industrial dishwasher. The trail of blood continued toward a heavy metal door in the back. A freezer door. Colton set his hand on the handle, took a deep breath, and yanked it open.

"Fuck."

"What?" Nova said, her voice loud in the empty kitchen. "What is it?"

Colton leaned back and looked at her.

"It's some dude. And he's all bloody."

20

BANNOCK WALKED ALONG THE SWITCHBACK HIGHWAY ONCE again, this time going slower and taking his time. His gut was heavy with the biscuits and gravy he'd consumed at the Cloud Vista diner and his forehead was already beading with sweat. As always, Gideon remained behind the wheel of their vehicle, watching the highway below for approaching traffic. He was supposed to honk once for any vehicle he saw coming from Scorpion Creek and twice for anything that looked like the authorities.

Bannock hoped to avoid further entanglements. They'd already taken enough detours on this assignment. First the police station in Scorpion Creek, then the old couple back at the ranch, and now here they were, back at Claw Heart. Too much tail chasing made Bannock uneasy. It'd taken more time and energy than he'd expected to find a suitable lake to dump their Honda with the old ranch couple still trussed up in the trunk. Every lake in Wyoming either seemed to have a couple of ugly new houses set around it or proved to be too shallow due to the summer drought, or too close to a significant highway. They'd lost several hours driving around in a ridiculous two-vehicle convoy, then another hour eating at the diner, and now half the day was gone before Bannock could properly begin hunting.

Ah.

But here was something.

About thirty feet from the crash site, Bannock found spots of blood on a clump of sagebrush. The blood cast led into the trees at the point that the highway switched directions and started to climb at a new angle. Sensing a lengthy search, Bannock looked back at Gideon, gestured to indicate his intentions, and stepped into the trees, entering the woods that clung to the mountainside.

Bannock wasn't the greatest tracker alive—he had in fact personally known several far superior trackers—but he was good enough to follow a trail so obvious it was clear whoever had made it had been more worried about speed than being followed. Branches were broken all over the place, and the farther the trail went, the more splotches of blood decorated the ground. A scrap of cloth, slick and artificial, was caught in a branch. Bannock plucked it without slowing and inhaled its scent, wondering if it had come from the van's driver or the passenger. He searched the ground for footprints, but the earth was hard and dry. He scanned the terrain ahead, noted the next trampled bush, and kept going.

Bannock understood that mountain terrain could be tricky. When you had the higher ground, a mountain was wonderful, made for concealment and clear sightlines, your friend in almost any combat situation. But when you had to go up an incline, even a slight one, you had to fight gravity as well as your enemy. Gravity never stopped. Gravity never forgave a misstep. Gravity pulled at everything, pulled at the unreliable ground itself, and gravity would bury you in rock if it had the chance.

The rugged mountains of Afghanistan were a good example. Bannock had spent several years there, serving first as a young and foolhardy soldier and later returning as a hardened security contractor making six figures a year. He'd used the mountains to his advantage many times and had also, more than once, discovered the mountains had turned against him and his company, abruptly morphing into a bloody shooting gallery he'd been lucky to survive. You had to respect the mountains, not simply endure them. The mountains could tell the difference between respect and disdain and would treat you accordingly. Bannock had known numerous men who'd gone up a mountain laughing and all gung-ho, believing they were immortal, and come back down again borne on a stretcher, their bodies pulverized and lifeless.

A mountain could tell what was in your heart. It could feel it in every step you took upon its surface, right through the soles of your boots, all the way up your spine.

The broken trail went on and on, climbing up the mountain at a steep, unlikely angle. Just when Bannock thought he'd finally lost the trail's thread, he would encounter yet another broken patch of vegetation, or more blood cast off. He still could not determine if he was tracking one man, two men, or even more. The mountain's dry soil was working against him, revealing nothing but a crumbled mess of dirt and rocky scree.

Was he walking into a trap? Was an entire den of armed thieves waiting for him at the top of the mountain? If so, why the hell would they have remained on Claw Heart Mountain in the first place? Had they missed their planned extraction? Were they so badly injured, so concussed, that they'd forgotten their plan entirely?

The van's crew was a pair of Russian cousins named Dmitri and Fyodor Sobol. Dmitri was forty-two. Fyodor was forty-one. Neither man was a genius, but supposedly the Russians weren't too stupid, either. The perfect underlings, the Sobols were dumb enough that they never got big ideas but smart enough to appreciate the significant money they earned with the Organization. Both were unlikely candidates to go rogue.

But perhaps the Sobol cousins had been drinking too much vodka lately or had accrued crushing debts they could not pay through conventional criminal earnings. Maybe they thought they could outrun the Organization and the Bannocks of the world, hired guns paid to hunt for them. Maybe the Sobols thought they were invincible.

Bannock followed the broken trail through a particularly dense and unpleasant thicket of spruce trees and emerged in a short clearing of cheatgrass. Ten yards away, on the other side of the clearing, was a sheer rock face rising a good fifty feet straight up. Bannock wanted to believe he'd lost the trail back in the spruce trees, but he could see a bloody print twenty feet up the wall. It was a 5.12-level climb at least, far beyond anything Bannock would have attempted even in his younger days. How one or two wounded men had climbed it with the weight of ten million dollars in cash was beyond him. Bannock closed his eyes and pictured the map of the mountain he'd studied on their drive from Utah. If he had his current position correct, somewhere up above was a ski resort.

Bannock stepped back a few feet from the rock face and shaded his eyes with both hands.

No signs of movement.

Not even a rogue elk looking to die on the highway.

Bannock fought the urge to announce his presence to any-one who might be watching. Instead, he turned back the way he'd come and headed for the stolen truck below, where Gideon wait-ed, as patient and single-minded as a spider pretending to lie dor-mant in its web.

21

NOVA STARED ACROSS THE KITCHEN AT COLTON. UNLIKE THE mellow lights out in the barroom, the lights in the kitchen were fluorescent white and made everything look harsh and dull. Even the blood on the floor was darker. Almost black.

"What do you mean, some dude is in the freezer?"

Colton shrugged. "Look for yourself. I've never seen him before."

Nova stepped closer. She stood next to Colton's big sweaty body and cautiously leaned into the freezer. It was cooler inside, but the freezer wasn't running. A white man with a black beard and black hair was lying on the floor, curled on his side, facing the doorway. His beard and chest were matted with dried blood, but he was still breathing. He looked about Nova's father's age, somewhere between forty and fifty. He had a receding hairline, bushy eyebrows, and a big, lumpy nose. He looked like a homeless person who'd murdered someone.

Nova stepped back and closed the door, careful not to slam it too loudly. She didn't know what to say.

Colton laughed and laced his hands behind his head. He started pacing around the kitchen. "Jesus. Look at that guy. He's a trespasser. He's trespassing, right?"

Nova nodded, picturing the curled-up man. Who could sleep like that covered in so much blood? A serial killer? An escaped mental patient?

"We need to call the cops," Colton said, pulling out his cell phone. "They can deal with this shit."

Nova didn't say anything. She remembered the night before, when the cop had stopped by Mackenna's cabin. How Mackenna had lied when she'd answered the cop's questions. She'd sounded natural enough, but Nova could only imagine what would happen if they spent more time talking to the police. How easily everything could unravel.

Colton dialed 911 and held his phone to his ear. He frowned as he listened for several seconds, then ended the call.

"What the hell? It's just a busy signal."

"Oh," Nova said, trying to keep the relief she felt out of her voice. "What about your dad? We could call him, right?"

"My parents left early this morning with my sister for a softball tournament in Bozeman. They're probably there already. Bozeman is, like, seven hours away."

"Shit."

They both stared at the freezer door, straining to hear any sounds coming from behind it.

"What are you guys looking at?"

Nova and Colton both yelped and leaped backward. Mackenna laughed as she stepped closer. Nova grabbed Mackenna's wrist and dragged her to the freezer, yanked its door open without saying anything.

Mackenna stared at the bloody stranger, her eyes wide and stunned. The stranger opened his eyes, and it was Mackenna's turn to yelp.

"Holy shit," Mackenna said. "Who the fuck?"

The stranger didn't say anything. Mackenna looked from the stranger to Nova and back again.

"Is that . . . like . . . blood?"

Nova nodded.

"Fuck this," Mackenna said, waving her hands in the air. "This is insane. I'm getting the other guys."

Colton and Nova stepped aside as Mackenna rushed out of the kitchen. The stranger watched Colton and Nova through the doorway, his dark eyes blank. He sat up on the floor and hunched forward. He was plump, with a little belly, but his arms were thick with muscles and his shoulders were broad. The dried blood covering the stranger's beard, shirt, and pants crackled when he moved.

"Hey," Nova said, giving the stranger a wave.

The stranger licked his lips.

"I'm Nova. That's Colton."

The stranger stared at Nova. He thought for several seconds, his dark eyes still flat. "I am Fyodor."

Nova looked at Colton, who was swaying from side to side on his feet with nervous energy. The stranger had a Russian accent and a Russian name. She'd never read it, but Nova knew a Russian named Fyodor Dostoevsky had written *Crime and Punishment*, which was supposed to be one of the best books ever.

"Are you hurt?"

Fyodor stared at Nova, his face blank.

"Hey," Colton said. "You're covered in blood, dude."

Fyodor looked down at himself. He raised his arms and examined them as if noticing the dried blood for the first time. He patted his stomach and thighs, taking inventory.

"It is not my blood."

Nova and Colton looked at each other.

"Whose blood is it?" Nova asked.

Fyodor grunted. Instead of answering the question, he pushed himself off the floor and got to his feet. He wasn't very tall. Maybe five-seven. He was wearing a white V-neck T-shirt, black track pants, and black sneakers. A golden cross necklace hung from his neck, resting in the curls of his thick black chest hair, which was also matted with dried blood.

"Is night over?"

Nova nodded, checking her phone.

"Yeah. It's almost one o'clock."

"It is bright out?"

Nova shared another look with Colton. Fyodor's questions were freaking her out. Everything about him seemed weird.

"Yeah," Colton said. "It's totally sunny out."

Fyodor exhaled and scratched his stomach. "Good. Maybe it will help."

Mackenna returned to the kitchen with Landon, Wyatt, and Isaac. She also brought a can of sparkling water for Fyodor, who took it and guzzled it while they all watched, still stunned by his presence. Fyodor looked reluctant to leave the freezer, but Nova managed to coax him out when she told him the kitchen sink was working.

The group parted as Fyodor emerged from the freezer, the smell of his sticky, burly body pungent, his steps unsteady. Everyone watched, enthralled, as he washed up in the sink, turning the water so hot steam rose off it. Pink water ran down the drain as Fyodor scrubbed his hands and his forearms with liquid soap, then dunked his entire head under the steaming water, clawing at his dark hair. The water must have been scalding hot, but Fyodor didn't seem to mind.

Nova wondered if the Russian worked nearby and had witnessed a horrific workplace accident. Maybe he was a lumberjack or worked for an electric company. The type of work where one little mistake could leave you mutilated. Or dead.

Colton found a towel in a cupboard and handed it to Fyodor when he finished washing. The Russian dried his hands and face and rubbed out his hair. He walked out of the kitchen and into the main barroom, where he stood with his hands on his hips, sticking his gut out. He looked at the front windows without approaching them. Nova and the others trailed after him like baby ducks following their mom.

Then the Russian started speaking. He spoke slowly and clearly, as if he were in a trance. Like he had to tell his story, whether anyone was listening or not.

22

"I DELIVER THINGS. MANY THINGS. YESTERDAY, I AM DRIVING with my cousin down this mountain to make important delivery to East Coast. I am not going too fast. I always obey speed limit. I am good driver."

The Russian coughed into his hand.

"But yesterday, my luck runs out. Something crosses our road. A great hairy beast. We hit beast and I lose steering control. Our van goes off road and rolls down. We roll many times and I think I am dead man. My sight goes dark. When I wake again, I can see ground below me. I am carried, like child, and whatever carries me is moving fast. I look over and see my cousin, also being carried, and then my sight goes dark again."

Fyodor fell silent. The bar glowed with sunlit dust motes. Nova glanced at Mackenna and realized they were both thinking the same thing—this was the van's missing driver. He was no longer an abstract hypothetical, a missing person. He was right here in front of them. Nova looked at the others and saw the same realization dawning in their eyes. Everyone except Colton, though he looked troubled by thoughts of his own, as if regretting bringing the others to the closed resort in the first place.

The Russian turned and looked at their group as if suddenly remembering he had an audience. He studied their faces, one at a time, as if searching for something inside their souls he needed to confirm before he could continue. He reminded Nova of a hairy woodland beast, wild and frightened.

"When I wake again, I am lying on ground in dark. The ground is hard and cold, like rock. All around, I smell rotting like bad meat. I keep my breathing steady despite the terrible smell. I don't move for many minutes because I think something is listening somewhere in dark. I feel it waiting. I pray to Virgin Mary. I have not prayed for many years."

Fyodor scratched his matted beard. Everyone else shifted on their feet, uneasy in the silence as they waited for the Russian to continue.

Though he was speaking carefully, Fyodor seemed to be vibrating with a strange energy that felt . . . unpredictable.

"I hear movement nearby and man groaning. I know it is my cousin, Dimitri. He is waking up, but I don't speak. I try to think where we are that is dark and damp and smells so terrible."

"A cave," Mackenna said, her voice monotone. "You were in a cave."

Fyodor nodded. "*Da.*"

"Shit," Landon said. "That's messed up."

Fyodor stared at Landon, who blushed and looked down at his shoes.

"I hear my cousin groan again. He calls for help. He is loud. He says his legs are broken. Still, I do not speak. I don't want listening thing to know I am awake. I want to see what it will do now."

Nova swallowed. Her throat had become so dry, it was as if Fyodor's story was soaking the moisture out of the air all around them.

"Soon, I hear clicking noise. I look closer at darkness. I see blue spot that could be light or trick of darkness. I focus on it, try to see deep into blue spot. When my cousin begins to scream, I start crawling toward blue spot. I hear loud grunting sounds, wet sounds, and a crunch of bone being snapped. Dimitri's screams grow much louder. It is terrible, this noise."

A sympathetic moan escaped from the back of Wyatt's throat. His eyes were wide and unblinking as he listened; he didn't seem aware that he'd made any noise at all.

"I feel hot liquid spray me. It is blood. I stand and run, no longer caring if I make noise. The blue spot in darkness grows brighter. Then I am outside, standing beneath stars and moon. It is cold, deep into night, but I am away from rotten cave smell, breathing cold fresh air. I look back into cave. My cousin's screams have stopped. I take deep breath, look around mountain, and run. I run like crazy man. I do not turn back to look. I keep running down mountain until I find this place."

Fyodor exhaled and looked up at the ceiling, as if a great weight had been lifted from his shoulders. He reached down and lifted his pant leg, revealing something strapped to his ankle. Nova heard the scratch of Velcro and suddenly Fyodor was holding a gun in his hand. He waved the weapon at all of them in a lazy, sweeping gesture. He looked tired and dangerous, his dark eyes glittering.

Did he know, somehow?

Could he sense they had his money hidden in the mountain?

"I must leave now. Give me all your wallets, car keys, and cell phones, or I will shoot. Put them on floor."

"What?" Mackenna said, her mouth falling open. "You're going to . . . rob us?"

"Yes. I will not ask again."

Isaac made a chuffing sound, as if he couldn't believe what he'd just heard. He stepped forward and raised his hand in the air, pointing at the Russian.

"Fuck you, dude—"

"Fuck me?!" Fyodor boomed, his chest puffing out as his back straightened and he rose to his full height. "No. I do not think so. How about fuck you?"

Fyodor pointed the gun and fired. The gunshot was so loud Nova's mind went blank. Fyodor said something she couldn't hear as Isaac crumpled to the floor, clutching his stomach, his eyes enormous with surprise.

23

AS DEPUTY SERRANO DROVE UP CLAW HEART MOUNTAIN, SHE
noticed a pickup truck parked along the side of the road. A pale
man wearing sunglasses and a forest camo shirt was sitting in the
truck, fussing with his cell phone. He didn't have his hazards on,
or indicate distress in any manner, but the vehicle's presence was
unusual. Nobody stopped near the bottom of the mountain, right
on the verge of hitting the open plains. Usually, if you stopped
on the switchback highway at all, it was because your engine had
stalled while trying to make the ascent. Also, the pale man was
parked close to where she'd discovered the armored van the day
before, which was . . . interesting.

Serrano slowed as she passed the truck, crossed over the oncoming lane, and pulled over twenty feet farther up the road. She
studied the truck in her rearview mirror and reminded herself she
wasn't a cop today. She was just a civilian, checking on the welfare
of another possibly stranded civilian.

That was all. She didn't even have her county-issued laptop to run his plates.

So what? a voice in her head said. *That doesn't mean you can't write it down.*

It was Sheriff Carson's voice.

"Oh, hell no," Serrano said out loud, peering up at the sky through her windshield. "Are you going to haunt me now, Sheriff?"

No reply. Nothing in her truck's cab rattled or moved like it was possessed. Serrano waited another couple of seconds, in case there was some kind of time delay with messages from the afterlife, before taking out her cell phone and texting herself the truck's license plate. She twisted in her seat and took a picture of the truck for good measure.

"Okay, that should make you happy, Sheriff."

Still no reply. Deputy Serrano slipped her phone back into her pocket. She opened her door and dropped to the highway. She unsnapped the button on her holster, patted her Glock for good luck, and strolled up to the parked truck. The driver had his engine idling and was sitting ramrod straight now, watching her approach in his rearview mirror. Serrano waved and smiled, hoping to reassure him, but her face felt stiff with grief and exhaustion. The driver's expression didn't change. Serrano scanned the bed of his pickup, saw it was empty, and knocked on the driver's window.

The driver turned and looked at her. Up close, he looked even paler, almost bookish, even with the dark sunglasses. After a long pause, the driver rolled down his window and a gust of chilled air blew out. He wasn't listening to music. He'd been sitting in dead silence, right on the side of a narrow switchback road.

"Hi there," Serrano said. "Do you need any help?"

The driver removed his sunglasses and stared at her. He had the strangest blue eyes she'd ever seen. Bright and dead at the same time.

"Why would I need help?"

Serrano smiled.

"Well, you're parked on the edge of a hazardous highway. Not an ideal place for a rest."

The driver turned and looked through the truck's windshield, as if pondering this statement. His hands were down at his sides, not ideal positioning. He could pull a gun without impediment.

"I guess I am. Thanks for letting me know."

Serrano noticed two plastic trash bags in the cab's backseat, stuffed full of something. Maybe clothes. Maybe not. "Haven't seen you around here before. You live on the mountain?"

The driver stared at her. He definitely gave off a creepy vibe. "Are you a police officer?"

"Yes, I am, but I'm off duty."

"Off duty but still packing heat," the driver said, smiling. "Must be expecting a wild Saturday night."

The driver's teeth were so straight and gleaming white they were distracting, like the blinding shine off the surface of a river.

"We had two officers in the area killed last night," Serrano said. "I'm just taking precautions."

"My, isn't that terrible. Two officers. I hadn't heard that."

Serrano didn't say anything.

The driver smiled again, wider this time. "Well, Officer, my name is Gideon, and I'm just passing through. I just have to make a phone call and I'll be on my way. You have a good night."

Gideon rolled up his window before Serrano could reply. Unable to think of an additional reason to continue pestering him, the deputy walked back to her truck. Right as she buckled her seat belt, her cell phone chimed. She'd received a text with a photo attachment.

The text was from Ted Knowles, another deputy in the Scorpion County Sheriff's Department.

Hey Serrano. Know you're on leave, but they finally pulled an image off the van's security camera. Looks like teenagers grabbed a chunk of the cash, but nobody recognizes them and nothing from NCIC yet. Anybody look familiar?

Serrano pulled up the image and enlarged it on her phone's screen. The photo was blurry and imperfect, but you could see five teenagers looming above the camera's eye. The camera had been mounted on the van's exterior, near the roof, so after the van was overturned, the camera was at ground level, making the teenagers look like giants. Two females and three males, all looking at something above the camera. Two Caucasian males, two Caucasian females, one African-American male.

Serrano studied the picture. She didn't recognize four of them, but the tall blond girl seemed familiar. She was beautiful, like a young Valkyrie. Like the girl last night. The fancy modern house on Hollow Drive, the one with all the windows.

Serrano slapped the steering wheel with her palm. She started her truck, glanced one last time in the rearview mirror at her weird new friend Gideon, and rolled back onto the highway, wishing she had her badge and a loud siren to blare.

24

THINGS HAPPENED FAST AFTER ISAAC WAS SHOT. WYATT IGNORED Fyodor and his gun and caught Isaac as he fell to the floor. Nova's ears rang from the gunfire and it took several seconds before she could hear anything. Fyodor's bearded face had gone blank, his gaze suddenly much harder than the stunned man Nova and Colton had discovered in the freezer.

"Empty your pockets," Fyodor said to the group. Nova looked at the others, still stunned enough that she couldn't understand what he was talking about. Mackenna, Colton, and Landon took out their phones, keys, and wallets and set them on the floor. Fyodor pointed his gun at Nova and its dark muzzle absorbed all her attention. Nova fumbled inside her canvas satchel and took out her wallet and phone. She knelt and dropped them beside the others.

Fyodor turned the gun on Wyatt.

"Now you."

Wyatt looked up from Isaac, who was sputtering in his arms. Wyatt's pupils were dilated and his nostrils flared, the tendons in his neck standing out. He looked ready to murder. "Do not fight," Fyodor said, keeping his gun steady. "Unless you want bullet in forehead." Wyatt's face held the murderous look for a few seconds until his brain caught up with his emotions and he deflated. He took out his cell phone and wallet and slid them across the floor.

Fyodor nodded at Isaac. "Jew boy too. I want all wallets and phones."

Wyatt scowled. He reached into Isaac's pockets, took out his phone and wallet, and slid them toward the others.

Isaac gasped, his eyes bright. "You . . . are . . . such . . . an asshole."

Fyodor grinned. "I did not escape from cave because I am hero."

Isaac took another sharp breath. It was painful just listening to him breathe. "What . . . makes . . . you think . . . you escaped?"

Fyodor's grin faded. "Everybody go back to freezer with arms in air. You run or fight, you end up bleeding like your bigmouth friend."

They shuffled to the kitchen with their arms raised, like the prisoners they'd suddenly become. Nobody tried to run. Landon helped Wyatt carry Isaac, who left a trail of blood as they went. Nova felt like she'd entered a nightmare, or a criminal TV show. She'd worried about a lot of things over the course of her eighteen-year-old life, but Nova had never considered the possibility she'd be taken hostage. She wasn't beautiful or famous. She wasn't important. She didn't even work at a bank. None of this made any sense.

Fyodor kept his distance as the group reached the freezer door. "Hey. Blondie. You open freezer door and hold it."

"My name's Mackenna."

"Good for you. Just do it."

Mackenna grabbed the door handle and yanked it open. She looked angry, like Wyatt.

"Big man, you go in first and stand back," Fyodor said, nodding at Colton. "We don't need you being hero."

Colton, who still seemed in shock, entered the freezer without saying anything, his broad shoulders slumped. Wyatt and Landon carried Isaac into the freezer and gently set him on the floor.

Nova looked at the fresh trail of blood Isaac had created, how it smeared right over the sticky blood trail Fyodor had left. She looked over her shoulder at Fyodor, who had his gun aimed at her. "Can we at least have some towels for Isaac?"

"No. Get in freezer."

Nova stared at Fyodor. "We gave you a towel. When you were washing the blood off your face. We brought you sparkling water."

Fyodor sighed. "Okay, Thumbelina. Get towels."

Nova went to the cupboard, grabbed an entire stack of dish towels, and took them into the freezer. She could feel Fyodor's eyes on her and wondered if she was going to be shot. She wasn't. Instead, Mackenna followed her into the freezer and shut the door behind her, sending them into total darkness.

"There's a light switch," Colton said. "Just inside the door."

Mackenna fumbled along the freezer wall until she found the switch and flipped it. A single bare lightbulb came on. They crowded around Isaac lying on the floor.

Nova handed Wyatt a handful of the dish towels. "Here. Keep those pressed around the wound. Try to slow the bleeding."

Wyatt took the towels and started pressing. Isaac groaned. Nova knelt beside him and stuck a couple towels under his head. A loud crash came from outside the freezer, making everyone flinch.

"What's that?" Landon said.

"Shh," Mackenna said. She put her ear to the freezer door and listened for several seconds. "I think he's gone."

Mackenna tried the freezer door handle. It worked, but the door didn't budge, even when she put her shoulder into it and pushed.

"That must have been one of the kitchen shelves that crashed," Colton said. "The freezer door doesn't lock, so he wedged us in here."

"Motherfucker," Isaac muttered, shivering though the freezer wasn't on. Everyone slid down the wall and sat around their wounded friend as if he were a Ouija board that could tell them their future. Nobody spoke. They just listened to Isaac shivering and muttering and replayed what had just happened in their minds. Trying to process everything. Trying to figure out what to do next.

The freezer was empty except for a bare metal shelf in back. Nova guessed the freezer was about six feet wide and eight feet deep. Colton and Landon stood up and tried to push open the freezer door together, heaving their shoulders and backs into it, grunting, but the door didn't move.

"Isaac's still bleeding," Wyatt said, his voice wavering. "He needs to go to the hospital."

Isaac's blood had started to puddle beneath him, despite the towels. Nova tried to remember how many pints of blood were in the human body. Eight? Ten? Isaac wasn't that big of a dude. He couldn't have that much blood inside him.

"This is so fucked," Landon said, leaning forward with his head in his hands. "I can't believe Fyodor shot him. Just like that. Bang."

"We were all there," Mackenna said, hugging herself. "We know what happened, Landon."

"I'm just saying. I can't believe it."

"We don't have any food or water," Colton said, still on his feet with his forehead pressed against the freezer door. "It could be days until anyone comes looking for us."

This idea made everyone go quiet again.

"Do you guys think he was telling the truth?" Landon asked. "About being carried away into that cave with his cousin?"

"No way," Mackenna said, shaking her head. "He was just messing with us."

"Why would he mess with us?"

"Because he's crazy, that's why."

Nova watched a fresh wave of blood leak out beneath Isaac and drew her legs further back, leaning against the freezer wall. "Fyodor had to get up here somehow," she said, staring at the tops of her shoes.

"It could be the Wraith," Landon said, scratching the metal floor with his fingernail. "From the campfire story last night? What was his name? Sutton? It could be him. It could be the Wraith. He could still be hungry."

"That's just an old ghost story," Colton said, turning from the freezer door to look down at them. "Nobody's ever really seen Sutton. I wouldn't be surprised if somebody on the town council made him up for publicity. You know, like the Loch Ness Monster, in Scotland?"

Nova stood and flexed her calves. She stood right next to Colton, almost touching him. "Why else would Fyodor be here?" she asked. "Why would he be sleeping in the freezer, covered in dried blood?"

"Who knows? He's obviously crazy."

"Maybe he isn't," Nova said. "Maybe he's telling the truth. I don't think he'd abandon his van just to come all the way up here and break into the Lookout Bar. Whatever he was delivering, it was probably valuable. He wouldn't just leave it like that."

Colton frowned. "His van? How do you know he was driving a van? He never said what they were driving."

Nova looked at the others. Everyone looked even queasier, if that was possible.

"What?" Colton asked, crossing his arms. "What is it?"

Nova could feel herself growing increasingly paranoid and wondered if Colton somehow knew more than he was letting on. She was saved from responding to his question by a loud metallic squeal outside the freezer. The freezer door opened about a foot wide and Fyodor appeared in the gap, holding his gun. Though he'd washed his face, his clothes were still dark with dried blood.

"I need two people to go down mountain with me."

"I'll go," Colton said, raising his hand. "My dad and I are the resort's caretakers. I can help you find stuff in the lodge if you want."

Fyodor made a clicking sound, thinking. He pointed his gun at Landon, then at Nova. "No. I will take Pretty Boy and Thumbelina. They are skinny. We will fit on chairlift together, like one big happy family."

25

NOVA SHUDDERED AND STEPPED FORWARD. SHE COULDN'T HELP but feel relieved to be leaving the freezer and its iron blood smell, even with a gun pointed at her. Fyodor prodded her and Landon outside to the front deck, which was still baking in the sunshine and windy mountain heat. The view down the ski runs and out across the grassy Wyoming hills was still beautiful, indifferent to what had happened inside the Lookout Bar and whatever might happen to them now. Colton's plastic cooler was open and one of the picnic tables was littered with balled-up plastic wrap and empty cans of sparkling water.

"Good food," Fyodor said. "Plenty of meat."

"We didn't make the sandwiches," Landon said, as if this mattered. "Colton's mom did."

Fyodor belched. Nova noticed their phones on a patio picnic table. Their screens were all smashed and their cases shattered, their plastic and metal guts spread everywhere.

"Our phones . . ."

"Yes," Fyodor said, grinning as he saw the sad look on Nova's face. "Now you cannot call for help."

They walked down to the lift's loading station, where the chairlift was still operating. Fyodor made all three of them cram into the same bench, with Nova wedged in the middle. He kept the muzzle of his gun pushed into her ribs and explained that if he fired, the bullet would rip right through Nova's body and into Landon.

"You understand? One bullet for two?"

They nodded. The chair began to descend the mountain along its cables, creaking with each gust of wind. Unlike going up the mountain, you rose high up in the air almost immediately when you were going down. They climbed twenty, thirty, forty feet into the air.

"It is nice up here," Fyodor said, turning his face to the sun, his gun still poking into Nova's ribs. "Relaxing, yes?"

Nova didn't say anything. She'd started to feel cold all over, even though it was hot in the afternoon sunlight. She leaned forward and vomited, her chest hitching so violently that both Fyodor and Landon grabbed hold of her to keep her from falling off. When she realized how close she'd just come to plunging to her death, Nova vomited up a second, deeper batch of what might have been her breakfast pancakes.

"*Tsch-tsch*," Fyodor said, leaning away from her. "Too much fun for Thumbelina."

Nova closed her eyes and leaned back in the curved bench. She tried to breathe despite the tightness in her chest. "Are you okay?" Landon asked, still gripping her arm. Nova nodded, though she wasn't okay. Not at all.

Fyodor laughed until he coughed and had to pound his chest. The dried blood stench coming off him was bad, even with the mountain winds.

"You Americans are all like child. You have never known hard life. Today is nothing. Your friend getting shot is nothing. You are weak because you have never lived between stone and scythe. You thought invisible virus was end of world. You have never been sharpened by true hunger."

Their bench rocked as the wind gusted. Nova leaned into Landon, who put his arm around her.

"It's going to be okay, Nova. I promise."

Nova opened her eyes, which were watering from the high winds. She wiped the water from her eyes and stared into the trees far below. The Russian was right, she thought. They were all a bunch of privileged brats. The hardest thing about their lives until today had been how easy it all was. How hard it could be to be comfortable and safe.

Then something moved in the trees up ahead.

Something big.

"Oh," Nova whispered to herself.

A hundred yards down the mountain, an enormous creature lumbered out from among the trees. Shaped like a man—with a head, torso, two arms and two legs—it must have been eight or nine feet tall, like a walking tree. Its body was covered in a thick bluish-green fur that blended into its surroundings, though patches of clammy white skin showed through here and there, as if it had mange. Despite its broad shoulders and muscular arms, it looked malnourished, not only its ribs but its entire skeleton prominent beneath its fur. Its head, which was pale and hairless, resembled a human head, but one that had been made out of wax and then melted by fire. Its mouth was stretched unnaturally wide, revealing a horrifying nest of jagged teeth, and its eyes were two pale orbs, pupilless, like the eyes of creatures who lived in the deepest parts of the ocean. It looked part woodland, part subterranean, and part hell demon.

"Landon," Nova said, sitting up and trying to catch her breath. "Landon."

"What?"

"Look. Down there."

The chairlift was already bringing them closer to the creature, which seemed to be sniffing the air through two gaps where its nose should have been, its chin tilted toward the sky. It had no ears—just two dark, possibly aural cavities where a human's ears would sit—and the pale skin on its face was pulled so tightly across its skull it looked like it didn't have skin at all. What looked like dried blood was caked around its mouth and splattered across its chest.

"Holy shit," Landon said. "Is that—"

"Shut up," Fyodor growled, his voice low. "It will hear you."

The chairlift kept moving, bringing them closer to the creature as it continued to smell the air. It was blind, Nova realized, hunting by smell and sound. Like a huge mole with long legs and claws for hands.

Nova stared at the creature's gnashing teeth, realizing that Fyodor had not been messing with them. She leaned toward Landon, bringing her mouth right against his ear.

"It's real," she whispered. "The Wraith is real."

Landon looked at her with wide eyes. He looked down at the creature. It swiped at the air around it with its claw-like hands, working itself into a frenzy. It was everything you could want from a nightmare.

Holy shit, Landon mouthed.

They kept moving.

Lower.

And lower.

When they passed above the Wraith, it was only ten or twelve feet below them. It must have caught their smell in the air, because it let out an ear-splitting shriek that made Nova jump in her seat. It was a primal noise unlike anything she'd ever heard before, a ravenous, aching sound that rose out of the depths of its emaciated body.

Nova, Landon, and Fyodor all turned to watch as the chairlift continued gliding down the mountain. The Wraith began to follow their bench, its long legs smoothly gliding along, covering the ground in huge strides. They were only halfway down, with about five minutes left, but already they'd dropped at least ten feet closer to the ground. In another two or three minutes, they'd be close enough to the ground that the Wraith could leap up and grab them, plucking them from the chairlift like ripe fruit from a tree.

"I think he knows we're up here," Landon whispered.

Fyodor removed the gun from Nova's ribs and reached behind her. She thought he was going to shoot at the Wraith, which was closing on them, but instead the Russian swung his arm around with force and cracked Landon in the back of the head with his gun. Landon made a small sound that might have been *O* and fell forward, dropping off the chairlift bench so quickly Nova didn't have time to grab him. She turned and saw Landon hurtling through the air, his arms and legs fluttering, plunging to the ground like a flightless newborn bird falling from its nest. He landed facedown on the grassy edge of the ski run, narrowly missing a cluster of rocks protruding along the run's edge.

"Landon!" Nova screamed. He didn't move. He just lay facedown on the ground, motionless, while the Wraith approached him, sniffing the air and gnashing its teeth. Nova turned to Fyodor, her heart bumping in her chest. The Russian was pulling out a tangled bungee cord from his pocket.

"How could you do that? It's going to kill him!"

"That was the idea," Fyodor said, calmly straightening the bungee cord. "A pretty boy makes nice bait, no? Everything likes something pretty."

Nova stared at the Russian, her mind going blank with rage. She wanted to plunge forward and strangle him until his fat head popped off his neck. Instead, Nova looked back as the chairlift continued to descend and saw the Wraith standing over Landon, looking down at him with colorless eyes. So absorbed in the scene, Nova didn't even notice as Fyodor grabbed her wrists and tied them together, knotting the bungee cord tight around them. The Wraith reached down with one long arm, scooped Landon up and threw him over its bony shoulder like a sack of dirty laundry.

Landon didn't fight back or try to escape. He just flopped around on the creature's shoulder, as if all his bones had been removed, his blond head bobbing back and forth. If he was still alive, he wasn't conscious. The Wraith let out another ear-splitting shriek and strode into the trees, disappearing as if it had never been there at all.

Fyodor grunted in approval.

"He is bait. You are bait. Why else I bring you down mountain?"

26

BANNOCK AND GIDEON SAT IN THE TRUCK THEY'D STOLEN FROM the old ranch couple. The truck's air-conditioning felt good to Bannock after his hike. He drank deeply from the 1.5-liter bottle of water he'd purchased earlier that day. He'd been stupid not to bring along any water on his hike, given the August heat and the unknown distance he'd set out to cover. It was a small mistake, relatively, but another reminder of the rust he'd been feeling on this job.

Or maybe it was just age. Bannock was getting too old for all this dicking around in the mountains, chasing Russian ghosts who could lose significant amounts of blood while somehow remaining capable of scaling great slabs of rock. Maybe he was approaching that inevitable moment when he should go to ground one final time, relocate to a truly untraceable location and destroy all the contact phones his clients had given him. He'd made more than enough money over the years, and it was mere pride that kept him working, pride in his abilities and the love of the hunt. If he could find the Sobol cousins and the stolen money, the three million he'd pocket in payment from the Organization would be more than enough to send him into a plush retirement. He'd always loved Argentina. Or maybe Thailand.

"So the wall went straight up the mountain?"

Bannock looked at Gideon. He'd almost forgotten the other man was sitting beside him.

"More or less. Only an expert could have climbed it."

Gideon held up his phone, showing Bannock a picture of the Sobol cousins. They both had beer guts and shaggy beards.

"These gentlemen?"

Bannock finished off the bottle of water, put its cap back on, and tossed it into the truck's footwell.

"Maybe they used some kind of winch."

"A winch?" Gideon said, looking again at the picture on his phone. "That seems like a lot of effort."

"They could have set it up ahead of time. Had a third guy waiting up there to lift them up. Another cousin, maybe."

"Right," Gideon said, smirking. "Or maybe they shot a couple of grappling hooks up the mountain, like Batman. Perhaps these two slobs were really highly trained KGB operatives all along."

Bannock shook his head. "The KGB doesn't exist anymore. They're called the Federal Security Service now. And they wouldn't necessarily have a skill set like that. It would be Russian Special Forces."

Gideon stared at Bannock. The younger man seemed visibly annoyed for the first time since they'd left Utah. "Dmitri and Fyodor Sobol aren't special forces. They aren't special anything. They might win a few barroom brawls, but that's it."

Bannock shrugged. "There's a ski resort. We could look there."

"All right."

Gideon put the truck in drive. They swung around the highway and headed back up the mountain. They passed the spot
where the dead elk had lain the day before. The highway was still
marked by a dark stain of blood and a few clumps of fur-covered
hide. The markings looked too messy for the usual roadkill crew.
Something big, like a bear or a mountain lion, had likely dragged
the elk carcass away, antlers and all. That would be a good feast,
Bannock thought, especially if you were getting ready to hibernate for winter.

"A nosy lady cop came by and buzzed me while you were gone,"
Gideon said, glancing into the rearview mirror.

"Oh yeah?"

Gideon grinned, revealing a sharp, enlarged right incisor.
What you might call a snaggletooth. He reminded Bannock of a
few mercenaries he'd known. The ones that looked clean-cut and
levelheaded but liked to beat whores and break everything in sight
when they got drunk.

"The cop was off duty. She was trying to play Nancy Drew. She
didn't even have her badge on her. She had a bee in her bonnet
about our visit to the Scorpion Creek station last night. Looked
like she hadn't slept much."

Bannock leaned forward in his seat, searching for the entrance
to the ski resort.

They had to be getting close.

"Which way did she go after you finished speaking?"

"Up the mountain."

"So she could be hanging around the area."

"I guess. Or she might be driving through. It's not like Cloud
Vista is the most exciting place on a Saturday night."

"Yesterday, fifteen million dollars in cash fell from the sky on
this mountain. An off-duty cop might find that interesting. She
could have called in the plates on our truck."

Gideon grunted and leaned forward. A sign for the Sunshine Lodge and Ski Resort appeared, and Gideon turned onto the lodge's access road without having to be told. They were immediately surrounded by trees on both sides, passing through patches of shadow and light. Bannock rolled down his window, letting in the hot air and the smell of pine so he could listen to what the woods wanted to tell him. The access road was in worse shape than the highway and the truck bucked its way through a variety of potholes.

"Hasn't been repaired since last winter," Gideon said, fighting with the steering wheel. "Maybe a couple of winters."

After slowly winding around the mountain for another bumpy three miles, the trees fell away and revealed a large parking lot. Above the parking lot was a series of faux-rustic buildings, the biggest of which must have been the lodge itself. The only vehicles in the lot were a black SUV and a brown pickup truck, both parked beneath the main lodge. A stout, bearded man was loading something into the back of the SUV and hadn't noticed them yet. The other parked vehicle, the brown pickup, looked empty and abandoned in the way vehicles parked at trailheads look abandoned.

"Stop the truck," Bannock ordered.

Gideon hit the brakes.

"Back up and park lengthways across the exit. Right between the trees."

Gideon threw the truck in reverse, backed up twenty feet, and swung the truck around so it was nearly wedged between two pine trees, creating a makeshift roadblock. Bannock unbuckled his seat belt and turned around. Behind them, covered by a blanket on the floor, was Bannock's duffel bag. Above the bag, sitting right out in the open on the truck's rear bench seat, was the five million dollars they'd taken from the Scorpion Creek police station, now packaged in two humble plastic yard bags.

Bannock unzipped his duffel bag, rummaged around its numerous contents, and selected the SIG Sauer P226. He tucked the loaded gun behind his back, into his belt. He pulled out the Berretta M9 and handed the weapon to Gideon. He turned around and faced the windshield.

The SUV was now approaching from across the parking lot. When its driver noticed their truck blocking the exit, he stopped the SUV about fifty yards away. Bannock squinted, trying to make out the driver through the SUV's gleaming windshield. Was this one of the Russians? Had their luck turned around?

"You might want to get clear of the truck," Bannock said. "This is the only exit to the access road. They might try ramming their way out."

Gideon squinted.

"What about the money?"

"It'll survive."

"All right."

Gideon exited the truck and walked down the resort's access road, slipping beneath the forest's shaded canopy. Bannock opened his passenger door and stepped down from the truck, already concocting a story about he and Gideon working as private security for the ski resort. The heat was dense in the parking lot, the pavement baking in the sunlight like the floor of a kiln.

Bannock waved hello at the SUV, making certain to show the driver both his hands were empty. He started across the lot, forcing a wide, shit-eating grin on his face as he studied the SUV driver's outline.

This was a dangerous moment. The greater the distance between them, the more speed the SUV could build, and Bannock wasn't exactly in the mood for playing matador. The driver fluttered his accelerator pedal a few times, revving the vehicle's engine, but he kept it in park as Bannock grew closer. The driver was likely confused, uncertain how much of a threat Bannock repre-sented, if he even was a threat at all.

At a distance of fifteen yards, Bannock was 80 percent cer-tain it was Fyodor Sobol behind the wheel. The beard, the hair, the overfed bulk of a long-haul driver. At ten yards, Bannock grew dead certain. He kept smiling, however, his hands empty and far from his sides. He'd come a long way for this opportuni-ty and didn't want any squirrelly behavior to mess it up. He had a ten-million-dollar question to ask.

Bannock stopped five feet from the SUV and made the twirl-ing, roll-down-your window gesture. Sobol stared at him like this simple request was a deep, ponderous question he had to really think about. Bannock kept smiling, like the suffocating heat was no bother, like he had all the time in the world for a little chat.

27

NOVA LAY ON THE FLOOR IN THE CARGO AREA OF MACKENNA'S SUV. Her hands were still bound by a bungee cord and her ankles were fastened together by a piece of T-shirt, which the Russian had ripped into long strips. Her mouth was gagged by another strip of T-shirt wrapped around her head and knotted in the back. She thought it must have been one of the dude's shirts, because it tasted like sweat and smelled like boy.

The SUV had started moving, then abruptly stopped only a few seconds later. Fyodor mumbled something and put the vehicle in park. Nova wriggled until she was able to sit up on the floor, glad she had flexible yoga skills. She shimmied her butt and legs until she was able to slide up the far backseat and peek above the seats in front of her, rising just far enough so she could see what was happening without being easily noticeable.

Fyodor's focus was straight ahead. He was looking at a truck parked sideways across the parking lot's exit. Nova felt a surge of hope as the truck's passenger door opened and a tall, lanky man walked across the parking lot toward the SUV. He wore sunglasses, a black windbreaker, and khaki pants. It was the same man she'd seen enter the diner back in town, the one who walked like a tiger conserving its energy. He crossed the distance between the SUV and the truck, smiling as he drew near. His tanned, lean face was pinched at the corners, like he wasn't used to smiling, and his arms hung loose at his sides. He came around to the driver's side of the SUV and stopped five feet away, gesturing to Fyodor to roll down his window.

He was dangerous, Nova realized. As dangerous as Fyodor.

Maybe more so.

Fyodor's gaze flickered up to the rearview mirror. He saw Nova watching from above the far backseat, but the Russian didn't say anything. His eyes had gone hard again, like when he'd first pulled his gun from his ankle holster and shot Isaac. Nova saw his shoulders shift as he rolled down his driver's-side window and realized he was about to shoot the man who'd approached. She dropped back to the floor of the SUV. She wanted to plug her ears, but her hands were bound, so she squeezed her eyes shut as hard as she could, as if this would help anything.

"Yes?" Fyodor said, his voice loud enough to reach Nova. "What do you want?"

"Hey there. I was just wondering what you were doing up here at the Sunshine Lodge. We're closed for the season."

"Who are you?"

"I'm Bannock. I'm the off-season caretaker for the resort."

Fyodor grunted, like this surprised him. Nova opened her eyes and shimmied back into a sitting position so she could hear better. So, Windbreaker Man's name was Bannock. Huh. That sounded like a good name. Maybe she was wrong and nothing bad was going to happen. Maybe if she could catch Bannock's eye—

"I took a wrong turn," Fyodor said. "I needed parking lot to circle back around."

"Is that so?"

"Move your truck and I will leave. It is not a problem."

Nova shimmied and peeked over the backseat. Bannock was still standing in the exact same place, his arms loose at his sides. He looked like the heat didn't bother him, as if he was a lizard basking in it.

"Do you know who that other vehicle belongs to?"

"What other vehicle?"

"That rusty Chevy truck over by the stairway."

"No, I do not."

"You don't have a buddy around here? Perhaps hiding out?"

"What?"

Bannock coughed into his hand and dropped his arm back down casually so it dipped behind his back.

"You know, like a cousin named Dmitri?"

Things began occurring at an accelerated pace Nova could barely track. Fyodor's left arm went up and his pistol appeared over the edge of the open window while at the same time a gun appeared in Bannock's hand, as sudden as a magic trick, and then a shattering bang as both men fired at the same time. The noise threw Nova against the floor and the ringing in her ears returned, worse than ever. Suddenly the SUV was moving again, shooting across the parking lot as Fyodor jammed the accelerator pedal to the floor and sent Nova rolling around. She screamed into her gag as she did her best to wedge herself under the seat in front of her and brace herself, her bound wrists raised to shield her face as the SUV picked up speed.

Fyodor roared so loud she could hear him bellowing over the ringing in her ears. A curse in Russian, something defiant and crazy.

And then they crashed.

The earliest dream Nova could remember went back to when she was four or five years old. In this first dream, Nova was even younger, about two or three years old, and strapped into a rear-facing car seat while her parents drove her somewhere. It was night, and she couldn't see anything except for headlights occasionally strobing across the seat in front of her, making strange, intriguing shadows. It was like a shadow puppet show, playing on the seat back just for her. One second, little Nova saw a cat, pouncing along, and then came a shadow bird, soaring through a shadow-clouded sky.

The plastic buckles that kept little Nova strapped into her car seat suddenly clicked open like magic and she was free to move around. She crawled out of her car seat, entranced by a shadow bear ambling through a shadow forest, and climbed into the shadow world itself. Nova felt happy and scared at the same time, the shadows swirling around her, forming all sorts of animals, all the creatures she loved, pigs and rabbits and monkeys and squirrels and dogs, and she could feel herself becoming a shadow, too. A shadow girl.

When shadow Nova looked back at the regular world, at the car she'd been riding in, she could see the backs of her parents' heads and bright lights beyond them. It seemed fake, the regular world, while the shadows around her seemed real.

In the dream, which she'd had so many times she lost count, Nova decided to stay in the shadow world and be a shadow girl forever.

Nova's mind came back online suddenly, with a rush of noise and input. She had no way of telling how long she'd been out. She was wedged hard into something, a small space that pressed upon her with significant force. She smelled something close to burning and realized it must have been gunpowder, though she couldn't remember ever having smelled actual gunpowder before. Wait. Maybe fireworks? Her dad loved fireworks. Every Fourth of July, he bought a huge bag of rockets and shot them off in their driveway, while Nova and her mother watched from lawn chairs in the front yard, amused as much by her father's boyish enthusiasm as by the fireworks themselves.

Nova heard someone groaning and cursing. Her vision came into focus. She was in a shadowy place but could see sunlight beyond. She looked up and saw the underside of a car bench. She tried to move and found she could, although her hands and feet were still bound together. She wiggled and wiggled and extracted herself, only to find gravity working against her and pulling her back—the SUV was tilted sideways.

Metal squealed against metal as a door was opened.

"Hello, Mr. Sobol. You look a little rough there, my friend."

This was a new voice. A man's voice but not Bannock. This voice was softer and more polished, like a college professor or a lawyer.

"Fuck you," Fyodor spit out.

"Looks like your leg is pinned. That cannot be comfortable."

Fyodor grunted, as if straining to move. He swore and made a gurgling noise that sounded like something in his chest was broken.

"My name is Gideon, Mr. Sobol. I believe you just met my associate, Bannock, who looks to be joining us shortly. Our employer is unhappy because your shipment failed to reach its intended location. Can you please explain what happened, precisely?"

Silence and heavy breathing. Nova brought her hands up to her face and pried at the strip of fabric gagging her mouth. The gag had come loose in the crash and she was able to work it enough so she could spit it out and pull it up over her head. From there, she started gnawing and pulling on the bungee cord binding her wrists together. It had been loosened as well.

"Ah," said Gideon. "Here's Bannock now. He doesn't look very happy, Mr. Sobol, and I happen to know he's an expert with a knife."

Fyodor coughed and let out a wheezing sigh.

"We hit animal and rolled down mountain."

"What kind of animal?"

Bannock's voice. He sounded pissed off. Nova chewed and tugged harder, loosening the bungee knot. She pictured herself as a rat, chewing its way out of a trap.

Chew-chew-chew.

"Who cares? Huge. Brown. A beast."

"Then what happened, Mr. Sobol?"

Fyodor let out another, louder sigh. "You will not believe me."

"Try me," Bannock said.

"We were dragged from van and taken up mountain by large monster into its cave. It devoured my cousin, but I escaped."

Gideon chuckled softly, but there wasn't any mirth in the sound. Nova loosened the bungee cord enough to slip her wrists free. For once she was glad for her thin wrists, her small but flexible body. She drew her knees up to her chest slowly, trying to be as quiet as possible, and started working on the knotted fabric binding her ankles together. She felt sore all over, but nothing seemed broken. She'd fit under the SUV's seat, which had probably saved her neck from getting snapped in the crash.

"Are you telling us Bigfoot kidnapped you and your cousin, Mr. Sobol?"

"No. More like giant from worst nightmares. Has bald head and mouth like piranha. Is close right now. Is hunting."

"What about the money?" Bannock asked. "The police found five million dollars, but ten is still missing. Where is it?"

Nova swallowed.

Holy shit.

Holy shit holy shit holy shit.

"I do not know," Fyodor said, sounding tired now, like he might pass out. "I have only been trying to survive since yesterday. I am not stupid. I would not steal from Organization."

Metal squealed again and Nova finished unknotting her feet. She could run when she needed to. Any second now and Fyodor would remember she was stashed in the back of the SUV.

Either Bannock or Gideon whistled.

"What's this in your car door?" Bannock said. "Looks like banded cash to me. About eighty thousand."

Everyone up front went silent. Nova clenched her hands together, squeezing her fear into them—the extra money Mackenna had left in the van. Shitshitshitshit—

"I do not know about that cash," Fyodor said, sounding weak and befuddled. "This is not my car. This is teenager car."

"Sure," Bannock said. "Teenagers."

A thudding sound and a new kind of silence. Nova winced, wondering exactly what had just happened.

"Why'd you do that?" Gideon asked. "Don't we need him conscious?"

"This is going to take more time," Bannock said. "He's talking gibberish. We'll take him into the lodge in case anybody shows up nosing around. I'll be able to work on him better there."

"Ah," Gideon said. "Ever the artist."

Bannock didn't say anything. The wrecked SUV began to rock back and forth as they extracted Fyodor from behind the wheel, complaining about how fat and sticky with blood he was. Nova kept squeezing her hands open and shut, open and shut.

28

WIND BLEW IN THROUGH THE SUV'S SHATTERED WINDSHIELD. Nova forced herself to wait until she couldn't hear Bannock and Gideon talking anymore. She could not believe she remained both alive and unnoticed and prayed her luck would hold. She thought of the others back up the mountain, trapped in a kitchen freezer without food or water, Isaac shot and bleeding, and knew she had to try to rescue them. Fyodor had only been the beginning of their trouble. These two men, Gideon and Bannock, were on the mountain now, hunting for the money, hunting for all of them.

Nova tried not to think about what was happening to the Russian. Bannock working on him sounded like a euphemism for torture. Fyodor might prefer being eaten by the Wraith.

Oh God.

For a few minutes she'd forgotten about the Wraith, gathering Landon in its spindly arms and throwing him over its shoulder. How could all this be happening? Only two days ago, Nova had been hanging around her house in the Denver suburbs, sick of her parents and bored out of her skull after a long, eventless summer. She'd never known how good she had it, being comfortably bored like that. How boredom could be a sort of privilege you took for granted.

When enough time had passed, Nova crawled over the backseat and looked around the SUV. The front of the vehicle, which was basically buried in tree trunks, had been demolished. She opened the SUV's rear driver's-side door and winced as it let out a long squeal. She slipped past the door frame and dropped to the ground, causing the tilted vehicle to rock onto its side. The SUV had made it maybe twenty feet past its collision with the truck blocking the exit of the parking lot before Fyodor had lost control and veered into the trees. Beyond the smashed truck was the resort's parking lot, saturated in sunlight, which seemed extra bright from the shaded road.

As she stood there staring at the smashed truck and the parking lot beyond, a hundred-dollar bill fluttered past Nova's face. She watched it rise in the air and float away, feeling oddly detached. Three more hundred-dollar bills flew past her, churning in the wind. Inside the wrecked truck's cab, even more hundreds swirled, dozens of them caught in the wind that flowed through one broken window and out the other. Nova walked toward the truck, wondering if she'd suffered a serious head injury in the crash. She opened the truck's driver-side door and more hundred-dollar bills fluttered past her.

Nova laughed. She stepped up into the truck and knelt on the front seat. She grabbed a handful of hundreds and held them close to her face. The bills crinkled in her hand—they felt real—and when she sniffed them, they smelled like money. She looked into the backseat and saw two stuffed yard bags. One of the bags had been torn open across the side and bundles of cash had fallen out.

Nova dug into the split garbage bag and pulled out a still-intact bundle. The bundle's paper band was white with yellow stripes and had **$10,000** printed on it in a yellow font, just like the bands on the armored-van cash.

"Did you escape from your hiding place?" Nova asked the bundle out loud. "Did you follow me here?"

The money didn't reply, which was both a relief and a disappointment. She noticed a blanket lying across the floor of the truck's backseat. She lifted the edge, expecting to find more magical cash, but instead discovered a large black duffel bag. Nova unzipped it and recoiled. The bag was filled with all kinds of crazy serial-killer shit, including a hatchet, a saw, a hammer, plastic zip cuffs, and even a bow and arrow set. The bow and arrow set looked cool, but Nova didn't know how to string the bow and it would take time to assemble. Nova picked up the hatchet and ran her thumb along the edge of its blade. It was extra sharp, as if it had been honed over a long period of time. She tried a few practice swings, slicing through the air. The hatchet felt both reassuring and dangerous on the end of her arm, like something she could use naturally, without hesitation in a fight. Nova dropped the hatchet into her canvas satchel, which was still strapped crosswise over her torso.

Good enough.

Nova felt like she'd been handed an extra-difficult problem in a math/logic class, like the extra-credit problem at the end of the test you could only hope you got right because you knew for sure you'd gotten some earlier problems wrong. She could walk down the access road back to the main highway and try to get help, but it was several miles to the highway, with woods on both sides, and it was easy to imagine the Wraith popping out of the trees and scooping her up. She could walk up the ski slopes, which would take forever and leave her exposed, an easy target if Bannock, Gideon, or the Wraith noticed her. She could get back on the chairlift and ride it to the Lookout Bar, but that would also leave her exposed. If the Wraith noticed her on the lift, like it had noticed them last time, it could simply track her progress and wait for her to arrive at the top of the mountain.

Nova adjusted her satchel's strap and looked out across the parking lot. Colton's truck was still parked near the staircase that led up to the Sunshine Lodge and the row of smaller resort buildings. Maybe his truck was unlocked and Colton had left a spare key in it. Small town peeps did that, didn't they? Leave things unlocked?

Nova peered down the shadowy gravel road that led back to the highway and then back across the parking lot baking in the sunlight, lit more brightly than any stage. She flexed her toes and bounced on the soles of her feet.

"Fuck it."

Nova ducked her head and started toward the truck, sprinting as if she were being shot at. She crossed into the blinding sunlight and kept going, expecting somebody to notice her and start shouting any second, her satchel banging against her hip. Nobody shouted. Nobody shot at her. She made it to Colton's truck and tried the handle on the driver's-side door.

It was locked. Nova shook her head.

"Goddamn it, Colton."

Nova crouched beside the truck and peered up toward the lodge. No signs of movement. She unshouldered her satchel and grabbed the hatchet's handle through the shoulder bag's fabric. She tapped the driver's side window with the canvas-wrapped hatchet, experimenting, before rearing back and smacking the window. The glass cracked into a thousand little webs but didn't shatter. She smacked the wrapped hatchet against it again, even harder, and this time the glass did shatter inward, busting into a million gummy pieces.

Nova unlocked the door and let herself into the cab, sitting on the broken glass without bothering to sweep it clear. She searched the cab, which was strangely neat for a vehicle owned by a teenage boy, but found nothing except a package of teriyaki beef jerky, a tire gauge, jumper cables, and a long-handled window scraper. She found no spare keys. No magically appearing spare cell phone. The only keys to Colton's truck were with Fyodor, which meant they might as well be on Mars.

Nova dropped the package of jerky into her satchel, got out of Colton's truck, and shut the door softly behind her. She circled to the front of the truck, still ducking low (as if ducking could make her invisible) and started up the staircase to the lodge. The lodge would have a telephone. Lots of telephones. People called resorts all the time, didn't they? They called to make reservations. They called to check ski conditions. They called to say hey, what exactly is your pet policy? Do you accept American Express?

Nova kept low as she ascended the stairs, her gaze turned upward, still expecting an unpleasant surprise to pop up at any second. She was sweating, her body tense and jittery, her throat tight with thirst. She made it to the top of the staircase and poked her ahead above the final set of stairs. The coast was still clear. The Sunshine Lodge was on her right and a row of several smaller buildings on her left. Nova tried to remember what Colton had said about the smaller buildings when he'd been giving them a tour earlier that afternoon, now regretting that she'd been giggling with Mackenna instead of listening.

A man emerged through the lodge's entrance, stepping through a doorway where the ground was covered in broken glass from the shattered door. It wasn't Bannock, so it must have been Gideon. He had a pale face, brown hair, and wore dark sunglasses. Even though he was dressed in olive cargo pants and a camo T-shirt, he looked like a librarian or middle-school teacher, not like a killer you'd hire to find your stolen money.

As Gideon turned to look up the mountainside, putting his back to her, Nova sprung up from the staircase and sprinted as fast as she could toward the row of smaller buildings across from the lodge. She ducked into the gap between the two nearest buildings, slumped against the wall, and paused to catch her breath.

She was doing it.

She was going to rescue everybody.

Nova peered out and saw Gideon walking down the parking lot stairway, passing through the exact empty space Nova had just been occupying. He crossed the sun-soaked parking lot, dug into the cab of the crumpled Ford truck, and pulled out the duffel bag full of murder tools. Glad she'd remembered to zip the bag up after taking the hatchet, Nova watched as Gideon recrossed the parking lot with the duffel bag, trudged up the stairway, and returned to the lodge. As he stepped back through the shattered doorway, a piercing scream came from inside the lodge. It was a terrible sound, even from so far away, and it made Nova shiver as if someone had thrown a bucket of ice water on her.

The scream trailed off. Nova pulled her head back and turned her attention to the small buildings around her, stepping out and peering down the row. Each building had its own sign, stamped with the same burnt-looking font. The first and largest building was DINING HALL & SKI RENTALS, which was two stories tall, followed by SPA, MEDICAL, and MAINTENANCE, which were all one story. Nova went down the row, deciding MEDICAL would be her best bet to find a phone. The medical building was locked, but after a few chops of the hatchet, the old door gave way and swung open.

The small building, which consisted of one main open room and a bathroom in back, reminded Nova of the nurse's office back at Pioneer Academy. It contained three canvas cots, a bunch of medical equipment covered by dusty sheets, and a desk with a landline phone on it. Nova tried the phone, but the line had been disconnected. She thought of Isaac, bleeding in the freezer, and grabbed a first-aid kit sitting on a shelf. Maybe it would be enough to stop the bleeding. Maybe she could save him if she got back to the Lookout Bar fast enough.

Nova left the medical building and broke into the maintenance building next door. Bigger than the medical building, MAINTENANCE was more like a garage. It had a phone on the wall, but it was also disconnected. A massive riding mower and a two-seat ATV were parked in the middle of the space facing a manual shed door. The ATV, which reminded her of a golf cart on steroids, had big wheels and looked like it could climb almost anything.

Nova sat in the ATV's driver's seat and dropped the first-aid kit in the passenger seat. The fuel gauge indicated the ATV's tank was full and its ignition already had the key right in it. It took Nova a minute to figure out that she had to keep her foot on the regular brake while releasing the parking brake for the engine to ignite, but as the engine rumbled to life, she grinned and pounded on the ATV's steering wheel.

It was time to go back up the mountain.

29

DEPUTY SERRANO SAT IN HER TRUCK, WATCHING THE WOLCOTT house. She'd pulled off the Wolcotts' driveway to park in the shade thrown by the pines surrounding the estate, about forty yards removed from the house itself. It was six o'clock. She'd been staking out the house for several hours, sweating in the afternoon sun even with the windows rolled down and the engine turned off, waiting for the Wolcotts' daughter to return with her friends. She'd already surveyed the grounds on foot, which were empty, and had done as much research on the home's owners as she could online.

Owned by Raymond and Heidi Wolcott, the house was worth 2.3 million dollars, give or take. The Wolcotts' oldest daughter, Mackenna, was about to be a sophomore at Colorado College, a private college in Colorado Springs. Mackenna's name popped up several times in local sports articles—apparently, she was a beast in both volleyball and softball, a star athlete on top of being a blond stunner from a wealthy family. Ray Wolcott was a hedge-fund manager and Heidi Wolcott owned a health-and-beauty-product company, which sold all kinds of lotions, oils, and facial creams that cost way too much.

Serrano checked her phone. Her husband had called twice, Deputy Ted Knowles had texted her five times, and various numbers she didn't recognize had called her several times each. Likely DEA and FBI agents, all wanting to grill her about finding Sheriff Carson and Deputy Heller. She was too exhausted to deal with any of them, even her husband, and she was worried if she talked to anyone, she'd find herself giving away Mackenna Wolcott's identity before she had the chance to talk to the girl first. Mackenna was nineteen, old enough to be charged as an adult, and stealing ten million dollars of what was likely drug money and not reporting it to the police would effectively derail her life. It would be better if Serrano found Mackenna and her friends first and advised them to turn the money in voluntarily before they'd officially been identified. That would go a long way with any district attorney in rectifying their dumb mistake.

Before moving to Scorpion Creek, Serrano had lived in Houston with her family. She had three brothers, all older than her. One was now a corporate lawyer, one owned a popular food truck, and one, Antonio, was in prison for armed robbery and felony murder. When he was only nineteen, his brain not even fully formed, Antonio had agreed to act as getaway driver for his criminal friends when they robbed a highway liquor store and shot the clerk. He'd gotten twenty-five years and still had ten years left on his term. Serrano still visited her brother twice a year in prison, in December and July, and she marveled at how she could still see the sweet boy inside the hard man he'd become. The way Antonio's eyes would go soft when he spoke to her, the regretful tone in his voice when he spoke about the night of the robbery, which he still thought of daily, playing the whole night over and over in his head.

He'd written several letters of apology to the liquor store clerk's wife, but she'd never replied.

It still amazed Serrano how a person's life could change in an instant, usually for the worse, and she'd seen this same surprise in the people she'd encountered in her work. The drunk driver who'd swerved into oncoming traffic, killing a pair of newlyweds. The doped-up mother who'd slept through a fire alarm and lost her house and two children. The carefree college boy who decided to dive headfirst into a shallow lake and ended up paralyzed for life. The people she crossed paths with on a daily basis were usually having a bad day, some the worst day of their life. Sometimes she felt less like she was serving and protecting and more like she was dealing with the whims of fate and mitigating their extreme consequences as best she could, trying to soften the hard punches life could pack.

Deputy Serrano got out of the truck and approached the Wolcotts' house. Once again, she considered breaking in and having a look. She didn't have a warrant, so nothing she found would be admissible in a court of law, and if she was caught creeping around off duty, she'd probably earn herself a healthy suspension.

Still. Ten million dollars and the knowledge she'd properly identified Mackenna Wolcott was a powerful draw.

Deputy Serrano tried the front door It was locked, as she'd expected. She went around to the back of the house. There she discovered another deck made of a beautiful dark red cedarwood and a full-size pool with all the trimmings, including a tiki-hut bar straight out of the 1950s.

The heat was draining from the day as the sun descended, but it was still hot, and Serrano felt an overpowering urge to dive into the pool. Instead, she knelt beside the pool and dipped a hand into the water. It was warm from the day's heat, but still cooler than the air above it.

Serrano's cell phone buzzed in her pocket. She stood up, crossed the cedarwood deck, and tried the glass sliding door at the back of the house. It opened smoothly, as if it had been waiting for her arrival. She stepped inside the house and went through it room by room, searching for any space or object that might be capable of hiding ten million dollars. It was a lot of money and would occupy a lot of space. If Mackenna and her friends were smart, they would have divvied up the cash as soon as they got into the house into smaller, more manageable amounts, likely with each one getting their own share of the spoils. Then they'd have each hidden the cash in their rooms. Either that, or they would have divvied up the money and then stored it in the same location together, a spot Mackenna would have likely recommended, since she knew the area and they did not.

Serrano didn't find any cash on the first or second floor. Every bedroom was messy, with clothes, toiletries, and electronics thrown everywhere. As she sat on the edge of an unmade bed on the second floor, Serrano took a deep breath and wiped the sweat from her forehead. She thought about the old fairytale "Goldilocks and the Three Bears" and what it must have felt like to be Goldilocks, entering a strange, unoccupied house and deciding to sample the owners' porridge, chairs, and beds.

Was she Goldilocks, looking for an ideal solution in a place she should not be? An outcome that would blunt the death of Marty Carson and Jeff Heller, two fellow law officers? Or were Mackenna Wolcott and her friends playing Goldilocks, trespassing in the criminal world and stealing porridge from some very dangerous bears? And how close were the bears, exactly? Were they about to return home and feed?

Serrano stood and walked out of the bedroom. She went down the hall and entered another bedroom that faced the driveway. The front yard was empty and the trees lining it looked peaceful as they swayed in the wind. This bedroom was less messy than the others, with a plastic bag filled with clothes and an empty leather weekend bag. Serrano picked up the plastic bag and examined its contents. The clothes weren't new, there were no tags still attached, so they weren't in a plastic bag because they'd been recently purchased. They were folded and clean, not dirty, like you might store soiled clothes in a bag when you were on vacation.

So why use the plastic bag when you had an empty, much nicer weekend bag? Serrano retraced her steps to the other three bedrooms. She found more plastic bags and no luggage. These were rich kids from the suburbs of Denver. They would have luggage. Nice luggage their rich parents might have given them for Christmas or a birthday.

Unless they'd emptied all their luggage to use for other purposes. Such as storing ten million dollars in cash.

Serrano laughed. It was a raspy, croaking laugh, maybe a little crazy sounding, but she didn't care. She still didn't know where the money was, but she knew it would be found in a pile of luggage somewhere. Somewhere . . . not in the house. Maybe they'd been spooked by her visit the night before, a cop dropping in unannounced, and they'd decided to hide the money ASAP. They could be hiding it right now, as Serrano stood there looking out at the woods, happy with their clever machinations, a bunch of teenage pirates burying the gold so they could dig it up later, when the cops were done looking for it.

Serrano's cell phone buzzed again in her pocket. She checked it this time, satisfied that she was gaining traction, that she now had enough momentum to turn away any requests for her to return to Scorpion Creek and account for her absence.

"Hey baby." Her husband, Miguel. Sounding tired, concerned, and relieved, all in two words.

"Hi sweetie," Serrano replied.

"You're on the job, aren't you? Even though they put you on leave."

"I can't confirm or deny that."

"I checked the second safe. Your gun and some bullets are missing."

"I took them for reassurance, that's all."

Her husband sighed. "You haven't fired your weapon during your entire career."

Serrano didn't say anything. This was true.

"You're not going to start using it now, are you?"

"I don't know. I hope not."

This was also true. Her phone went silent and Serrano checked the screen to see if the call had been disconnected.

"I'll feed the boys dinner," Miguel said. "Be safe."

"I will. I love you. Kiss the boys for me."

"Okay."

Her husband ended the call. Serrano slipped her phone back into her pocket. Her stomach gurgled and she felt lightheaded. She realized she hadn't eaten all day, not even breakfast, and now it was catching up with her. She could check the Wolcotts' kitchen for something to eat, but that would make her Goldilocks. Better to go back into Cloud Vista and eat at the diner, where she could monitor any passing traffic from a window booth.

She wouldn't miss anyone heading toward the Wolcott house.

Her eyes were wide open now.

30

THE SUN DROPPED BEHIND CLAW HEART MOUNTAIN, COVERING the mountainside in muddled blue shadow. The ATV was rolling along at a steady pace that felt both exhilarating and scary. Nova kept expecting the vehicle to tilt upward and tumble back down the mountain, crushing her in the process. She kept the accelerator pedal pressed to the floor, urging the vehicle to go as fast as it could. She doubted she was moving faster than the Wraith could travel (she could still picture its long, spindly legs rapidly striding along), but at least Nova felt more in control driving a vehicle than she would have been up in the chairlift, dangling like a piece of fresh meat in a butcher-shop window.

The ATV went over a bump and its front end bucked into the air, reminding Nova of Landon being thrown over the Wraith's shoulder. She glanced at the dense tree line on her left, a blur of green and brown in the deepening twilight gloom. About halfway up the final stretch of the ski run, the ATV's engine took on a new, high-pitched whine. Nova imagined the noise carrying across the entire mountainside, like a dinner bell for the Wraith, and she wondered if she was better off ditching the ATV and going the rest of the way on foot. But the mountain slope was steep and only getting steeper, while her breathing already felt shallow and quick at such a high altitude.

So Nova kept driving.

The ATV climbed the last slope and managed not to die until Nova reached the Lookout Bar, its high-pitched whine cutting off a second after she killed the engine. The resulting quiet was startling. Nova grabbed the first aid kit and ran up the steps to the patio.

Colton's plastic cooler was still there, along with the cell phones Fyodor had smashed. Nova examined the pile, trying each phone in turn, but they were all dead and useless now, including her own.

Looking at the plastic mess, she felt a surge of anger and was suddenly less troubled by whatever was happening to the Russian down at the lodge. Fyodor could have gotten away without being such an asshole.

Nova hustled around to the back of the bar, entered, and went into the kitchen. The stainless-steel prep table was still lying on its side, its tabletop pushed against the freezer door. Nova set the first-aid kit on a counter and pulled at the table's end with all her strength, grimacing as the steel screeched across the linoleum floor and reluctantly allowed itself to be moved.

The freezer door popped open before Nova could even touch its handle, bashing into the table. Mackenna slipped through the gap between the door and the doorway, looking stunned.

"Nova. You came back."

Nova grinned. She was about to say something badass, like "of course I did, bitch," but Mackenna darted forward and hugged her before Nova could say anything.

"We tried, Nova. We tried our best."

Mackenna squeezed Nova so hard the air went out of her lungs. She smelled like blood. Nova allowed the punishing hug to go on for a few seconds before she extracted herself and took a deep breath. Mackenna's eyes filled with tears.

"Isaac's dead."

———

Colton and Wyatt peeled out of the freezer and looked at Nova but didn't ask any questions. They both went over to the cupboards, dug out four pint glasses, and poured water for everyone. Nova, suddenly remembering how thirsty she was, accepted a glass and guzzled the entire pint before coming up for air. Everyone else did the same, then poured themselves a second glass and drank that as well.

"Well?" Mackenna said, looking at Nova. "Aren't you going to look?"

"Huh?"

Everyone stared at Nova. She realized they wanted her to go into the freezer and look at Isaac—that they somehow *needed* her to look at him—so Nova set her glass on the counter and stepped forward, poking her head into the freezer. She'd only seen two dead bodies before—her grandfather on her mother's side, and her grandmother on her father's side. They had both been old, dressed up, and prepared by a funeral home for public viewing, their cheeks rosy pink with blush.

This body was not like that. It was Isaac, yes, but Isaac with the life drained out of him. He was lying on his back, his eyes shut.

His T-shirt was soaked with dried blood, not just the area around his stomach where he'd been shot. His summer tan was gone, his face extra pale in contrast with his dark hair. He looked . . . inanimate, like an object you did not expect to move on its own, something that would freak you out if it *did* move.

Isaac would not be moving again.

Isaac was dead.

Nova's eyes filled with tears. She wiped her eyes with the back of her hand and turned to the others. Colton and Wyatt looked at her with dumb hope in their eyes, as if she might have come to a different conclusion or could resurrect the dead boy. Mackenna was looking around the kitchen, her forehead wrinkled in confusion.

"Where's Landon?"

Nova looked at the concrete floor. Two different trails of blood were now smeared across it, leading to the kitchen's doorway. Isaac's trail of blood was brighter and damper, but it would dry soon. Nova swallowed and looked up, making eye contact with Mackenna.

"The Wraith took him."

Both Wyatt and Colton inhaled sharply. Mackenna simply stared back at Nova.

"Fuck you, Nova. Really. Where is he?"

Nova looked at the guys.

"Fyodor wanted us as bait. That's why he took us."

Mackenna shook her head.

"Nope. No. No way."

"We went down the mountain on the chairlift," Nova continued. "The Wraith came out of the woods and started following us. It was enormous. Like, nine feet tall. Fyodor hit Landon in the head and pushed him off the chairlift. The Wraith scooped him up and carried him into the woods."

"Oh shit," Wyatt whispered, his eyes widening. "It probably took him back to its cave."

"The Wraith isn't real," Colton said, rubbing his arms. "It's just a local ghost story. Max was just trying to freak everyone out last night."

Nova took the hatchet out of her satchel and waved it at Colton. "It's real, Colton. Really real. It's huge. It has pale eyes and bluish-green fur. Its body looks all, like, emaciated, and it has this wide, freaky mouth and claws for hands."

"Claw hands?" Wyatt said. "Like Bigfoot?"

"Yeah," Nova said. "Except the Wraith is real. I saw it. I saw it carry Landon away."

Nova dropped the hatchet back into her satchel, deciding she'd made her point. Mackenna paced back and forth without looking at anyone. She had streaks of dried blood in her hair—as if her blond ponytail had crimson highlights. Nova stepped forward and touched her shoulder.

"Mackenna—"

Mackenna whirled around and slapped Nova with an open hand, hitting her so hard Nova staggered backward and wavered on her feet, nearly collapsing. White lights fizzed and strobed across Nova's vision. She touched her face where she'd been slapped, astonished. She could feel the heated imprint where Mackenna's hand had connected with her face. She'd been bonked by a few kickballs and Frisbees, but no one had ever actually hit her before.

"Jesus," Wyatt said. "Goddamn, Mack."

Mackenna's blue eyes flared. She pointed at Nova, her pretty Nordic face transformed into a mask of rigid, ugly rage.

"This bitch. This bitch is lying to us."

Colton stepped forward, holding his hands up like a boxing referee prepared to break up a fight. Nova gaped at Mackenna, still trying to process the slap, and this seemed to make Mackenna even angrier. She whirled around and stormed through the kitchen doorway, its swinging doors flapping behind her. Nova lowered her hand and looked at Colton and Wyatt.

"I'm not lying."

"Okay," Colton said, nodding. "We believe you. But how'd you make it back?"

Nova told Colton and Wyatt about Bannock and Gideon. How they'd stopped the Russian from escaping, and how Nova had escaped while they dragged the Russian away.

"Why would they do that?" Colton asked, crossing his arms. "What do they want?"

Nova looked at Wyatt, calculating how much to tell Colton. "Fyodor and his cousin were delivering money in their van. Millions in cash, I guess."

"Holy shit," Colton said, laughing and shaking his head. "Really? And they think it's still around here?"

Nova shrugged. "I guess. They can't find it. They're torturing the Russian right now. I mean, I heard him screaming."

"Bannock and Gideon," Wyatt said, massaging his shoulder. "They don't sound Russian."

"They're not. They don't have accents."

"Then what are they doing—"

"Hunting," Nova said, interrupting Wyatt. "Hunting for their money."

Colton laughed again. "Seriously. Millions of dollars? Around here? On Claw Heart Mountain?"

Wyatt looked toward the kitchen doorway, avoiding Colton's eyes. Nova shrugged and tried to look nonchalant. "Fyodor and his cousin had to be transporting something."

"If there even *was* a cousin," Colton said, rolling his eyes. "If Fyodor wasn't just some crazy person who broke into this place with a gun."

Nova opened her mouth, intent on making Colton and Wyatt understand how serious this was, that killers were now all around them, but a loud scream interrupted her. A piercing scream, the kind that escaped your lungs before you could even think about it.

Mackenna.

31

EVERYONE LOOKED AT THE KITCHEN DOORWAY, THE WARM AIR crackling with an ominous new energy. The swinging doors burst inward as Mackenna plunged into the room, her eyes wild. She scanned the kitchen and darted toward a knife block on one of the kitchen counters, pulling out a butcher knife and holding it in the air, her arm trembling.

"It's here. It's outside."

Wyatt and Colton stared at Mackenna. Nova pushed past her and went through the swinging doors. She threaded her way through the maze of barroom tables and peered through the dusty windows at the front of the bar.

There it was. The Wraith. Looming like a tree beyond the bar's deck, standing beside the ATV and sniffing the air, its eyes pale and milky, its teeth numerous and sharp. Its bluish-green fur fluttering in the wind.

The kitchen's swinging doors creaked.

Nova could sense the others walking up behind her. She didn't look back at them. Her gaze was 100 percent focused on the Wraith. Its presence was terrible and magnetic. "You were right," Mackenna whispered over her shoulder. "I'm sorry, Nova. I'm sorry I slapped you."

Nova had already forgotten about the slap. The slap didn't even register in a world where the Wraith existed, standing outside, a mere thirty feet away. The Wraith was the slap. The Wraith was the slap in the face of reality. It was the Hunger in the Mountain.

The others came up and stood beside Nova . . . four freaked-out teenagers, looking at the impossible.

"I wish I had my cell phone," Wyatt said. "I would take so many damn pictures right now. Like, so many."

"Oh," Mackenna said, still sounding dazed. "I didn't even think of that."

They all kept staring. The Wraith reached out with one huge arm and swatted at the side of the ATV, causing it to rock on its shocks. Nova remembered how loud the ATV's engine had whined before it died outside the Lookout Bar.

"That's not some old-timey dude cursed by a witch," Colton said, leaning his forehead against the window glass. "Look at all those teeth. That thing is something else. Something way beyond a curse. Something . . . prehistoric."

The Wraith turned its pale, horrifying face in their direction as if it could hear what Colton had said. Its jaws opened and closed slowly, tasting the air. Nova reached her arms in front of her friends and backed up from the window, ushering everyone backward. The Wraith turned to the ATV, slid its ropy arms beneath the vehicle, and lifted it above its head, as if the ATV hardly weighed anything at all.

"Holy shit," Wyatt said. "Dude is JACKED."

Nova backed everyone up several additional feet, until they were deep in the building's gloom, away from the windows. "Lie down," Nova whispered. "Now." For once, everyone listened to her without arguing.

All seemed quiet except for their shallow breaths. Then the ATV crashed through the front of the building, as loud as a bomb. Shards of glass and wood flew everywhere, covering them from thirty feet away, and the ATV rolled twice before coming to a stop. Nova shuddered but fought back the urge to scream—and thankfully, the others did too. Nova looked at Mackenna, lying to her left, and they stared into each other's eyes as they listened for signs of movement outside. Nova could feel her friend's terror as strongly as she could feel her own. Suddenly she and Mackenna were fully connected, more connected than she'd ever been to anyone in her life, even her parents, and Nova felt as worried about her friend's life as she did her own. They shared the same life now, the same fate.

They all did. Either they'd all get away, or they'd all be dead and devoured by morning. It was that simple.

Nova mouthed the word *kitchen* and started to crawl. She turned her back to the front of the building and headed for the kitchen's swinging doors, crawling through the shattered glass and wood on her elbows, trying not to make a sound. Nova could hear the others doing the same, inching forward slowly, as she listened for something much bigger to enter the building.

After what felt like an hour, or maybe an eternity, Nova made it to the kitchen and crawled beneath the swinging doors. The others followed her and Nova put her finger to her lips as everyone got to their feet. She walked back to the freezer and opened its door, waving toward the others to go inside. Everyone stepped into the freezer and Nova closed the door behind them, though she didn't latch it fully.

"We're not safe in here," Colton whispered, lacing his hands behind his head. "You saw how strong that thing is. It'll tear the freezer door right off its hinges."

"Is there some kind of trail from here?" Nova asked. "A mountain trail?

Colton nodded.

"There's one that goes into town, actually. It's rough and steep, but we could take it."

"You want to leave?" Wyatt said, brushing the broken window glass from his shirt and pants. "You want to leave this building?"

"It'll hunt us," Mackenna said, clutching herself and blinking too much. "It'll hunt us down."

"I know," Nova whispered back, putting her hand on Mackenna's shoulder. "That's why we need Isaac."

They all looked down at the dead boy on the freezer floor. He looked even deader than before, but he still looked like Isaac. Isaac, who'd been alive only a couple of hours earlier. Who'd gotten the huevos rancheros with hash browns and a caramel roll at Al's Griddle.

"What for?" Mackenna whispered.

Nova pushed the freezer door open a few inches and listened.

"Bait," Nova said. "We need Isaac for bait."

32

BANNOCK SURVEYED THE ENTRANCE HALL OF THE SUNSHINE Lodge as he wiped the blade of his knife clean. Clearly built in the 1950s, the hall was a clumsy, earnest American take on a resort in the Swiss Alps. Built on a large scale to impress visitors, the hall had an enormous limestone walk-in fireplace, a check-in desk composed of lacquered pine, and a high ceiling dominated by a massive antler chandelier.

A full-sized, taxidermied black bear stood in one corner, its face frozen in a snarl and its claws extended. Faded mountain landscapes and black-and-white photos of skiers smiling hung on the walls in fake gold frames. A big wooden stairway with an ornately carved handrail led up to the second floor.

Bannock slid his knife into the sheath on his belt and took a deep breath. The lodge smelled like dust, mold, and time. Bannock looked at Gideon, who was sitting in a chair he'd pulled up to the hall's entrance so he could keep an eye out for visitors. "I feel like

I've been here before," Bannock told him. "Maybe when I was a child."

Gideon examined the gun he was holding, peering down its sight. "Perhaps you've visited this lodge in a dream. A dream of premonition."

The Russian groaned. Fyodor Sobol was tied to a chair in front of Bannock, quietly bleeding onto the lobby's polished wood floor. Bannock had worked him over pretty good with the knife. They could untie the Russian now.

He was no longer a threat. He wouldn't run.

Most of his major tendons and muscles had been either severed or carved into.

He was still alive, though, which impressed Bannock. He'd known far bigger men to die much more easily.

"My family liked to travel all across the West when I was a child," Bannock said, pulling up a second chair to sit across from the Russian. "My father was obsessed with the Old West. He loved reading Louis L'Amour and Zane Grey. He read Western paperbacks as frequently as most people used to read the paper. If he had the day off, he'd start reading a Western at breakfast and by dinnertime he'd be finished. It would drive my mother crazy, how my father focused on those books and ignored the rest of us. He worked for the electric company as a line repairman. He'd served in World War II, in the Pacific Theater. He fought on Okinawa. He saw his best friend's face blown off by an artillery shell. He said his buddy kept living for five minutes after the explosion, even without a face. His buddy reached out and squeezed my father's hand. He used Morse code to convey 'Kill them all' before he died."

Fyodor grunted and opened his eyes. "We were allies in World War II, American. Twenty-six million Soviets die in battle and starvation. Not even half million Americans. But you think you are great heroes."

"That's a fair point," Bannock conceded. "Without the Red Army, the Nazis would be in the White House right now. So, I guess I should thank you for that before you die."

Fyodor chuckled and spat blood. It dribbled down his matted beard and mixed with all the other layers of blood. "We both die today, Mr. Knife Man. You should know this."

Bannock stared at the Russian. He'd been told many times he was going to die, in various amounts of time, but Sobol had said it with less emotion than was common. Usually when someone predicted your demise, they said it with anger and fear in their voice, or at least a trace of annoyance. The Russian, on the other hand, only sounded amused and certain.

"You're referring to the scary monster you mentioned?"

"*Da.*"

"The one who took our ten million dollars and brought it to his cave?"

The Russian didn't say anything. They'd gone over his ridiculous story several times already while he was under the knife. The driving accident on the mountain, the dark cave, the Russian's escape to the bar at the resort's peak. The teenagers he'd locked in a freezer and the two other teenagers he'd used as bait while they rode down on the chairlift. It was an unlikely story, the ravings of a madman, but on the other hand, Bannock had never known his knife to fail to produce the truth before. Either everything Sobol was saying was true or the Russian didn't register pain at the same level most human beings did.

Which was much more likely than Bigfoot roaming loose in southern Wyoming and snatching people up.

"The money we found in your van matches the rest of the cash," Bannock said, lacing his hands behind his head and nodding at the two yard bags of cash Gideon had hauled up from the truck. "Same yellow-striped currency straps, same general condition. I've never met a teenager who carried eighty grand in banded hundreds before."

Sobol didn't respond. His eyes were closed and his breath was slowing. Bannock leaned back in his chair and glanced at Gideon, who was staring out a window in a trance. "He said there were two kids, Gideon. He fed the boy to the monster, but the girl was supposedly in the back of the SUV, all trussed up. Did you see a girl when you brought up the cash, Gideon?"

"No," Gideon said, his voice distant and flat. "I did not see a girl."

Bannock touched the side of his head, which still burned from the sizzle of the Russian's bullet. Their little parking-lot duel. Well, Bannock supposed it wouldn't hurt to check out the Russian's story. It wasn't like they had any other good leads to chase down. They still had access to the rusty Chevy in the parking lot and the set of Chevy keys Bannock had found in Sobol's pocket. He could drive up the mountainside and look around while Gideon cleaned up the interrogation site and buried the Russian in the woods.

Sobol inhaled sharply and held his breath for a long time. Bannock thought this might be the Russian's final breath, his death gasp, but Fyodor Sobol opened his eyes again and grinned, revealing a mouthful of black and yellow teeth.

"Tonight, Mr. Knife Man. You join me in death tonight."

With this proclamation the Russian finally died, his bearded chin slumping to his chest. His heavy body relaxed, straining against the tight network of ropes that kept him from falling out of his chair. Bannock took the elk's antler tine from the pocket of his windbreaker and twirled it in his hand. He pressed it between his fingers like a claw and ran its point across his cheek, wondering what waited for him higher up the mountain.

He felt a buzzing in his bones.

33

NOVA SLIPPED BACK INTO THE KITCHEN AND SEARCHED BENEATH the counters until she found the cleaning supplies. She grabbed an eighty-ounce jug of industrial clog remover and brought it back to the freezer, gently closing the freezer door behind her. She set the jug on the floor and everyone looked at her as if she'd lost her mind. Maybe she had.

"We need to sit Isaac up and pour this down his throat."

"What?" Mackenna said, still blinking too much and too fast.

"Colton and Wyatt, prop him against the wall and hold him up by each shoulder. I'll pour. Mackenna, you massage his throat so he can swallow."

"What . . . the . . . fuck?"

"Poisoned bait," Colton said. "You want to fill him with poison and give him to the Wraith."

"Jesus," Wyatt said, leaning forward and crossing his arms. "This is messed up. I mean, really, really messed up."

"C'mon, guys. We don't have much time."

Colton moved first, grabbing Isaac by the shoulders and lifting him into a sitting position. "Wyatt," Colton said, keeping his voice low. The other boy snapped to attention and helped drag Isaac's body over against the cooler wall. Nova uncapped the jug of clog remover, which was almost full. It smelled strong and toxic and made her eyes water. She tilted Isaac's head back and squished his mouth open by pinching his cheeks and loosening his jaw. He felt cool and rubbery to the touch.

"Mackenna, get over here."

"No. I don't want to. This is, like, desecration."

"I'll do it," Wyatt said. He knelt on the other side of Isaac and started massaging Isaac's throat while Colton kept the boy's body propped up. Nova started pouring the clog remover slowly, so Isaac's mouth and throat didn't fill up too fast and overflow. The clog remover's chemical smell overpowered the smell of dried blood, filling the entire freezer, and Mackenna started to gag. "Keep massaging," Nova said, though Wyatt hadn't stopped. Nova felt like a nurse on the world's most messed-up TV show. The whole thing felt oddly intimate, her touching her dead friend with two live friends beside her, helping her.

"It's working," Wyatt said. "I can feel it going down."

Mackenna gagged again and threw up this time, a wet splatter Nova didn't look at. She kept her eyes focused on dead Isaac's face, not wanting to spill the clog remover if she didn't have to. Isaac's hazel eyes had rolled open and were locking past her shoulder, unfocused and cloudy. "I'm sorry," Nova told him. "I know we weren't besties or anything, but you deserve way better than this."

Mackenna heaved some more, but this time it sounded like nothing came up. Both Colton and Wyatt had gone stone-faced, just enduring what was happening, trying to tune out Mackenna and everything else. Finally, when the jug was about half empty, the liquid cleaner started to overflow in Isaac's mouth and spilled down the front of his bloodstained shirt. His stomach was so distended you could see it puffing out.

Nova stopped pouring and capped the jug. "Okay. That's enough. Let's get out of this fucking freezer once and for all."

Mackenna made an urping sound as Wyatt opened the freezer door. He peeked through the doorway into the kitchen. He looked back at them and mouthed the word *empty*. Colton picked Isaac up beneath his arms and Wyatt grabbed him by his feet. They carried Isaac out of the freezer and Nova and Mackenna followed behind. Mackenna looked wrecked, like all her fuses had blown. She still had puke in the corner of her mouth and flecks of it on the front of her shirt. Nova took the older girl's hand and gave it a squeeze, trying to reassure her, but Mackenna only gave her a freaked-out look, like the squeeze had startled her.

Colton and Wyatt stopped before the swinging doors and Nova darted ahead. She peeked beneath the doors, checking for the Wraith. The coast was clear. She pushed the swinging doors open as slowly as possible, so they didn't make noise, and stepped into the barroom in front of the guys, holding one panel of the doors open as they came through with the body. Mackenna followed, exiting the kitchen last, and headed toward the building's rear door without even glancing at the overturned ATV or the smashed windows.

Nova held back as Colton and Wyatt carried the limp body up to the gap in the front wall, glass crunching beneath their feet. They crossed the threshold of the damaged building and stepped onto the deck. Colton and Wyatt swung Isaac between them, building up momentum as they counted silently to three, and threw him as far as they could. Nova watched Isaac's body clear the deck railing and disappear beyond it.

Now. Now it was time to run.

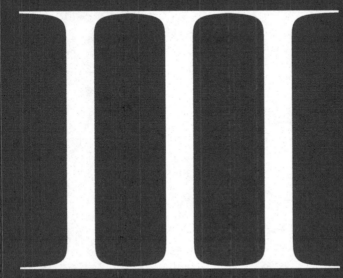

III

THE HUNGER
IN THE
MOUNTAIN

34

DEPUTY SERRANO ATE DINNER AT AL'S GRIDDLE AND WATCHED the highway from her window-booth viewpoint, searching for vehicles with Colorado plates. The diner was bustling; this was the main place to eat in town on a Saturday night, even if it wasn't ski season. Serrano had a bacon cheeseburger, fries, and coleslaw, devouring everything with a gusto that surprised her, then ordered a slice of cherry pie for dessert. She also drank an entire pot of coffee, fueling up for what she expected to be a long night.

Her thoughts jangled and her nerves raw, Deputy Serrano felt as if she were dining with the ghosts of Sheriff Carson and Deputy Heller, sitting invisibly across from her in the opposite booth. They were watching her stuff her face and guzzle coffee in ghostly silence, waiting to see what she would do next. Which was a crazy idea, of course.

Maybe Serrano was turning into her beloved abuela, who sensed ghosts all around her.

When the waitress, a big-bosomed woman whose name tag read 'Pam,' brought her cherry pie, a thought suddenly bubbled up in Serrano's mind.

"Excuse me, Pam. When did your shift start today?"

Pam wiped her hands on the front of her apron. "At breakfast, honey. We have a girl out sick today."

"Have you served any teenagers?"

"Oh yeah," Pam said, nodding. "They eat, too."

"These would have been from out of town. Rich kids from around Denver."

Pam thought a minute.

"Yep, a group of out-of-town kids did come through for lunch. They about ordered one of everything too."

"They pay in cash? Maybe a hundred-dollar bill?"

Pam's eyes widened.

"How'd you know that?"

"Lucky guess. Did you happen to hear what they were up to today?"

Pam thought some more. The diner clattered behind her, a bubble of noise and light. A slow-moving elderly couple exited through the diner's front door, linked arm in arm. Soon the diner would close for the night and Pam could go home and rest her tired feet. Maybe drink a glass of wine and watch her shows.

"They said something about the ski resort, but that's closed until November, so who knows about that?" Pam said. "Maybe they were going to smoke in the resort's parking lot. Sometimes the local kids like to do that. They skateboard too."

Deputy Serrano nodded. "Thanks, Pam. I appreciate it."

Pam laughed. She had a big, easy laugh that passed through her entire body. "Heck, that was nothing compared to some of the gossip that passes through this place. Some of it would make your ears burn, honey. Heart to God."

Deputy Serrano nodded, exhausted by Pam's cheerful energy. The waitress walked away, and Serrano took a large bite of the cherry pie. She opened her purse, dug out her wallet, and dropped a twenty on the table before getting up and leaving the diner, still swallowing the pie as she hustled for her truck, trying to ignore the feeling that her ghosts were coming along for the ride.

The access road to the Sunshine Ski Resort and Lodge was longer than Deputy Serrano expected, several miles of tight winding roads that circled the mountain. She drove fast but kept scanning the tree lines, worried about animals leaping out, and because of this it took her an extra second to notice the vehicular wreckage up ahead on the road, blocking access to what looked like a parking lot beyond it. Serrano clucked her tongue.

"Well, well. This is interesting."

The deputy slowed as she approached the wreckage, scanning the road for human shapes and movement. She instinctively reached for a CB radio mic, but of course there was none in her civilian truck. She parked twenty feet from the wreckage and took out her cell phone, deciding enough was enough, that it was time to call Deputy Knowles and let him in on her private investigation, to call in the cavalry.

Of course, in the shadow of the mountain her cell phone had no reception. Serrano cursed the saints, slipped the phone back into her pocket, and turned off the truck's engine. "You still here with me, Carson?" Deputy Serrano asked out loud, peering through the truck's windshield. "You think I should approach the scene immediately, or drive back to the diner?"

The sheriff's ghost didn't answer. Maybe he wasn't even listening.

"Okay. Fuck it."

Serrano opened her door and approached the wreckage with her weapon drawn. She called out to indicate her presence and received no response. The two vehicles were a black Mercedes SUV with Colorado plates (bingo) and an old Ford F150. The SUV's front end had been demolished and the passenger side of the truck's cab had buckled inward, indicating a sidelong collision, as if the truck had been parked across the exit and the SUV had tried to drive through it. The SUV's driver's seat was covered in dried blood, but otherwise the vehicle appeared empty.

There was no one in the truck either, but Serrano found a loose hundred-dollar bill tucked between the windshield and the truck's console like a temporary parking pass. She felt the tiny hairs on the back of her neck stick up. A trail of blood ran out of the truck and across the parking lot, headed more or less for the lodge's stairway. A large wooden building with a triangular roof loomed large above the parking lot—the main ski lodge, most likely—along with a row of additional wooden buildings running to the left of the lodge like little lodge children. The only other vehicle in the parking lot was a rusty brown Chevy Silverado with Wyoming plates parked directly beneath the stairway.

Serrano left the two-vehicle wreckage and headed for the lodge, feeling exposed, out in the open. Instead of moving in a diagonal line, the shortest path between the two points, Serrano walked along the tree line on the edge of the parking lot before taking a right angle and moving along the grassy embankment at the front of the parking lot. The Chevy truck had a broken driver's-side window and looked like it had been tossed—someone had been searching for something.

Moving on, Serrano took the stairs fast (there was no ideal way to go up a flight of stairs in a tactical situation, especially if you believed a gunman had the drop on you from above), popping up at the top of the stairway as suddenly as she could, hoping for any small advantage the element of surprise might give her. However, nobody was waiting for her at the top. No one was in view at all. The main lodge was on the deputy's right and the smaller buildings were on her left. Dwarfing all of them were the wide, grassy ski slopes running up the mountain and into the darkening sky above.

Serrano had never been skiing or even visited a ski lodge. She had to admit the slopes were a beautiful sight, even in the summertime, and that the old lodge and its ancillary buildings had a simple rustic charm to them. She could imagine visiting in the winter and drinking hot cocoa before a roaring fire, all cozied up in flannel pajamas. Maybe she could take Miguel and the boys here for a Christmas surprise. The boys, who loved anything dangerous and potentially bone-snapping, would probably love skiing.

Deputy Serrano approached the lodge's main entrance, deciding to check the biggest and most obvious destination first. She noticed a chairlift in operation, its enclosed bench seats empty as they moved up the mountain. Two sets of glass sliding doors were set into the lodge's entrance. One door had been shattered, leaving a mess of broken glass beneath it. Serrano paused outside the shattered door, peering into the gloom beyond, listening while allowing her eyes to adjust to the lower light. She thought about announcing herself but kept quiet, deciding any shouting might get her head blown off. She stepped through the broken doorway and entered the dim lobby.

The first object Serrano's eyes were drawn to in the large space was an empty chair, placed in the center of the lobby, surrounded by nylon rope and covered in blood. She thought of Sheriff Carson, bound and carved up in the police station's evidence locker. The second and third objects she noticed in the lobby were two black plastic yard bags, leaning against the far wall. Deciding to skip investigating the bags until the site was secure, Serrano tried the phone at the front desk. She found the line had been disconnected, though the lodge still had electricity. She performed a fast search of the premises, checking each floor door by door, but all the guest rooms were locked and the hallways themselves gave off a dusty, unused vibe. Serrano made her way back to the first floor and reentered the front hall, prepared to move on and search the resort's other buildings, but noticed a sign on her left that read:

THE

UNDERGROUND

LOUNGE

LODGE GUESTS ONLY!

A set of stairs led downward. Deputy Serrano went to the top of the stairs, flipped on the lights, and listened for movement below. She felt another urge to announce her presence, to ask whoever might be lurking in the basement to come upstairs with their hands raised in the air, pretty please, but she descended the stairs instead. The deputy pictured finding Mackenna and the other teenagers from the security photo, tied up but alive, frightened but unharmed, having learned a valuable lesson about stealing millions of dollars from folks with nefarious intent.

If you envisioned things, sometimes they came true. Isn't that what people said?

Serrano reached the bottom of the basement stairs. It was pitch black beyond the stairwell and utterly silent. Unable to find the basement light panel, Serrano was forced to reach into the darkness and pat along the wall for it. She had a brief, irrational moment of panic as she imagined something grabbing her arm and yanking her into the dark, but she finally found the light switches and flipped them all on, flooding the basement with light.

Nothing. Just a lounge with thick orange shag carpeting and light globes with yellow, blue, and red stained-glass panels hanging from the ceiling. A bunch of low, round tables surrounded by those brown leather rolling chairs everybody used to have in the seventies, the kind with tombstone shaped backs and low-slung arms. On the opposite side of the room was a bar decorated in silver mirrored tiles, which somehow glittered even in the mellow lighting, with several shelves of liquor bottles set up behind it. If the lodge's entrance-hall theme was classic Swiss ski chalet, the Underground Lounge was a sleazy, late-1970s bar where you should watch your drink.

Deputy Serrano took one pass through the lounge, making sure it was as empty as it felt, and headed back up the basement stairs, turning off the lights behind her. She fell into deep thought as she climbed the stairs, her chin dropping to her chest as she recalled the chairlift, appearing extra creepy as it moved along without riders. Was heading further up the mountain her inevitable next step? Still deep in thought, she reached the top of the stairs and noticed a man standing in the entrance hall, seemingly surprised to see her. It was the strange pale man she'd spoken to earlier, sitting in his truck, the truck Serrano only now realized was the same Ford F150 that had been involved in the parking-lot accident. How had she missed that? She was exhausted. What was his name? Gideon. He'd said his name was Gideon.

And now Gideon was pulling a gun from his pocket.

Looked like a Berretta.

Which he was now pointing at her.

Trying to catch up to all this information, Deputy Serrano raised her own weapon, shouting the word *police*, but she was too tired and slow. He fired.

And then she was tumbling back down the stairs, where the dark basement was waiting.

35

NOVA, WYATT, AND MACKENNA ALL FOLLOWED COLTON, RUNNING out the back of the Lookout Bar and sprinting toward the woods. Colton paused at the edge of the tree line, scanning the surroundings. For an unsettling moment, Nova thought Colton might have been wrong, that there was no path into town at all, but then he darted forward again, leading them into a narrow gap in the woods. Tree shade fell over them, cool and concealing. They hurried down the path and Nova tried to keep her mind blank, pushing aside an image of Isaac's body flying through the air like a rag doll over the deck railing at the Lookout Bar.

Or Landon, lying motionless on the ground as the Wraith approached.

Or—

The Wraith shrieked in the distance, causing everyone to pull up and freeze. Nova, the only member of their group who'd heard the Wraith scream before, was the first to shake off the deep, primal fear trying to lock up her body. "That's it," she announced, breathing hard as she set her hands on her hips. "That's the Wraith."

Everyone looked back through the trees and listened. The woods around them had fallen totally silent. "Fuck," Wyatt said, slapping his knees. "That fucking scream, man. It tears right through your soul."

"What even is it?" Mackenna asked. "I mean, like exactly?"

"It's hungry," Nova said. "That's all we need to know."

"Fuck," Wyatt said, repeating himself.

"We need to keep moving," Colton said. "It might not take the bait. It might just keep looking for us."

"You mean Isaac," Mackenna said, glaring at Nova. "It might not take our friend Isaac."

"Yeah," Colton said, his face blank as he nodded. "That's what I mean."

Wyatt slapped his cheeks. "FUUUUCK."

Colton started moving again and everyone followed. The path was composed of packed dirt, loose and embedded rocks, and exposed tree roots. It was difficult to run, but they maintained a decent hustle as they went along single file. Nova followed Colton, with Mackenna following her, and Wyatt bringing up the rear. Nova was suddenly glad for her short legs and small feet, which made it easier for her to pick her way over the uneven terrain. The others, with their long legs and wider bodies, were laboring more than she was, their arms and shoulders getting scratched by the branches she mostly avoided. Desperate to fight the terror itching at the back of her mind, Nova imagined she was a tiny forest elf, capable of skipping undetected through the woods.

The path tilted as it gained elevation and everyone had to slow to a walk. Sweat dripped into Nova's eyes and she was already thirsty again, even though she'd just drank two glasses of water back in the kitchen of the Lookout Bar. She wondered how long they'd be able to keep moving like this, without water or food, already exhausted by everything that had happened. She wished she could call her mom.

Twilight turned into night. They'd been on the mountain path for a while now, maybe hours. They'd slowed to a trudging speed, putting one foot in front of the other with grim determination, pine needles clinging to their socks and shoes. The temperature was cooling off, but the air remained dry and soaked up every ounce of moisture it could. Mackenna was the first to stop walking, which made everyone else stop too. They'd only left the cabin that morning, everyone freshly showered, but already their group looked like they'd been wandering around the woods for a week.

Mackenna undid her ponytail and shook her blond hair out. "How far is it to town, Colton? I mean, for real?"

"I don't know," Colton admitted, shrugging. "We still have to go all the way around the north ridge, then go up through the woods and come down the other side. It could take six or seven more hours. I've never been on this trail before."

"What?" Wyatt said. "Never?"

Colton wiped his forehead and flicked the sweat away into the trees. "Nope. It's supposed to be really hard. There's a big elevation change over a short distance, plus there's lots of chances to break your ankle."

"So how do you know this trail even goes into town?"

"People say."

Wyatt bent over and folded his hands together. "People say?"

"Yep."

"Shit."

"Yep."

Mackenna exhaled and wiped her hands on her dirty white shorts. "Well, at least it's dark. The Wraith won't be able to find us in the dark, right?"

"Actually, I think it might be blind," Nova said, slapping a mosquito on her arm. "I think it hunts by sound and smell. Did you see its eyes? They're, like, milky white, like some kind of underground creature."

"Like a mole," Colton said. "Or a deep-sea lobster."

"Oh great," Mackenna said. "So we're mostly blind out here, but it can hunt us like normal?"

"We're not going to make it to town in the dark," Wyatt said. "Will we, Colton?"

Colton looked upward, past the treetops to the vague outline of the mountain peak looming above them. You could feel the mountain's entire weight pulling at you, challenging you to remain standing upright, much less keep climbing.

"We have to keep going," Colton said. "We have to try."

Nobody cheered.

Nobody said anything.

They started moving again, because Colton started moving again, and it took another hour of hiking steeply upward before Nova's legs threatened to give out on her. She was getting so dehydrated that her calves had begun to cramp and knot up. Nova started humming to herself, some low-key inspirational humming, but Colton turned around and told her to be quiet. "It might hear you," he said, which was fair enough, so Nova stopped humming, only to start again a minute later, the noise starting low in the back of her throat and slowly growing louder without her even noticing she was humming at all.

After this second round of humming, Colton just stopped and stared at her. He was breathing hard and covered in sweat. Nova was so thirsty she considered leaning up on tiptoe and licking the sweat off Colton's freckled face, which made her realize she was getting close to delirious, if she wasn't already. Still, she *did* wonder what his sweat would taste like—

"Nova."

"Yeah?"

"Please. Stop. Humming."

"Okay. I'm sorry."

Colton stared at her for another few seconds. Nova could see the defeat in his eyes, even as the woods grew darker and darker around them, the only light coming from the growing stars and the crescent moon. He knew they weren't going to make it over the mountain and into town. He was trying to be the brave leader, the big man, but the path to safety he'd suggested had turned out to be hard, uncertain, and nearly as dangerous as waiting for the Wraith to find them cowering in the Lookout Bar freezer.

Fifteen minutes later, their luck seemed to change for the better as they came to a stream running across the trail. It was only three feet wide and two feet deep, but its waters were cold and flowed reasonably fast. Nova and the others dropped to their knees alongside the flowing water as if preparing to worship. "We shouldn't drink it," Colton said, scooping up the stream water with his hands and splashing his face. "Streams and rivers have E. coli bacteria in them. They can make you sick."

Nova splashed her face and arms with water. She drenched the entire front of her shirt and felt cool relief trickle down her back. It seemed impossibly cruel to be so close to water and not be allowed to drink it.

"How sick?" Mackenna asked. "Like COVID-19 sick?"

"Sick enough," Colton said, peeling off his shirt and wringing it out in the stream. "Stomachache, diarrhea, you might puke a lot. It's not worth it. Even if you're really thirsty."

"Fuck dude, I don't care," Wyatt said, slurping water from his hands. "I can handle the squirts. I'll take my chances."

Mackenna looked from Wyatt to Colton and back to Wyatt again. Mackenna started slurping the stream water too, which actually helped Nova fight the urge to join them. Instead, Nova focused on drenching herself with as much cool water as possible, closing her eyes as she dipped her head into the stream and focusing on the external relief it brought her. She stayed under for ten, fifteen seconds. She heard a loud splash above the waterline but didn't think much of it. When she raised her head and opened her eyes, Colton was floating in the stream, facedown and motionless.

"Colton!"

Nova grabbed Colton's arm, dragged him out of the water, and turned him face up. She looked for help from Wyatt and Mackenna, wondering why they hadn't said anything, but she couldn't see anyone else.

It was as if they'd magically disappeared.

Nova looked down at the stream, wondering for a crazy second if the water had some kind of curse of its own, a vanishing curse, before noticing two huge footprints in the mud. Nova whirled around, searching the dark trees for movement. She heard branches snapping in the distance but couldn't see anything.

Nova crouched over Colton and patted the side of his face. She begged him to wake up, wake up, and watched his chest, which rose and fell slowly, maybe too slowly. Did you ever need CPR even though you were already breathing? She couldn't remember. They'd all gotten certified in her health class during her junior year at Pioneer Academy, but she'd only paid partial attention in class, attaining the certificate by the skin of her teeth. She'd been distracted by Tennyson, who'd sat beside her, brooding in a hot way while writing strange poetic phrases in a notebook. Tennyson, who sometimes wore a dark-blue silk scarf to school wrapped loosely around his neck. Tennyson, who could look right back at you without flinching.

Nova pounded her fist against Colton's chest, skipping all the CPR training and going with pure emotion. The redheaded boy gasped and sputtered, spitting up water. Nova stepped back, expecting Colton to sit up and explain everything, but his eyes stayed closed and his breathing remained slower than normal. Nova knelt over him again, examining him more closely, forcing herself to take a deep breath and calm down. Combing through Colton's hair with her fingers, she discovered a dark bruise forming on the side of his head and a trail of blood trickling out of his ear. She pictured the Wraith, emerging from the woods, clubbing Colton unconscious, and snatching both Mackenna and Wyatt while they drank from the stream. Maybe it had clubbed them too, so they hadn't even made a sound while it carried them away, just like it had carried off Fyodor and his cousin.

Which meant it would be taking Wyatt and Mackenna back to its cave right now. Perhaps even the Wraith could only carry so many people up the mountain at once.

Which meant it might be coming back for them too.

"Colton, please! Wake up!"

Nova slapped his face hard, again and again, but Colton didn't wake up. He was totally out. He might not wake up for hours.

Nova rubbed her face in her hands. The stream water that had felt so good just minutes earlier was now chillingly cold and made her clothes cling to her body. She felt heavy and tired, and it was so dark. The question was, should she keep going on the path for as long as she could and abandon Colton where he was? Should she use him the same way the Russian had used Landon on the chairlift? This was probably her best option, if she wanted to stay alive and make it back into town. Colton was too big for her to move on her own and there was nowhere safe to move him to, even if she could.

Nova took one last look at Colton, lying immobile in the starlight, and crossed the stream in one quick leap, landing lightly on the other side. She studied the ground, sticking to the lighter parts of the darkness to guide her, and went about twenty yards down the trail before stopping and looking up at the stars through an open spot in the forest canopy. She took slow, deep breaths. She listened to the surrounding woods and felt a crushing sadness unlike anything she'd ever felt before. She turned around and returned to the stream, leaping back across, and sat down on the ground beside her unconscious companion.

Nova pulled the hatchet out of her satchel and set it beside her. If the Wraith came back, at least they'd face it together.

36

THE DRIVE UP THE RESORT'S SKI SLOPES TOOK LONGER THAN Bannock had expected. This did not surprise him, given that near-ly every aspect of his current commission had ended up being more involved and time-consuming than he'd expected. The truck he'd taken from the lodge parking lot, an old Chevy Silverado, had to chug against the slope's sharp incline, barely capable of muster-ing fifteen miles per hour as it bounced on its paper-thin shocks. Also, the truck's air-conditioning didn't work, so even with the windows down, the cab remained a hot, windblown experience that slowly drained Bannock's energy and patience.

By the time Bannock was two-thirds up the mountain, the truck's engine finally overheated and died altogether. Bannock dug through his duffel bag and pulled out a mini-flashlight and the carrying case for his takedown recurve bow. Bannock slung the case over his shoulder and started up the slope on foot, abandon-ing the piece-of-shit truck with the keys still in it. He had a knife sheathed on his ankle and his SIG Sauer P226 holstered on his hip. Using the bow would be a luxury he'd afford himself if he had time—he wasn't going to assemble the bow now and carry it up a mountain like some kind of asshole.

———

The steep hike up the final grassy ski run was grueling and uncomfortable, with the strap of the carrying case digging into Bannock's shoulder. The hum and creak of the chairlift kept him company as the sky darkened. As Bannock finally approached the Lookout Bar, he noticed the unmistakable figure of a dead body lying in the grass. Interesting. Was this the teenager the Russian claimed he'd shot in the stomach?

Bannock unbuttoned the holster attached to his belt but did not draw his gun. He studied the supine body from a distance of ten yards and the building beyond it for a long minute, noting the broken front windows and some kind of wreckage beyond it. He waited for movement—any kind of movement. The stars had come out, along with a sliver of moon that drifted in and out of cloud cover, and the temperature had dropped significantly.

Bannock approached the body and looked it over more closely, shining his flashlight on it. It was a white male, eighteen or nineteen. He was lying on his side, with his arm wedged beneath his head, as if he were at home taking a nap on the couch. The boy's shirt was stained with blood and he was covered with loose dirt. Bannock lifted up the boy's shirt and noted a single gunshot wound to his stomach.

"Must have been slow and painful," Bannock said, talking to himself and the dead teenager. He noticed the ground beside the teenager's body had been torn up. It looked like an animal with significant claws, such as a bear or a mountain lion, had swiped at the ground beside the teen and thrown dirt over him, like it was trying to bury its scat or cover something that smelled displeasing. Bannock bent to examine the claw marks in the ground and noticed a chemical smell rising from the teenager's body. A cleaning agent, he decided, like bleach or drain cleaner. Strange. Had the boy been drinking it? A desperate, delirious attempt at counteracting a gunshot wound to the gut?

Bannock walked past the dead boy and surveyed the chaos of the Lookout Bar. It appeared someone had driven an all-terrain vehicle through the front wall at great velocity, though it was hard to imagine how, exactly, given the limited confines of the deck railing and the apparent head-on angle of the impact. Bannock stepped through the sparkling broken glass that lay everywhere and entered the Lookout Bar, following his flashlight's illumination. The building was deserted—its emptiness was palpable—but Bannock did find blood cast, which led him to the kitchen, which led him to the walk-in freezer, which was covered in blood and smelled like death and chemicals. He found a bottle of drain cleaner, uncapped and half empty, set aside in a back corner.

Bannock returned to the Lookout Bar's main room and examined the ATV. The vehicle was lying on its driver's side, its front end crumpled. Bannock examined the floor with his flashlight but couldn't see any fluid cast. Either the driver had leaped clear of the vehicle before the moment of impact or had been incredibly lucky. Bannock stood in the ragged opening at the front of the building and tried to imagine someone driving the ATV along the deck and turning into its front wall, head-on, at the last second, while still maintaining a high velocity. It seemed improbable at best, and Bannock wasn't certain this particular ATV could break thirty miles per hour in the best conditions. It was almost as likely that the vehicle had fallen from the sky, like a meteorite, and crashed into the building.

Bannock reexamined the bar's main room, shining his flashlight into every dusty corner. He noticed the back door of the building was ajar. The door appeared to have been forced open, which also matched up with what the Russian had said about breaking into the building. So, where were the other teenagers the Russian had mentioned? They'd obviously escaped from the freezer, somehow, and they hadn't come back down the mountain, at least not on the chairlift. Mythical Bigfoot monster or not, they appeared to have been dealing with extreme circumstances of one kind or another, the kind of trouble that caused you to run like hell.

Bannock heard a branch snap in the woods behind the bar. Small game, likely a rabbit or a deer. He stepped down from the bar's deck and approached the trees edging the clearing. He shined his flashlight back and forth and noticed an opening among the trees. Bannock smiled and stepped into the opening. It was the start of a trail, leading farther up the mountain along the north ridge, perhaps eventually turning in the direction of Cloud Vista.

Bannock adjusted the strap of his bow's carrying case and started along the trail.

This would be a unique and challenging hunt.

Perhaps his greatest.

37

THE MOUNTAIN COOLED AND SETTLED WHILE COLTON REMAINED unconscious. Nova could sense all the birds tucking themselves into their nests while the night sky thickened with bats, flitting around as they feasted. She recalled a memory from early childhood when she was four or five. Her mother, chasing a bat around their house with a broom and finally knocking it to the floor. Victorious, her mother had swept the stunned bat into a dustpan and brought it out to their garage. She'd dumped the bat into a plastic ice cream pail, where other previously trapped bats, many still alive, clawed wildly for freedom before Nova's mother got the lid snapped back on.

This had been at their old house, the one they still called the Bat House because bats kept getting in somehow, sneaking in through a gap nobody could find. Almost every night, a bat would appear and start fluttering around, scaring the crap out of everyone, and her parents would have to chase it around until they could subdue it. They started putting the bats in the plastic ice cream pail so they wouldn't just fly back into the house. Her mother, an animal lover and wimp when it came to killing live things, hadn't wanted to kill the bats, so she'd put holes in the ice cream bucket's lid and started collecting them instead, with the idea that eventually she'd drive out to the country and release them all at once.

It must have been terrible, Nova thought, to be one of the bats trapped in the pail. Had her mother given the bats water? Bugs?

Had she ever released them into the countryside at all?

These questions somehow haunted Nova now, while she shivered and froze and waited for a monster to return and do what monsters did. The night was mostly clear, but the trees surrounding the stream obscured the sky, allowing Nova to see only a few stars through a small gap in the canopy. Even so, her eyes had fully adjusted to the night, and she could make out various degrees of darkness. The stream's surface glinted faintly with motion and reflected starlight, making it the brightest thing around. Sitting next to it was like sitting next to a nightlight.

Her knees bent and her legs sprawled apart, Nova sat in the dirt like a child in a sandbox. She dug around with her stolen hatchet, cutting through tree roots and looking for rocks, distracting herself from both the present and the future. She could barely see the rocks she found, but she wiped the dirt off each one anyway and felt it closely with her fingers, trying to picture it in her mind.

The night grew colder. Nova's clothes were still damp, which made her feel cold to the bone. She gave up her semi-delirious digging and crawled off the path a few feet, as far as she dared in the near dark. She searched blindly with her hands until she found a few fallen branches with pine needles still on them. She dragged the branches back to Colton, covered him as best she could, and lay beside him with the hatchet's wooden handle clutched in her hand.

Nova draped her right arm and right leg over Colton's body and focused on the warmth shared between them. She slowed her breathing until it matched his. His chest sounded like the ocean. His skin was pale in the starlight, the freckles on his face tiny spots of darkness.

The blood that had been trickling out of his ear had stopped, thankfully, and was now dry. Colton muttered gibberish in his sleep and Nova stroked his forehead with the back of her hand, trying to sooth him as her mother had soothed her during childhood fever dreams. She murmured softly to him, telling him it would be all right.

She listened to the nocturnal animals rustling in the forest undergrowth, wondering if each little crackling noise signaled the Wraith had finally returned to collect them.

Colton stopped muttering. The forest returned to a deep state of calm, as if they'd slipped into a magical fairy-tale bubble. Nova felt warm and cozy, cuddled beside Colton's large, radiator-warm body, covered by her makeshift quilt of pine tree branches, and finally she drifted off to sleep.

When she woke again, Colton was staring at her. A faint amount of dark blue light now permeated the forest, slightly brighter than starlight.

What was it called again?

False dawn?

Or was this false false dawn?

"Hey," Colton said.

Nova rolled her tongue in her mouth, trying to loosen it. She was so thirsty.

"Hey."

Colton touched the side of his head, where a dark purple splotch had formed on his temple and cheek. He winced and drew his hand back like he'd touched fire.

"Shit."

"Yeah," Nova said, pushing herself up on her elbows. "Be careful with that."

Colton stared at her. "I can feel the mountain spinning under me. I might throw up."

"Okay. Just don't throw up on me, okay?"

Colton closed his eyes. He groaned and turned flat onto his back. "Jesus."

"Do you remember what happened?"

Colton exhaled and smacked his lips. The stream burbled beside them. Nova realized you never really thought about what streams did in the dark. How they kept on burbling and flowing, even when nobody was around to watch and take pics.

"We were hiking? On the path into town?"

"What's the last thing you remember?"

"Trees. A lot of trees."

Nova nodded. She was glad that was the last thing Colton remembered. He'd probably need less therapy if they managed to survive.

"We found a stream right when it was getting dark," Nova said, pointing at the stream on the other side of Colton. "When I was dipping my head into the water, I heard this splashing noise. When I looked up, you were lying facedown in the stream, and Mackenna and Wyatt were gone. Like, vanished gone."

Colton slowly rose to a sitting position.

"The Wraith. It found us."

"Yeah."

"It might come back."

"Yeah."

Colton's head dipped between his knees. Nova reached out and massaged his back. She rubbed in a circular motion while pressing hard with her palm. Colton's shirt felt damp and clammy, but his back was warm and solid beneath it. Guys were always so warm, even when they shouldn't be.

"You stayed with me," Colton said, raising his head and looking at Nova. "Even though you knew it could come back."

Nova grinned and squeezed Colton's shoulder. "Hey. I never said I was a genius."

Colton coughed into his hand and turned to look at her. His eyes gleamed in the faint light, and Nova suddenly realized she was alone with a handsome man, miles from civilization.

"Fuck, Nova. You're kind of a badass, you know that?"

Nova smiled as her face flushed with pleasure. She looked back at Colton and felt a crackle between them that seemed filled with ... possibility. She imagined inviting him back to Mackenna's cabin after they returned to town. They could strip off their muddy clothes and take a long, hot shower together. Colton crawled over to the stream. He propped himself up by his elbows and dunked his entire head under the water, holding it under for a surprisingly long time.

Nova joined him at the edge of the stream and splashed her face—after what had happened last time, she wasn't going to dunk her head underwater anytime soon. The water was cold and invigorating and she decided she no longer gave a flip about bacteria; she drank from the stream with cupped hands. Colton, head thoroughly soaked as he came up for air, watched her drink without saying anything before dunking his head a second time, this time with his mouth open.

When they'd both had enough water, they sat back and looked up at the sky poking through the forest canopy. False dawn was over. The sky was dark again except for a scattering of stars.

Nova patted her belly, which was sloshing with the stream water and slightly less hungry. "How do you feel now?"

"Better," Colton said, gingerly touching his head bruise. "The cold water numbed the pain."

"That's good."

"Yeah."

Colton turned and Nova could feel him watching her. The early morning was so dark. He could have been any young man illuminated by starlight, but she could still tell it was Colton Morgan sitting beside her. He had a reassuring presence, even now.

"Do you think you'll be able to keep hiking?" Nova asked, pretending like she couldn't feel him watching her.

"I guess I don't have any choice, do I?"

"No. I guess you don't."

Neither of them made a move. The hike still loomed in front of them. It was such a long way into town. Nova stuck her hand into her satchel, digging around for mints or gum or anything she could chew on and distract herself from being hungry. She discovered a small plastic bag lying at the bottom of her satchel and pulled it out, amazed.

"Ha. It's your beef jerky."

"Huh?"

Nova waved the bag in Colton's face. "I stopped by your truck earlier and took this."

"Oh. Score."

Nova opened the plastic bag and dug around. She counted six pieces of jerky by touch. She handed Colton three and took three for herself. She started gnawing on the first piece and felt an explosion of sweet teriyaki flavor on her tongue. It tasted better than anything she'd ever eaten in her life, and she normally didn't even *like* beef jerky. Her stomach gurgled with gratitude. She tried to eat her three pieces slowly, really chewing them. Colton ate his pieces so fast it seemed like he barely chewed them at all, swallowing them like a pelican.

"I also broke your window," Nova admitted. "To get into your truck."

Colton laughed. "No shit?"

"I used a hatchet. There's glass everywhere now."

"Well," Colton said, burping. "Shit happens."

Nova shivered and squeezed Colton with her arm and leg. Her whole body, actually. "It must be terrible," Nova said. "To be hungry like the Wraith all the time, no matter how much you eat. It would make anyone insane."

"Yeah. It would."

Colton turned and looked at her, his face open and serious. A bird warbled somewhere in the trees above them, waking up. It sounded like someone playing the flute.

"Do you mind if I kiss you, Nova?"

Nova raised her head. Her breath felt caught in her chest. "I don't know. Is that you, or your head wound asking?"

Colton grinned. "All me. I promise."

Nova leaned toward Colton and they kissed. It was a good kiss. Colton was just there, letting the kiss be, allowing it to exist between them as a simple connection. Nova felt the good kind of shivers pass through her body and leaned toward him further, pressing into him with the full weight of her body. She wanted to wrap his warm body around her like a heavy comforter and combine their heat into a single unifying force.

Then, Nova felt something else. Something like . . . being watched. She pulled back and looked down the trail, back in the direction from which they'd come. A creepy-crawly feeling passed up and down her body.

"What is it?"

"Shh."

The murky outline of something was standing in the middle of the trail, watching them with obvious intelligence. Hoping it was just a deer, come to drink at its favorite stream, Nova waited for her eyes to determine the shape.

It wasn't a deer. It was a man in a dark windbreaker and light pants. He was carrying something over his shoulder. He could see Nova watching him and nodded in greeting. Nova dredged up the man's name from the muddy bottom of her memory, though she'd only learned it the day before.

The sunburned man.

Bannock.

38

THE SUNSHINE LODGE WAS AS SILENT AS A CATACOMB, AND
Deputy Serrano's otherwise useless phone told her it was now
3:08 a.m. She was in the dark, but she could see artificial light filtering down the stairway to the Underground Lounge. She sat in
a chair with a good view of the stairwell, with a table in front of
her so she could rest her gun on it. At fifteen feet, she was close
enough to the stairway that she'd have a decent chance of hitting
Gideon with a rushed shot, but distant enough that she could protect herself if he decided to throw a grenade or some other type of
explosive down the stairwell.

Serrano checked her cell phone, begging it for at least two
reception bars but couldn't even get one. All her attempts to call
out had failed and her phone's battery was draining. She'd found
a landline phone in the back of the bar, but it didn't have a dial
tone. All communication between herself and the outside world
was effectively cut off.

After Gideon had surprised Serrano in the entrance hall and shot at her, she'd fallen down the basement stairs awkwardly and retreated into the dark. He'd missed hitting her, somehow, but Serrano had sprained her right shoulder during the fall. She'd scrambled backward into the dark basement and drawn her weapon with her left, nondominant, hand, waiting for Gideon to rush down the stairway, gun blazing, to try and finish her off.

Instead, Gideon had remained upstairs. He didn't call down and taunt her. He didn't demand that she give up her gun and come upstairs with her hands raised. He didn't set the whole lodge on fire and try to smoke her out. He did the hardest thing for someone in a high-pressure situation to do. He remained calm. He sat tight.

This behavior was confounding, to be sure. Deputy Serrano could charge up the stairs and take her chances, but she was injured in a way that would hinder her shooting abilities, and Gideon had the high ground. She'd probably get her head blown off before she could even sight him. So, no. No charging uphill like a lunatic. Better to defend a stable position and wait for reinforcements to eventually arrive.

And arrive they would. Her husband would be worried that she hadn't come home and would sound the alarm, if he hadn't already. All kinds of law agencies would come looking for her, sooner or later, and they'd comb the mountain until they found her. It was only a matter of time.

The lodge was so quiet Serrano could hear Gideon breathing at the top of the stairs. She pictured him sitting in a chair of his own, his own gun resting on his knee, his flat blue eyes watching the stairwell with the patience of a circling vulture. Serrano stood up, stretched, and silently padded over to a corner of the lounge. She pulled down her pants and peed while still keeping her gun pointed toward the stairwell. When she was finished, she pulled her pants up with her right hand, wincing at the pain flaring in her sprained shoulder, and returned to her chair to maintain her vigil.

As she waited, Serrano went over every observation she'd made since finding the armored van near the bottom of Claw Heart Mountain. She thought about the attack on the police station in Scorpion Creek. The arrows sticking out of Deputy Heller and Sheriff Carson. She considered the fact that Gideon had shot at her and missed from a relatively short distance. When she'd run into him earlier that day, sticking out on the side of the highway, Gideon had been killing time in his truck, as if he were waiting for something. Or someone.

Recovering millions of dollars was a big job, especially if the police had already seized a portion of it. Gideon probably had a partner. A true heavy, someone so good at killing that normal gunplay bored him, even when he was attacking a police station. Someone who liked using traditional kinds of weapons, like bows and knives. Someone who fancied themselves a true caveman hunter. Maybe this mysterious partner had been hunting on the mountainside while Gideon waited, and maybe his hunt had led them here, to the lodge, where they ran into the armored van's crew. Gideon and the mystery hunter had won a pitched battle in the lodge parking lot, only to find the crew didn't have the remainder of the money, because Mackenna Wolcott and her friends had tucked it away somewhere.

Serrano recalled the chairlift, strangely in motion although the resort was closed. Going up a mountain at a closed resort would be the kind of thing a group of teenagers might think was fun. Teenagers celebrating becoming instant millionaires. The hunter would have also noticed the operational chairlift. He would have followed it up the mountain, leaving Gideon to deal with the van's crew and clean up.

So . . .

Gideon was waiting for the hunter to return. He probably wasn't allowed to leave without him. He would have orders. And, bonus, the hunter would be able to deal with the nosy cop who'd showed up to the party uninvited. The cop who was trapped in what was basically a windowless concrete bunker without cell phone reception. The cop who'd been foolish enough to go rogue, who hadn't even told her own husband her current location.

Serrano stretched her arms and yawned, silently, arching her back until it cracked. She wondered if this would be the last day of her life. She could feel her ghosts gathering around her, keeping her company in their own solemn way.

39

NOVA STOOD UP, HIDING THE HATCHET BEHIND HER BACK. COLTON also tried to stand, but his concussion made him dizzy and he sat back down again before he could even make it halfway. The sun-burned man watched them both without moving, sizing them up. He had a holstered gun on his belt in addition to whatever he was carrying over his shoulder.

Nova could sense the importance of this moment and knew she had to be careful. She wasn't just looking at a man. She was looking into her own future grave, yawning wide open in front of her. Every word and movement counted now.

Every second.

"Hello, Bannock."

The sunburned man took a step forward and entered a patch of starlight. He had a dark scorch mark along his right temple. Nova recalled his conversation with the Russian and the gunfight. So the Russian had come close, at least.

"How do you know my name?"

"I'm Nova," Nova said, ignoring his question. "This is Colton. He's hurt."

Bannock tilted his head. "You don't say."

"Is that a bow case you're carrying?" Colton said from the ground, sounding groggy but amused. "Who the hell are you, Robin Hood?"

Bannock grinned, which made him only look more dangerous. "Funny you should ask, Colton. I'm here because somebody stole from the rich and now the rich want their money back. You could say I'm their paid representative."

"Oh," Colton said. "You must be looking for the Russian."

Bannock took another step forward and Nova shifted on her feet. He was only four or five feet away now. Almost within chopping distance.

"I already found the Russian, actually. He told me what I thought was a tall tale about a monster and some teenagers, but I'm beginning to suspect he was telling the truth. I believe I found your friend a few hours ago. He had a gunshot wound in his midsection."

"He wasn't"—Nova began, glancing at Colton—"eaten?"

"No. He wasn't. The ground beside him had been clawed at, though. Like something was trying to cover him with dirt."

Nova nodded.

"That was the Wraith. It lives on the mountain. It has a cave somewhere. It eats people."

Bannock scratched his chin. "Interesting. The Russian told me a similar story. Said he'd managed to escape its cave."

"Did you kill Fyodor?"

Bannock nodded. "Yes, ma'am. The subject died during interrogation. The question is, what are we going to do about the two of you?"

Nova's hand clenched tighter around the hatchet's handle. Maybe she could cover the distance between them faster than she thought, using the element of surprise.

Maybe not.

"The Wraith took our friends. Mackenna and Wyatt. It hurt Colton and took them."

"Really? Yet it left you unharmed."

"I'm small," Nova said. "I'd barely be a snack."

Bannock chuckled. "Small and lucky, I guess."

"Lucky enough. I was in the back of the SUV when the Russian rammed your truck. He had me tied up. He was going to use me as bait. Like he'd done with Landon in the chairlift when the Wraith started hunting us. I got away twice."

Bannock rubbed his hands together and blew into them. His eyes never left Nova. "My, my. I missed discovering you in that SUV? I must be rusty."

"Well. You'd just been shot in the head." Nova smiled. "Can you help us find our friends?" she asked, shifting her weight from one foot to another, trying to look cute and pathetic. "The Wraith is going to kill them."

Bannock stared at her, saying nothing.

This was it. Time to roll the dice.

"We have the money," Nova said. "We were on our way to our friend's cabin when we discovered an armored van that had crashed near the bottom of the mountain. Nobody was around and the money was just sitting there. We took most of it and buried it in case the police came looking for it."

Bannock drew his gun. He pointed it at Colton's head, his eyes still locked on Nova. Colton laughed from the ground. His eyes were closed and he'd rolled onto his side, with his arm stretched out as a pillow. He was so out of it, the significance of what Nova had just said seemed to go right past him.

"How much money did you bury?" Bannock asked. "Round figure."

"Over ten million," Nova said. "It was in little packets of hundred-dollar bills bound together with paper bands."

"What color were the bands?"

Nova pictured the money all piled together in Mackenna's living room before they started to divide it, heaped like dragon's treasure.

"Yellow."

Bannock's arm drifted in Nova's direction, pointing the gun at her. "Why couldn't I just force you to show me where the money is?"

"Because I don't know. Not really. Yeah, sure, I was there when we buried it, but I'm not from around here. I'm not, like, a camping person. All I know is that we walked a long way through the woods in the dark, up and down the mountain, before we buried it. Mackenna's the one who knows the mountain. It was her hiding spot. She can help you find the money." Nova took a step closer to Bannock. "If you help rescue them, we'll give it all to you. I promise."

Bannock raised his arm in the air, pointing his gun at the sky. He kept his eyes fixed on Nova, scanning her like he could read every thought she'd ever had. "All right," he said. "We'll wait until first light and track the beast to its cave. I have to admit, I'm curious to see this thing for myself. I thought I'd already hunted everything there was to hunt."

Nova exhaled, some of the tension dropping from her shoulders.

"And you can put the hatchet away," Bannock said, holstering his gun. "You're not that lucky, kid."

After drinking from the stream, Bannock lay down on the stream's opposite bank with his hands laced behind his head and closed his eyes. He lay so still Nova couldn't tell if he was asleep or dead. He looked like he was used to sleeping in the open and untroubled by it. Still exhausted despite the adrenaline circling through her body, Nova lay back down beside Colton and shared the warmth radiating from his body, covering them both again with pine branches.

Nova couldn't sleep, though. Trying to sleep near Bannock felt like sleeping beside a poisonous snake. He was coiled and motionless now, sure, but he could uncoil and strike at any moment. He could change his mind, kill both of them, and search for the cave and the money by himself. He didn't really need either of them, did he? Unless, like the Russian, he thought he was going to need bait.

Or maybe he wanted an audience for his battle. Maybe Bannock was *that* confident he could kill the Wraith.

By dawn, Colton had still not awakened. His breathing was steady, though, and when Nova checked his pulse, it seemed strong enough. She realized he wasn't going to be able to travel for several hours, if not days, and that they'd need to leave him by the stream if they were going to find the cave or go anywhere else. There was still a danger the Wraith could return and attack him if they left Colton by the stream, though the arrival of Bannock seemed to have changed the atmosphere of the mountain somehow, like the Wraith would be paying more attention to them hunting for its cave than a sleeping young man.

At least, that's what Nova hoped. Every choice she had was dangerous now, and none of them really felt like a choice at all. More like inevitable steps triggered by their group's collective bad choice two days earlier, when they'd discovered the van.

That stupid vote.

Bannock sat up as the sky lightened. He drank from the stream and washed his face, scrubbing at his skin with his fingernails. Nova did the same, trying to ignore Bannock's presence. Her stomach lurched with hunger as the stream water went down. At least it was cold and tasted clean. She hadn't started E. coli-puking yet, either, which was a bonus.

Bannock stood up and shouldered his bow case.

"Your pal looks rough. The beast must have clubbed him good."

"I found him floating in the stream," Nova said, standing up. "Wyatt and Mackenna were just gone, like they'd teleported somewhere. I'd only stuck my head under the water for a few seconds."

Bannock whistled. "Big and fast. It must be something special."

"You really think you can kill it?"

Bannock shrugged and spat on the ground. "Everything alive can be killed."

"What if it's not alive? What if it's, like, supernatural?"

Bannock grinned. "I guess we'll cross that bridge if we come to it."

Nova looked down at Colton.

"We're going to have to leave him here."

"Agreed. In his condition, he'd be a liability."

Bannock started circling around, examining the ground and stepping over the stream when he needed to. He reminded Nova of a dog sniffing for a particular scent. After five minutes of searching, he murmured to himself and bent closer to the ground.

"Okay. This could be a print."

Nova slipped on the strap of her canvas satchel, which was heavy with the hatchet's weight, and cautiously came up beside the older man. He pointed at a wide, flat imprint in the dirt that was speckled with squashed pine needles. It looked like something, but not necessarily a footprint. Bannock headed deeper into the trees and nodded again. "Second print," Bannock called back, pointing up the mountain. "Looks like it headed toward that crest."

Nova looked where Bannock was pointing, but it just looked like more mountain to her. He seemed satisfied, though, and started moving into the woods with confidence. Nova looked back at Colton and considered waking him up to say good-bye, but decided he was better off asleep and dreaming. She followed Bannock into the trees, adjusting the strap of her satchel across her torso, saying a little prayer that they'd all survive.

40

CLAW HEART MOUNTAIN GRADUALLY WOKE UP AS THE SUN ROSE in the sky. The pine trees and the scrubby undergrowth beneath them all puffed upward, battling for sunlight, while the air grew warmer, first easing the nighttime chill, then erasing it altogether. Rocky-mountain squirrels rustled among the dry pinecones on the forest floor, raced up and down tree trunks, and scampered along branches, causing them to waver before the squirrels leaped recklessly from branch to branch. The air smelled fresh and sweet, the mountain scented with pinesap warming in the sun, the sky through the tree canopy a dazzling blue.

It would have all been so beautiful and relaxing, Nova thought, if she wasn't hunting for a monster with the help of a hired killer. Bannock was leading the way up the mountain, silent as he studied the ground, looking for the next track the next sign the Wraith had come this way with Mackenna and Wyatt. Nova stayed several feet behind, giving Bannock space to work and glad for the distance between them. He was so . . . intense. He had a way of not only looking through you, but through *everything*.

Nova studied the bow case slung over Bannock's shoulder and thought back to a summer camp she'd attended in middle school, where they'd done traditional camp activities like crafts, canoeing, hiking, and archery. She'd enjoyed archery, even if she hadn't been very good at it. She liked notching an arrow and pulling the bowstring back, the tension that created. It felt like pure possibility when you prepared to shoot an arrow, like you might hit anything, like you might become a hero and lead an entire mighty kingdom to victory. You sighted your target, held your breath, and then let it fly, sending your arrow through the air at high speeds, maybe hitting your target, maybe not. Nova wondered if Bannock felt like that too, if this was why he carried a bow case while he also wore a handgun on his hip. Maybe he felt like a gun was too easy.

Bannock stopped and snatched something from the ground. He turned to Nova and held up the object for her to look at. It was a plastic tube of watermelon lip balm. Pink and bright, it was obviously out of place in the forest's greens and browns. "Mackenna," Nova said, feeling a cold prickling along her forearms. "I think she uses that kind."

Bannock grunted and tossed Nova the lip balm. She tried to catch it, but the little tube bounced off her hand and fell to the forest floor. She reached down and plucked it up, brushing off a single red ant that had somehow already started crawling across it. She uncapped the lip balm and smelled it.

Sweet, waxy watermelon. Nova rubbed the balm on her chapped lips and tasted it. Her eyes went misty with tears. She felt more connected to Mackenna now, a little closer to finding her and Wyatt.

"You should wipe that off your lips," Bannock said, scowling. "This thing can probably smell crap like that from two miles off."

Nova blinked and wiped her tears away. She felt her jaw setting and a new rage toward Bannock blooming in her heart. Hard, stubborn, and bossy, he wasn't that different from her workaholic dad. Just more efficient and homicidal.

And a lot skinnier.

"This 'crap' makes me feel closer to my missing friend. You have friends, don't you?"

Bannock shook his head. "No. I don't. The few I had all died a long time ago."

"So you don't care about anyone?"

Bannock shrugged. "You can learn to live without all that. It helps you survive. Friends can weigh you down. Same goes with caring what people think and expect from you."

Nova licked her lips, absorbing as much of the sweet watermelon taste as possible. She wondered if the balm had any nutritional value. She could gobble it down fast and maybe it wouldn't taste too bad.

"That sounds sad," Nova said. "And lonely."

Bannock grinned. "What about your friends, kid? They helped lead you here, didn't they? They've brought you right up to the edge of getting killed a few times over."

Nova tucked the lip balm into her pocket. "They're barely my friends, I guess," Nova admitted. "I just know them from back in high school. We live in the same suburb. Mackenna invited me because all her real friends were busy."

"Yet here you are, looking for them in a monster's cave. That just proves my point. Even fragile connections can drag you down."

Nova shrugged. "It's the right thing to do. They're human beings, even if they're annoying. We can't just let them get eaten."

Bannock rubbed the back of his neck, smirking like he thought she was the biggest idiot in the world. His tanned face even looked red in the shadows, as if decades of accumulated sunshine glowed beneath it. He was human beef jerky, with an emphasis on the jerk. Nova wondered what he'd been like as a child. If the child version of Bannock had always been headed toward the killing machine the adult version seemed to be.

Whenever she'd watched a serial-killer documentary on TV with her mom, Nova wondered at what moment, exactly, you were supposed stop feeling sorry for someone who'd endured a terrible childhood and harden your heart toward them because they'd turned out so evil.

Was it when they killed their first frog at the age of six? When their parents abused them at the age of nine? When they lost a family member to drugs or violence at thirteen?

Bannock stepped forward, dipped his hand into Nova's satchel, and pulled out the hatchet, moving so quickly she barely had time to register his movements. He stepped back and examined it, running his thumb along its sharp blade.

"Hey. Give that back."

"What's the biggest thing you ever killed?"

"I don't know. I ran over a squirrel once when I was in driver's ed."

Bannock looked at her, his smirk gone. His eyes were flat, like all the light had been sucked out of them. He smelled like woodsmoke.

"You kill enough people, you can see how we're just animals, like all the other critters in the woods. We forget that because of our big brains, but it's as true as true gets. You get sentimental about human beings, they'll pull you under the dark water with them, sooner or later."

Nova crossed her arms. "Or they might pull you out."

Bannock turned and threw the hatchet, again moving with stunning speed. The hatchet flashed through the air, its metal edge glinting as it passed through a patch of sunlight and halted with a sudden *thuck* as it stuck into the trunk of a tree.

"Nobody gets pulled out of the dark water," Bannock said. "Not really."

Bannock turned away and began studying the ground again. Nova stayed back a few seconds, until he was almost out of sight, before running over to the hatchet. Its blade was planted deep in the tree's fibers. It took all her strength just to yank it free.

They went far enough around the mountain that the view changed below, though the path leveled out and the trees grew sparser, making the hiking easier. Bannock continued to study the ground, but Nova couldn't tell if he was following new tracks or just guessing as he went along. She kept her mouth shut, not wanting to annoy an armed killer. She was about to give up on ever finding Mackenna and Wyatt when Bannock stopped abruptly and peered into a clump of spruce trees on their left. They looked like all the other spruce trees on the mountain, nothing unusual about them that Nova could see.

Bannock unshouldered his bow case and laid it on the ground. He unzipped the case and assembled his bow, first clicking the main three sections of the bow together and then stringing the bow with what looked like a second string, which he stepped on to make the bow flex and tighten, setting the first string into the bow's string groove. After returning the stringer to the carrying case, he put a leather armband on his left arm and slipped an archery glove onto his right hand. He removed five arrows from their clips inside the case and slid four into a slender, tube-shaped quiver that he strapped across his body. He notched the fifth arrow onto the bowstring.

"Looks like the cave is in that ravine. You ready?"

"Really? I don't see anything."

Bannock blew into the arrow's fletching, ruffling the feather.

"Look hard. You see that darker section among the shadows? At the back of the ravine?"

Nova shielded her eyes and stared. It took a few seconds, but the shadows began to separate themselves.

"I think so."

"That's the cave entrance. If you pay attention, you can always see gradations, even in darkness. You just have to clear your mind of all the usual chatter. You have to look with clear eyes."

Nova took the hatchet out of her satchel and swung it a few times, rolling her shoulders and loosening up.

"Okay, Mr. Clear Eyes. I'm ready."

Bannock smirked, studying her for a long moment.

"What?"

"You just reminded me of someone I knew once. When I was much younger."

"They must have been pretty awesome."

"Yes," Bannock admitted. "She was formidable."

Bannock stepped forward into the trees, ending their conversation before Nova could ask questions. She followed behind, crouching low, ready to chop anything that might jump out at her. They pushed through the spruce trees and stepped into the ravine. The walls on both sides were sheer rock and rose straight up. At the end of the ravine was the patch of darkness, which, as promised, transformed into the mouth of a cave as they approached.

Nova stopped, her legs locking up beneath her. She'd wanted to find the cave, but she wasn't ready to go inside. She'd wanted to rescue her friends, but she wasn't ready to see the Wraith again. It was too . . . terrible. Bannock looked back at her. He didn't scowl. Didn't grin. His expression remained flat. He wasn't feeling. He was thinking. Like the dark cave with its monster waiting inside was nothing but a problem to solve, rot a horrifying nightmare scenario, the kind of dangerous encounter that stretched back thousands of years in the genetic memory of humankind.

Bannock lowered the bow and arrow, releasing the tension in the bow. He dug into his back pocket and pulled out a slender mini-flashlight. He held it toward Nova, his eyes calm and expectant. He needed her help, but he wasn't going to order her around. It was up to her.

Take the flashlight.

Or not.

Nova stepped forward, feeling pulled toward Bannock and the cave's entrance like water circling a drain. She took the flashlight and clicked it on. It seemed like a loud noise, though it was so quiet, and Nova realized they couldn't speak again until it was all over, one way or another; otherwise, the Wraith would hear them and pinpoint their location.

It dawned on her that she might already have spoken her last words, had her final conversation. Had she told her mom and dad she loved them enough? Did Tennyson realize what an asshole he was and how hurt she'd been by his text cumping? Would he even care when he heard she'd died? Would he ugly cry? Was it possible to come back from the afterlife and haunt the living? Had her short life meant anything at all?

To Nova, the end of her life had always seemed so far away, so distant, but now it could be only a minute or two away. Maybe it had always been hovering nearby, waiting for her to open her eyes and notice it.

Bannock pointed at the mini-flashlight and then at his eyes. Nova nodded. She understood what her job would be when they entered the cave.

You needed light to hunt in the dark.

41

THEY APPROACHED THE CAVE, WHICH WAS ALREADY GIVING OFF a disconcerting odor of rotting flesh. Bannock thought of his father, a tough, brutal man who'd fought in World War II as a teenage army infantryman.

A veteran of multiple ugly battles in the Pacific, where violent death and physical maiming had been a frequent occurrence, Bannock's father had believed overcoming your opponent involved willpower as much as it did tactics and logistics. He'd beaten this message into Bannock and Bannock's two older brothers over and over again, both physically and verbally, pitting the three brothers against each other in their backyard in day-long contests of mental and physical endurance. They did calisthenics; ran endless sprints; performed thousands of sit-ups; wrestled and boxed to exhaustion; practiced orienteering, fire building, and knot tying; low crawled beneath strings of barbed wire; engaged in tugs-of-war until their hands bled from rope burns; and trained with a variety of weapons on the elaborate firing range their father had constructed behind their house.

Bannock's family lived ten miles from town, in the middle of an isolated patch of Maine woods. Bannock's mother had died in a car accident when he was only five years old, so theirs was a household of four men. Twice a year, once in summer and once in winter, Bannock's father would drive Bannock and his brothers fifteen miles, deep into the woods, blindfolded the entire time like hostages, and then turn them loose to find their way back to civilization on foot, with only a bowie knife and a canteen of water each. Bannock and his brothers would starve and endure all manner of physical discomfort—bug bites, ticks, leeches, snakebites, broken bones, frostbite, diarrhea, heatstroke—but the three of them would always make it home, eventually, if only to spite their old man.

The central proving ground of Bannock's childhood had been the "Pit." Constructed of hay bales piled in a circle two-high, the Pit had a dirt floor that was either dry and cracked, churned into mud, or frozen into a cement-like toughness, depending on the season. Every Saturday, the three brothers fought each other hand to hand, and the winner won the chance to fight their father.

Bannock, as the youngest brother, usually didn't make it to this final round. The brother who did make it could use either a billy club or a length of chain, while their father fought with only his bare hands. Bannock had seen his older brothers lose many, many times to their father, sometimes to the point of being knocked unconscious, while their father demanded they believe they could win, to trust that their willpower was stronger than his. Finally, one spring day, Bannock's oldest brother, recently turned seventeen, got lucky when their father slipped in the mud. He struck the older man hard in the temple with a billy club, causing him to drop instantly to the floor of the Pit.

The whole world went quiet. Bannock's oldest brother stood above their father in triumph, his chest heaving, both eyes blackened, until it was clear their father was out for the duration. Bannock's oldest brother didn't shout and exult, didn't say anything at all, but he tossed aside the club and spit on their father. The next day, both Bannock's older brothers left home, never to be heard from again, while Bannock was left alone with the old man for a few more years of seasoning, until one day he also beat the old man in the Pit and left home himself, enlisting in the army as soon as he turned eighteen and graduated from high school.

Bannock often wondered how long his father had lived on after Bannock left home. The old man would be ninety-some years old now, maybe over a hundred. He would undoubtedly be skinny and tough as a nail, his eyes still gleaming with anger at the world, his body existing via the force of willpower alone, and each day would be another the old man clawed away from Death itself. Bannock, who was not normally a mystical individual, had always assumed he would feel something change in the universe when his father died. So far, however, he had felt nothing and was wondering if this long-held assumption was mistaken. Human beings were just walking, talking bags of meat, held together by skin and propped up by bone. How could one bag of meat call out to another across great gaps of space, even given the amplification of death? Where was the logic in that?

Bannock glanced back at the teenage girl following him into the cave. She was small and sloe-eyed, with a set to her jaw Bannock admired in such a situation, especially given her youth. What had her name been? Nova? Bannock had heard worse names. Astronomically, a nova involved a white dwarf star stealing gas from a neighboring star until the gas built up to such an extreme that it triggered an explosion, causing the white dwarf's entire local star system to shine a million times more brightly than usual.

And now Nova was holding a flashlight, set to guide them into the darkness.

Fitting.

As if this hunt had already happened thousands of times before.

The entrance to the cave was taller than most cave entrances—over seven feet high—but narrow enough that only one person could enter at a time. Bannock went first, crouching low with his bow pulled at half draw. He listened for movement in the dark, prepared to draw fully and let fly at anything that rushed forward.

Nothing rushed forward. Bannock stepped aside and made room for Nova to enter the cave with the flashlight, which had seemed small and useless in the daylight but now shone brightly, throwing light across the cave's ceiling, walls, and floor. The cave's dimensions were roughly twelve feet wide and ten feet high. Bones littered the chamber's floor. Bannock identified deer, wolf, bear, rabbit, fox, beaver. Nothing too small, like birds or squirrels. Only larger bones. Bones even a large creature might not necessarily want to swallow and pass through its system.

Nova folded at the waist and started retching, causing the beam of her flashlight to dance among the bones. The smell of rotting flesh, of meat in various states of decomposition, was much stronger here than it had been outside the cave, like a river of stench that had been released and now flowed over them. Bannock remained still, eyeing the darkness beyond the flashlight's dancing reach, until Nova gathered herself and wiped her mouth. Bannock expected her to speak, either complain or apologize, but the girl held her silence. Bannock nodded to her in approval and pointed at the opening at the back of the cave. She nodded back, visibly steeling herself, and they continued deeper into the cave, leaving the last of the natural daylight behind as they picked their way among the bones, trying to make as little noise as possible.

The next section was an extensive tunnel, four feet in width and eight feet in height. Blood smeared the walls on both sides of the tunnel, which also had extensive scarring, resembling claw marks, and the tunnel floor was sticky with dried blood and chunks of pulpy gore. This wasn't a new home for the beast. It was a den that had known much feasting over a long period of time, and it was well embedded here. Bannock moved along slowly, minding his feet, and Nova trailed a few feet behind him, still holding the flashlight aloft. They reached the end of the tunnel and a gust of wind buffeted them, carrying more carrion stench laced with a hint of cold water on stone.

Bannock heard a scraping sound in the next chamber. He glanced at Nova, whose wide eyes indicated she'd heard it as well, and found himself grinning, the predator inside his heart assuming its normal forward-facing position. He moved ahead at a slight crouch and entered the next chamber, drawing the line of his bow to peak draw weight. The chamber remained dark a few moments before the girl followed behind with her light.

This second chamber was similar to the first, only larger and filled with more bones and several animal carcasses with flesh still on the bone. The beast—the improbable beast—was perched on a mound of bones and carcasses in the middle of the chamber, like a king upon his throne, gnawing on what looked like a man's detached leg, holding the limb by the ankle. The leg itself was bare, but the leg's foot still wore what looked like a sock and a man's hiking boot, still tightly laced.

The beast itself was magnificent, well worth the efforts Bannock had made over the past few days, from the moment his contact phone had chirped in his study outside of Salt Lake City and set him in motion toward Claw Heart Mountain. The beast was like a man merged with bear and wolf, with some vampire bat thrown in. Its patchy bluish-green fur was dark with bloodstains and gore, its hulking frame bigger than anything Bannock had ever seen walking upon two legs, though it somehow appeared emaciated as well, its skeletal structure protruding through its fur. Areas of fish-belly pale skin poked through its fur, like spots of snow on a mountainside, and its sickly white head was totally hairless.

Good Lord, its head. A ghoulish visage straight out of a child's most scrabbling nightmares, the creature's head appeared both human and alien at once, its boney forehead as flat and monumental as Hoover Dam, its mouth stretched wide to an alarming degree, its thorny nest of teeth exposed to the air (the word *dinosaur* popped into Bannock's mind). It was missing both ears and a nose, that soft cartilage one associated with a human head, but small holes did seem to be located where you'd expect them to be, indicating it could still hear and smell. Its eyes were milky white, without pupils and obviously sightless. The girl pointed the flashlight straight at it, her hand trembling, and the beast took no notice of the light as it continued gnawing.

Bannock took three cautious steps into the chamber, while Nova remained in the chamber's doorway, rooted to the spot. What had the girl called the beast? The Wraith? Bannock had to admit it was a fitting name. Even from twenty feet away, it radiated hunger in a palpable way Bannock could feel all the way into his bones, almost as if it were already drawing molecular nourishment from Bannock's physical presence. He studied it for a few additional moments, searching its body for weak spots, as it bit through the leg with its monstrous teeth, shattering the femur with a sickening crunch.

The Wraith reminded Bannock of his father, hunched over a plate of ribs at the dinner table, his face slathered in barbecue sauce, no wife around to tell him not to eat like a pig. For a man who preached self-control and determination, Bannock's father ate like a beast in the wild, feeding with the abandon of a starving wolf in winter.

Bannock's arm started to tremble from the effort of maintaining full draw weight. He aimed for where he assumed the beast's heart to be, held his breath, and released the drawstring, letting fly. The arrow whistled through the air and struck the beast in the chest, dead center. The beast stopped gnawing on the leg and stood up to full height, its head scraping the cave's ceiling from its throne of carnage.

Bannock reached back and grabbed a second arrow from his quiver, notching it without taking his eyes off the beast. The beast raised the leg into the air above its head like a club. Staring straight at Bannock, it let out a shriek that eclipsed all other sounds in the world, a sound that poured forth from its enormous body in exponentially louder waves as it echoed off the walls. Bannock found himself on his knees, his bow and arrow reflexively dropped as he clamped his hands over his ears. Nova must have done the same, because the angle of the flashlight's beam changed, rolling across the cave chamber's floor and throwing shadows across the ceiling. Liquid poured through Bannock's clamped hands and he realized it must have been blood leaking from his ears. He sank to the ground, putting his back to the beast, and curled into a ball until the shrieking finally, mercifully, stopped.

Bannock, now effectively deafened, groped for the gun in his belt holster, his blood-slick fingers struggling to find purchase on the leather. He turned over onto his back and saw the beast, the Wraith, striding toward him, bones and carcasses rolling out beneath it, churning like waves on the ocean. Bannock saw a pair of human eyes, open and wide, peering out at him among the carnage, pleading, and realized at least one person was still alive among the piled dead. He found the trigger on his gun and sighted as best he could while lying on his back. He fired as the beast loomed above him, its arms upraised as if summoning the full depth of its rage, its gnawing hunger; a lifetime of shooting experience reflexively took hold in Bannock's body, allowing him to fire in a tight grouping into the creature's chest and head, into its many, many teeth, which exploded in puffs of bone dust. The beast kept coming, however, and fell upon him with its claws and hungry rage.

So, Bannock thought. *My final hunt.*

42

NOVA FELT AS IF SHE'D BEEN EXISTING OUTSIDE HER BODY. MAYBE since they'd entered the cave, when the first wave of rotten-meat stench had engulfed them and made her dry heave. It was possible that a part of Nova—what you could call her soul—had checked out when she'd followed Bannock into the cave. What remained behind seemed to be a robot version, Nova 2.0, going through the motions of walking and thinking and holding a flashlight so they could see all the terrible things the cave held, things she'd never wanted to see and would never forget. Things she knew would visit her brain at night when she was trying to sleep, knocking around like tennis shoes in a dryer.

The Wraith's angry screeching had dropped her to her knees. Nova was trying to return to her body while she still could, before it was too late. She'd been prepared for the screeching at least, since she'd heard it before, and had managed to cover her ears a second before the sound struck her in the chest, the handle of the hatchet clamped between her hand and head, the wood vibrating right into her skull. Gasping, she saw Bannock lying on the ground, curled into a ball. The screeching grew so loud her eyes watered and her body ached with the noise of it. She saw a light rolling on the ground and realized she'd dropped the flashlight. Her one job. When the Wraith finally stopped screeching, Nova shouted Bannock's name as loud as she could.

Bannock uncurled and turned onto his back, messing with something on his belt. The Wraith, about twenty yards away from him, started thumping across the heap of bodies and bones, which snapped and crunched beneath its weight. It made progress toward Bannock with the same surprising speed Nova had seen the day before on the mountainside. Bannock raised his arm and Nova saw he was holding a gun. She pressed her hands even tighter against her ears as several shots rang out, so loud inside the cave. The Wraith staggered backward, puffs of white powder exploding around its head. As the Wraith was clearly wounded, Nova expected it to collapse, to fall like a chopped tree, but it shook off the gunshots and started swiping at Bannock with its long arms and sharp claws.

Bannock got off a few more shots before it tore the gun away and tossed the weapon somewhere into the dark behind it. The Wraith shrieked again as Bannock rolled toward the right and got to his feet. Bannock roared back at the creature and started to laugh. He was already clawed and bloody, his shirt in shreds, but he'd pulled out a large knife and looked ready to fight, a crazy grin on his face, as if he was enjoying himself. He circled farther to the right, causing the Wraith to turn as well, its many teeth clicking as saliva dripped from its mouth. Nova, realizing she only had a small window while the Wraith's attention was occupied, circled carefully behind the monster, keeping a distance of about ten feet, until she was fully behind it.

The Wraith lunged, rushing Bannock head on, grabbed him with its long arms, and pulled him to its body in a crushing hug, trapping Bannock's arms at his side. Bannock remained helplessly immobile as the Wraith lifted him into the air, bent its massive head downward, and clamped its huge, toothy mouth around Bannock's head.

Bannock roared from inside the Wraith's mouth. Nova ran forward, hatchet raised, and buried the hatchet's blade as deep as she could in the side of the Wraith's neck. The Wraith released Bannock and staggered backward, thrashing as it clawed at the sunken hatchet, knocking Nova to the ground with a swipe of its arm. The Wraith pulled out the hatchet and a dark geyser of blood spurted from its wound. The Wraith stumbled across the cave, screeching in pain, and disappeared into the tunnel connecting the cave's two chambers.

Nova remained on the cave floor as the shrieking grew fainter and then faded away entirely. She gasped for air, finally remembering to breathe.

Holy shit.

The Wraith had run away.

She'd hurt it bad enough to make it run away.

———

Nova retrieved the dropped flashlight and went to Bannock. He was gravely wounded. His chest and arms were slashed, with blood everywhere, and he had teeth marks on the sides of his head, as well as two puncture wounds where his neck met his shoulders, one on each side. These neck wounds were pumping out a serious amount of blood, way too much blood, and Nova could tell it was hopeless even as she set the flashlight down and pressed each wound with her hands, trying to slow down the bleeding.

Bannock swallowed. He was still conscious and looking up at her with his pale gray eyes.

"It's gone?"

Nova nodded. "I chopped it in the neck."

Bannock grinned and swallowed. Blood kept pouring through Nova's fingers. It felt hot and alive and precious.

"Good work, kid. You've got some steel inside you."

Bannock reached into the pocket of his windbreaker and offered Nova what looked like a bony tooth, broken off at the end.

"Here," Bannock said, a gurgle in the back of his throat. "A little memento."

Something rustled among the bones and dead animals. Nova reflexively glanced in the direction of the rustling and when she looked back Bannock was dead, his eyes already unfocused and flat. The blood stopped pumping through her fingers and became only a trickle, propelled by gravity instead of Bannock's heart. Nova pulled her hands back and wiped them on her pants. She took the bony tooth from the dead man's hand and dropped it inside her satchel. She was trembling and the seat of her pants was wet. She'd peed herself sometime between entering the second chamber and now.

"Is he dead?"

Nova screamed and shot to her feet. She swept the flashlight's beam across the chamber, sending shadows flying everywhere. A shape stepped into the light.

Wyatt.

Nova sprinted forward and hugged the older boy. He smelled terrible, but his body was warm. He was alive. They were both alive and they still had bodies to hug.

"Hey, Nova," Wyatt said, his voice soft in her ear. "Good to see you."

Nova pulled back. "Mackenna?"

Wyatt turned and looked at the heap.

"She's here somewhere, I think."

They started digging, teaming up to lift the bigger dead animals, chucking everything aside while trying not to look too closely at what they were touching. The smell was so overwhelming, tears streamed from Nova's eyes and she worked half blind. They finally found Mackenna near the bottom of the pile. She'd fallen into a crevice somehow and curled into a ball. She was unconscious but alive.

Nova felt a flood of gratitude toward the universe.

Wyatt was alive.

Mackenna was alive.

Not everything was horror and death.

Wyatt grabbed Mackenna beneath the armpits and dragged her out of the bone heap and laid her out on the floor. Nova slapped the side of Mackenna's face until her eyes fluttered open and gained focus. She stared at Nova and Wyatt for several seconds before recognition appeared in her eyes.

"Hey," Nova said, kneeling over her. "How do you feel?"

Mackenna stared past Nova at the cave's ceiling. "I had the weirdest dream."

Nova glanced at Wyatt. He was looking foggy himself.

"Can you walk? We need to get out of here."

Mackenna stared at the ceiling for a few more seconds, as if puzzled by something, before her gaze returned to Nova.

"I think so."

Nova and Wyatt helped Mackenna to her feet. The flashlight flickered a few times. Nova slapped it until the LED beam was steady again. Nova draped one of Mackenna's arms around her shoulder while Wyatt took the other side. The three of them started walking through the chamber, kicking their way through the bones, avoiding the largest dead animals, each person helping prop up the other two. They passed Bannock's corpse and approached the chamber's exit. Nova's flashlight beam swept across the front of the space, falling on a body she hadn't noticed before, lying up against the wall. It was a young man, not a deer or an elk, and he had a huge chunk of his midsection missing and both legs torn off.

His face was perfectly intact, however. His eyes were closed. He looked like he was sleeping. Peaceful.

"Oh," Mackenna said, going limp between Nova and Wyatt. "Oh."

"Don't look at him," Nova said, fighting to keep her friend standing. "Don't think right now. We need to leave. We can't think about anything else."

"Landon," Mackenna said, gasping. "Oh."

"Nova's right," Wyatt said. "Don't think about anything but walking."

"But—"

Nova and Wyatt hustled Mackenna out of the chamber and into the connecting tunnel. It was tighter here, barely wide enough for the three of them to pass through. The floor was sticky with fresh blood that squished beneath their feet. Mackenna grew steadier and began to carry her weight. Nova imagined daylight and fresh air. She pictured the Wraith, lying dead somewhere on the mountainside, not lurking in the shadows. She pictured her mother and father, welcoming her home with huge smiles on their faces, their arms open wide to lift her into the biggest hugs.

They reached the end of the tunnel and paused to listen. "I can stand now," Mackenna said, straightening further. Nova and Wyatt extracted their shoulders, allowing Mackenna to stand on her own. The flashlight started flickering again, went out, and wouldn't recover no matter how much Nova smacked it. She wanted to curse but swallowed the urge, thinking of the Wraith with its head tilted, listening. She stepped ahead of the others and poked her head out of the tunnel's exit.

The outer chamber was dark and silent.

Nothing moved.

Nothing rattled or skittered or slurped.

Far across the chamber, like a portal to another universe, was a circle of glowing daylight. Nova reached out, took Mackenna's hand, and together they made their way through the dark, Wyatt following close behind. The three of them went slowly but steadily, stumbling a few times on loose bones. Nova followed her own advice, clearing her head and thinking of nothing at all. Nothing but the light, waiting for them to arrive.

43

IT HAD BEEN A LONG WEEKEND FOR DEPUTY SERRANO. SHE'D already endured one night of poor-to-little sleep and now she'd fought through a second without any sleep at all, knowing that at any moment Gideon might change his mind, sneak down the basement stairs, and shoot her in her sleep.

All morning, the deputy had started drifting off to sleep. The only way she could stay awake was picturing Sheriff Carson's mutilated body in the evidence locker while thinking *This Could Be You* and then picturing her husband's face when he discovered what had happened to her, when her children discovered Mamá all carved up.

Horrible images, horrible imaginings, and they worked like ice water thrown on her face.

Even so, sometimes Serrano allowed herself to drift off deeper than she should have. Sleep was welcoming. So enticing. Sometimes she would fall asleep for real, for five or ten minutes, before

snapping awake in a panic, thinking she'd heard Gideon or somebody else walking down the stairs.

But no one came, and nothing happened.

It was like being trapped in amber.

Or a tomb.

For the fifth or sixth time, Deputy Serrano retreated to the bar
area in the Underground Lounge. The lounge didn't have a kitch-
en, or even a microwave, but the sink worked and she'd been
drinking from it every few hours, running it as quietly as possible,
filling the same pint glass she'd found in a cupboard while she kept
her gun handy.

She'd just filled her newest glass of water when she heard a
gunshot upstairs. Dropping the glass of water, Serrano ran across
the dark lounge toward the daylit stairwell, zigzagging around the
lounge's chairs and tables. She heard a man shouting and several
more gunshots. She paused, wondering if this was a tactic to get
her up the stairs, but then a primal scream erupted, a sound that
could not be faked. Serrano went up the stairs, not running, but
not moving too slowly either, arms raised in a classic shooting
stance, the pain in her sprained right shoulder overwhelmed by
adrenaline. Taking a deep breath, she popped above the last few
stairs, leaning against the wall to her right to make as small a target as possible.

What Deputy Serrano saw defied her wildest expectations, a
scene that sucked all the air from her lungs. Dominating the entrance hall was a hairy monster with a pale, hairless head, milky-
white eyes, and a freakishly wide mouth. It was holding Gideon
sideways in its claws, like he was a piece of corn on the cob, casually chewing on the man's midsection while Gideon thrashed in

pain, uselessly flailing his arms in the air while he screamed. The monster was immense, like a fairy-tale giant sprung to life, and it smelled like the rancid floor of a slaughterhouse.

This was a demon escaped from hell.

Bigfoot.

Chupacabra.

Gideon screamed again as a large bone snapped in his leg, probably his femur. His eyes found Serrano's and pleaded with her, conferring raw, animal pain all the way from across the hall. Serrano swallowed, wishing she'd brought something bigger than a compact Glock 19, something more like a shotgun, or a ground-to-air missile launcher. She scanned the monster and noted it was already bleeding, especially from the neck, but it didn't look particularly discouraged, even with the shaft of an arrow sticking out of its chest.

Serrano would have shot the creature in the head, if it hadn't already been chewing on Gideon. She didn't want to kill the hostage by accident, even if the hostage had been keeping *her* hostage for nearly twenty hours. Instead, Deputy Serrano aimed for the monster's lower stomach and crotch and began to fire, trying to keep her shots in a tight grouping.

It took three shots for the monster to stop chewing and swivel its head in her direction. It opened its mouth and let out an otherworldly shriek, a sound so loud it made Serrano reel toward the stairwell, but she gritted her teeth and kept firing, keeping her shots low. The monster threw Gideon aside and charged, moving with surprising speed. Serrano placed three shots to its chest and then three to its skull, aiming for its milky white eyes, but even the headshots glanced off its forehead, which must have been made of some seriously dense bone.

The monster shrieked again, swiping at the air in front of Serrano, as if it still couldn't quite locate her.

It was blind.

It was hunting by sound.

Serrano pulled the trigger again, but the Glock's clip was empty. She turned and looked down the basement stairs, wondering if retreat was once again her best option. She noticed a red fire-alarm panel set into the wall beside the stairwell. A warm bloom of hope rushed through her. The resort's owner was obviously a cheap bastard, but even he wouldn't be so cheap he'd leave his shuttered resort without protection from a fire. Serrano pulled the alarm and it began braying from several speakers in the entrance hall, as loud as she could have hoped. The ceiling sprinklers kicked on, spraying water everywhere.

The monster shrieked and clutched its head, aggravated by the noise and the sprinkler deluge. This shriek, this shocking noise, was unlike anything Serrano had ever heard. It sounded like a bottomless well of rage and suffering, like hunger and thirst and endless, soul-crushing loneliness. It was the sound of suffering itself. Giving up its attack, the monster staggered toward the front hall's wrecked entrance, stomping across a carpet of broken glass as the fire alarm continued to bray.

The last Serrano saw of the monster was the bluish-green fur on its back as it ducked through the doorway, blending into the grass beyond it.

Serrano approached Gideon and took off her belt. Gideon was still alive, but it looked like he was going to lose his left leg, at least. She could see bone sticking through the skin, jagged and broken, unhappy to be in open air. She looped her belt around his upper thigh. She pulled the belt as tight as she could and tied it into a makeshift tourniquet. Gideon screamed one last time and passed out. Serrano turned her face toward the sprinklers and felt the water fall upon her like a saint's blessing. She closed her eyes and listened for the sound of sirens wailing beyond the fire alarm's racket. She prayed the alarm had triggered something, somewhere, that alerted the proper authorities to trouble on Claw Heart Mountain.

Enough people had died already.

Enough was enough.

44

NOVA, MACKENNA, AND WYATT EMERGED FROM THE RAVINE outside the Wraith's cave and stood blinking in the sunlight. The air smelled fresh and clean and chased the cave chill from their bones. None of them had any idea where exactly they were on the mountain, but it felt high up and the sun was behind them. Nobody had a cell phone or a watch, so they couldn't even tell what time it was. Nova, the only one of them who'd not been knocked out and dragged away into cave darkness, thought it was probably around one in the afternoon.

Nova scanned the woods for signs of the Wraith. She didn't have her hatchet anymore and missed its reassuring weight, though it had already served her well.

"It's still out there," Mackenna said, shivering as she rubbed her arms. "It could still hunt us down."

"Nova hurt it bad," Wyatt said. "She went fucking samurai on it. You should have seen all the blood spurting from its neck."

"No thanks," Mackenna said. "I've seen enough blood for the rest of my life."

"I think it went to find shelter," Nova said, taking the lead as they started downhill. "Like, another cave or something. Somewhere it could hide and lick its wounds."

Wyatt picked up a long branch and pounded the ground with it. Nova thought it would make a decent walking stick.

"It'll still be hungry though, right?" Wyatt said. "It's the Wraith. That's its thing."

"The Hunger in the Mountain," Mackenna said, waving off a horsefly. "Yeah, it's a real actual thing that killed Landon."

"We'll worry about it if we see it again," Nova said, stepping over an exposed branch. "Right now, we need to focus on getting off this mountain. Bannock and I hiked all morning from the stream. We went up and to the right a lot, so I guess we should go down and to the right to find the trail again."

"Bannock," Wyatt said. "That's the guy the Wraith killed in the cave? The dude you said showed up at the lodge looking for the money?"

"Yeah," Nova said. "I told him we'd give him the money if he helped me rescue you guys. He found Colton and me at the stream. Colton was still hurt from the Wraith's attack and couldn't come with. He's got a bad concussion. We need to try and find him, but I don't even know which direction we'd start looking, other than down and to the right."

"Colton's tough," Wyatt said. "He's from here. He'll find his way home."

Nova stared at Wyatt. He hadn't seen Colton lying on the ground, groggy from his concussion. Colton hadn't been so tough then.

"Maybe we'll run into him on the way down," Mackenna said, setting her hand on Nova's shoulder. "You never know."

Nova sighed, unable to think of a better plan. They kept going down, down, down. The incline wasn't too steep, but it was steep enough you had to keep your weight back and make sure your feet didn't slip out from beneath you. All three of them smelled like blood and rotting flesh, and the flies were starting to discover them, buzzing around in larger and larger numbers. Nova noticed how neither Wyatt nor Mackenna complained about the flies or paid much attention to them at all.

Two days ago, everyone would have been bitching. Even the scratching thirst in the back of Nova's throat wasn't so bad. It was just there. The thirst. Like it had always been there and always would be.

***

After roughly two hours of downhill and "to the right" hiking, while occasionally shouting Colton's name, they came across a stream. They couldn't tell if it was the same one they'd found the day before or a different one. They didn't care. They dropped to their knees and scooped water into their mouths until they couldn't drink any more. They stripped off their bloody, smelly clothes and stepped into the stream naked. Nobody checked anybody else out. Nobody cared what anybody looked like naked. They scrubbed themselves raw in the cool water, using mud for soap, and Nova felt herself returning to something a little more human.

"Oh my God," Wyatt said, rubbing his bare chest with mud and pebbled sand. "This feels so good it's crazy."

Nova grinned back at him, scratching at her scalp with her fingernails. She'd almost forgotten how it felt to be happy, even if it was just for a few seconds. They washed their clothes in the stream as best they could and put them back on wet, which wasn't so bad in the afternoon heat, though Nova's wet capris chafed as they started hiking again. They followed the stream down, as if it were a path cut into the mountain for them, and after twenty minutes they came to a trail leading both to the left and to the right. Nova, remembering Bannock's advice, allowed her mind to go blank and looked at the ground with clear eyes.

"This is it!" Nova told the others, her breath catching in her throat. "This is where the Wraith attacked us."

Wyatt and Mackenna frowned as they looked around the clearing, clearly not recalling anything. Nova knelt and pointed at two depressions in the mud, one big and one smaller. "This is where Colton and I slept. He must have gotten better and started hiking again."

"Or," Wyatt said, "the Wraith came back . . ."

Nova shivered and circled the clearing, trying to think like Bannock would. She didn't see any fresh blood or signs of struggle. If the Wraith had snatched Colton, it hadn't left a trace.

"Which way now?" Mackenna asked, looking at Nova. "Left or right?"

Nova examined the ground. She couldn't be sure, but it looked like there was a fresher footprint heading back toward the Lookout Bar. It was a big print made by a regular human shoe. Would Colton have decided to go back to the resort? It would be a lot easier than hiking up over the mountain summit and going into town. The other bad guy might still be lurking down there, but maybe Gideon had taken off by now. It'd almost been twenty-four hours. He wouldn't wait for Bannock forever.

Or would he?

"Let's vote," Nova said. "Who wants to take the easier path back down the mountain, where a bad guy may or may not still be waiting for us, and who wants to take the longer, harder path up the mountain, which probably has no bad guys, but could be another hunting ground for the Wraith?"

Mackenna snorted. "Wow. Such great choices."

They listened to the burbling stream and thought for a few seconds. The trees whispered to each other as the wind gusted through them, holding their own kind of wind-based deliberation.

"I guess I vote for going back to the bar," Wyatt said, breaking the silence. "We should bring Isaac down with us."

Mackenna flinched.

"God. I forgot about Isaac."

Nova pictured Isaac's clammy face as they massaged clog remover down his throat. How would they ever explain doing that to anyone? Explain it to his family? How would they explain anything that'd happened?

"Okay," Mackenna said. "I guess I vote for going back to the bar too. But if anything seems janky there, we can come back this way and try the death march over the mountain."

Nova nodded.

It was settled, and she hadn't even needed to vote.

———

They took the trail to the Lookout Bar. The hiking allowed Nova to let her troubled mind go blank. She put one foot in front of the other, watching out for exposed roots and loose rocks, as the sun warmed the back of her neck. She felt an overwhelming heaviness in her bones. It was like being tired but beyond tired. The feeling was not just in her body but also in her soul. The day was so bright, the sky so blue, but now she could see death lying behind everything, waiting for its chance to take it all away.

They arrived at the Lookout Bar in the middle of the afternoon, thirsty and exhausted. They circled around the bar from the back, half expecting to be ambushed, and came around to the building's front, which was all smashed up by the thrown ATV.

Miraculously, the chairlift was still running, electricity humming through its lines as it circulated through an endless rotation of benches. Isaac's corpse was lying in front of the bar. Clumps of dirt covered the body, and the ground beside it was torn up, just like Bannock had said. The Wraith hadn't taken the poisoned bait, but it had at least been distracted by it for a few precious seconds.

"Fuck, man," Wyatt said, speaking for all of them as they stood around the body, the sun revealing too much of everything. Nova's stomach roiled, but she pushed the pain away. She was alive. She wasn't going to complain about anything in Isaac's presence.

Glass crunched and popped inside the Lookout Bar. They turned toward the noise as a group, exposed on the open hillside. A large shape emerged from the shadows, draped in white. Nova smiled, her chest expanding with happiness. It was Colton, carrying a white linen tablecloth that glowed in the sunlight. Everyone cheered and ran across the lawn, hugging Colton, laughing and shouting. Happy. Colton was alive. This was one good thing. Colton Morgan was still alive.

The happiness died down when Wyatt asked him what the tablecloth was for. "Isaac," Colton said, nodding toward the body lying in the grass. They all turned and walked back to Isaac. Colton brushed the dirt off Isaac's face and chest. He draped the tablecloth over the body and rolled it over inside the fabric until Isaac was on his back again, all bundled up. Colton lifted Isaac into his arms and started walking toward the ski lift, moving slowly but steadily. Colton looked better than he had that morning, though his eyes were still glazed. Nova walked beside him and told him about Bannock helping her find the cave and rescuing Wyatt and Mackenna. How Bannock had died after she chopped the Wraith in the neck.

"The guy looking for the money?" Colton said, squinting and adjusting his hold on Isaac. "He's dead?"

"Yeah. He's in the cave still. With Landon's body."

Colton exhaled.

"Well . . . shit."

"I know." Nova glanced at Colton's face, trying to figure out his strange expression. "Hey, why'd you come back this way, anyhow? I thought you'd keep going into town."

"I wanted to get my truck back," Colton said. "It's still in the lodge parking lot."

"Your truck? What exactly are you planning on doing about Gideon? You know, the other guy looking for the money? You going to go all action hero when you get down there?"

"I don't care about some out-of-town asshole," Colton said, scowling. "It's my truck and I want it back."

Nova nodded. She couldn't argue with that, though it sounded like Colton's brain was still a little scrambled.

They reached the loading area for the ski lift with Wyatt and Mackenna following close behind.

"Are you going to set Isaac on a bench by himself?"

Colton shook his head.

"No. I'm going to ride down with him on my lap."

Nova looked at Wyatt and Mackenna. They both looked like they might fall asleep standing up. "I'll ride down with Colton and Isaac," Nova told them. "You guys come right behind us." Wyatt and Mackenna nodded. The next bench came around and Colton and Nova fell into it, sitting with Isaac stretched out on their laps. Nova expected the dead boy to smell bad, but she couldn't smell anything coming from him except a chemical tang. She had Isaac's legs stretched across her knees and his feet pointed straight up beneath the sheet. She felt a weird urge to take off his shoes and massage his feet, as if she could massage life back into his body.

They rose into the air as their bench made the turn and headed down the mountain. Colton stared straight ahead, lost in his thoughts. After about five minutes, they passed a brown truck parked on the mountain slope. "My truck," Colton said, sounding unhappy but not surprised. "Somebody ditched my truck on the mountain."

"It must have been Bannock," Nova said. "He came up the mountain somehow. I just thought he'd used the chairlift."

Colton closed his eyes and leaned back against the bench. Nova peered into the distance and noticed fire trucks and police cars in the parking lot of the Sunshine Lodge, their lights flashing. The emergency vehicles looked small from so far away, like toy cars. Nova leaned against Colton's shoulder and pointed down the mountain.

"Look, Colton. We're saved."

Colton opened his eyes but didn't say anything. He didn't seem to care much. They continued their smooth ride down the mountain, the chairlift humming and creaking, and by the time they reached the lodge, it felt as if they'd come from another dimension back into the reality they'd always known. As they got closer, a woman emerged from the lodge and waited for them at the chairlift's disembarkation point. She was pretty, with dark hair and olive-colored skin, but she looked exhausted and her clothes were stained with blood.

Working together, Nova and Colton lifted Isaac into the air as they dropped from the chairlift and hit the ground. They carried his body several feet before setting him down off to the side. The dark-haired woman eyed them and the body wrapped in the tablecloth but didn't say anything.

Mackenna and Wyatt arrived a few seconds later, jumping off their own bench.

"Mackenna Wolcott?"

Mackenna stared at the woman.

"Yeah?"

"I'm Deputy Serrano. We spoke when I stopped by your house on Friday."

Mackenna swallowed, recognition dawning in her eyes. She looked at Nova, and Nova felt a familiar sinking feeling in her stomach, like all her guts were about to drop out of her body.

It wasn't over.

45

THEY FORMED A LARGE GROUP ON THE NARROW MOUNTAIN TRAIL.
Mackenna led the way, followed by four DEA agents, then Wyatt
and Nova, with Deputy Serrano and two more deputies from the
county sheriff's office bringing up the rear. Which made ten people, total. It was seven o'clock, about two hours from sunset, and
Nova couldn't stop peering into the darker patches in the trees,
expecting the Wraith to appear at any moment. Part of her—the
darkest, most despair-filled part—almost hoped it would. Dying in
one last attack would be easier than explaining all this to her parents. Better than going to court and getting sent to juvie, or whatever terrible shit was going to happen to them now.

How had it come to this?

And so fast?

Isaac's body had been taken away by the county coroner, and
Colton had been sent to a hospital in Rawlins for further medical
evaluation. The police had found Fyodor buried in a fresh, shallow

grave in the woods near the lodge. Their parents had all been called and they would be in Cloud Vista soon. Mackenna, Wyatt, and Nova had all confessed to stealing the money after Deputy Serrano showed them a security camera image from the armored van. You could clearly see Mackenna and Nova talking to each other in the picture, with Landon slightly fuzzy in the background, peering over Mackenna's shoulder. Deputy Serrano said the police had the entire theft on video, not just the one image, and told them if they turned over the money immediately, it could be a mitigating factor in their case. The sheriff's deputy said she didn't want their lives ruined by one rash incident, but the DEA would hound them and hound them until the money was all turned in.

"Nope, I think we should get lawyers," Wyatt had countered. "We shouldn't say shit to anybody."

Mackenna, Wyatt, and Nova had been sitting on cots in the resort's medical building. Another police officer had already brought them water bottles, granola bars, and blankets. They'd all wrapped up in the blankets, even though it was warm and stuffy in the building. It felt comforting, to be cocooned. Nova had eaten three granola bars and was thinking about a fourth. Her stomach growled and churned, excited to be reintroduced to food.

"Lawyers would complicate things," Deputy Serrano said. "For instance, right now, you're being treated as witnesses. If you ask for a lawyer, we'll have to officially arrest you for stealing evidence and take you into custody. Is that what you kids want? Do you want to spend the night in the Scorpion Creek jail?"

"Not really," Mackenna said, glancing at Wyatt and Nova.

"What if we take you to the money ourselves?" Nova said. "Would you still have to arrest us then?"

Deputy Serrano nodded. "I think that would be a good start to all three of you going home tonight. First, let's do statements, okay?"

They agreed. Two DEA agents, a man and a woman, came to the medical building and took Mackenna, Wyatt, and Nova away, one by one, to give a statement in the spa building next door. Nova went last. She told the DEA agents everything she could remember, talking for almost an hour into a digital recording device they'd put on the table in front of her. Nova expected the DEA agents to laugh when she first mentioned the Wraith, how she'd described its freakish body and crazy teeth, but the agents' faces remained serious and they just scribbled in their notepads. At first, Nova thought this was because Mackenna and Wyatt had already given them the same report, but the longer she sat in the spa building with the agents, the more Nova wondered if something else had happened that she didn't know about.

"Hey," Nova said, when she'd finished giving her statement. "Why were you guys all swarming around the lodge in the first place? Why were there fire trucks in the parking lot? Why does Deputy Serrano have blood on her clothes?"

The DEA agents looked at each other. "There was an incident in the lodge this afternoon," the female agent said. "Deputy Serrano was involved."

"What happened? What incident?"

"Sorry, we can't tell you that," the male DEA agent said. "We're not at liberty to discuss the details of an open investigation."

"Right," Nova said, crossing her arms. "I tell you everything, but you guys tell me nothing. That figures."

The DEA agents didn't respond. They were busy writing in their notebooks again, ignoring her. Nova reached out and turned off the tape recorder herself. She realized the agents hadn't seen the Wraith and would never believe in it without actual proof.

"What about its cave? Are you going to find it? Landon's body is still in there. And Bannock. And probably the other Russian, too. Fyodor's cousin."

The lady DEA agent looked up from her writing and nodded. "We'll find the cave," she said. "If it exists, we'll find it."

The way the lady DEA agent said this, half confident and half dismissive, made Nova realize they would never find the Wraith's hiding place, not even if they looked with an army of helicopters, dogs, and highly-trained searchers.

"Don't look so despondent, miss," the male DEA agent said, closing his notebook and slapping it on his knee. "We're getting food delivered from the diner in Cloud Vista. Burgers, fries, and soda for everybody. The world always looks better on a full stomach, right?"

Nova pictured Isaac, his pale stomach bloated. She closed her eyes and focused on not throwing up.

———————

They kept hiking along the trail to where they'd hidden the money as the sun drifted toward the mountain's ridgeline. Deputy Serrano fell in beside Nova. She was almost as short as Nova and their strides matched step for step. Nova inspected the woman from the corner of her eye, deciding that she looked as exhausted as Nova felt. The deputy had changed clothes since their confessions back at the Sunshine Lodge. She was wearing an old navy-blue Scorpion Creek police department T-shirt and black jeans. She must have kept extra clothes in her car or something.

"What happened at the lodge?" Nova asked the deputy. "Why did you have blood on your clothes earlier?"

The deputy glanced at her but kept walking. "I encountered one of the men sent to retrieve the money," she said, her voice neutral. "He was badly hurt and I had to provide medical assistance. It was his blood."

"You mean Gideon."

The deputy nodded. "Yes."

"Did he die?"

"Not on scene. He was taken to the hospital in Rawlins about thirty minutes before you arrived at the lodge. The medic said he'd likely live, though he may lose a leg."

Nova nodded, processing this. She recalled the Wraith, standing on its pile of bones and bodies, chewing the leg with the hiking boot still on it. "The Wraith," Nova whispered, stopping and turning toward the deputy. "The Wraith came to the lodge, didn't it?"

Deputy Serrano looked at her. "You're a smart girl, Nova. How did you get mixed up in all this?"

Nova shrugged. "When we found the van, we voted whether we should take the money or not. I lost."

Deputy Serrano winced. "That's no excuse for not contacting the police later. You were in the house when I stopped by that night, weren't you? You could have come out and told me about the money then. You might have saved the lives of your friends."

Nova didn't say anything. She remembered listening to Mackenna talk to Deputy Serrano in the front hall of her cabin. Though against taking the money at first, by that time Nova had been swept up in the frenzy. She'd agreed to hide the money on the mountain like everybody else. She'd convinced herself she'd done all she could, when she'd really done nothing at all. She'd just wanted to soothe her conscience so she could enjoy being rich without feeling guilty. It was the American way.

The other sheriff deputies caught up to them on the trail, and Serrano and Nova started walking again. "You're still young," the deputy said, pushing a branch away from her face. "You'll still have your life ahead of you after this. You'll have the chance to make better decisions. I have a younger brother, Antonio, who's been in prison for fifteen years. His entire adult life has been spent in prison. Can you imagine that?"

Nova tucked her chin against her chest and looked at the ground. She noticed a furrow in the dirt, a track that might have been made by a luggage wheel being dragged along. She remembered the way Bannock studied the ground, his movements steady and fluid as they picked their way up the mountain. He'd been a bad guy, obviously, but there'd been something about the way he carried himself she admired. How he'd been ready for the world and not intimidated by it—not even the worst of it.

"It's there," Mackenna announced from the front of their large group, stopping and pointing down the hillside to their right. She was standing by the massive boulder Nova remembered from Friday night, the one that looked like an avalanche waiting to happen. Mackenna started down the steep mountainside first and the four DEA agents followed closely behind. Nova and Wyatt went next, together, while Deputy Serrano and the two other deputies followed last.

They'd kicked up a cloud of dirt during their scramble down to the rocky shelf, but Nova could still make out the piled branches covering the entrance to the hole in the ground. The camouflage looked a lot more obvious in daylight, especially if you were looking for it. Mackenna knelt and tossed away the branches, revealing the cave's opening. "We called it the Cave of Wonders when I was a kid," Mackenna said, her voice flat as she backed away from the opening. The normal sparkle was gone from her blue eyes and she looked pale, even with her summer tan. Like the rest of them, she obviously needed to sleep for a long, long time.

The DEA agents converged on the opening, dropping to their knees and pulling flashlights from their belts. The female DEA agent—the same lady who'd taken Nova's statement earlier—leaned into the hole with her flashlight.

The agent was silent for several seconds before she grunted and came back up.

"It's empty."

Mackenna blinked. "What?"

"The hollow is empty. The ground looks disturbed by recent traffic, but it's empty now."

Mackenna looked at Nova and Wyatt, her face blank with disbelief. She pushed her way between two burly DEA agents and stuck her own head into the hole. Her shoulders disappeared from sight as her torso twisted back and forth, looking. Mackenna began laughing while she was still inside the opening, a loud, cackling laugh, but by the time she pulled back into the light she was crying, her face twisted in fury and unhappiness. Wyatt knelt beside her, cooing as he rubbed her back and tried to console her. Nova stood over both of them, feeling nothing at all as Mackenna looked up at her with damp, red eyes.

She looked so much smaller now.

Like nothing special.

Nova turned her back on Mackenna and everyone else gathered on the ledge. Somehow, she was not surprised the money was gone. She dug into her satchel and examined the bony tooth Bannock had given her before he died. It wasn't made of tooth enamel, she realized. It was some other kind of bone, with almost a woodgrain look to it. She'd have to ask her dad what he thought it was. She hoped it wasn't human.

Nova slipped the mystery bone back into her satchel as the wind picked up, gusting with almost a winter chill to it. It would be dark soon. Nova raised her head and peered into the pine trees farther up the mountain's ridgeline. She thought she could make out a large, unusual shape among a patch of shadows, a shape that could have been something big and alive.

Something hungry.

Epilogue

THE KEY

ALONE IN HER HOUSE, NOVA GATHERED HER POETRY NOTEBOOK, her lucky blue pen, and a thermos filled with iced tea and went into her backyard. It was another warm August day in Colorado. The sky was blue and cloudless. Nova sat in one of the two matching Adirondack chairs on their patio and let her body go loose, sprawling her limbs in the sunshine and flexing her bare toes. She'd grown a surprising two inches during her first two years at Colorado College, and she liked her new, longer legs, which made her an inch taller than her mom.

After basking in the sunshine for a while, Nova opened her notebook and started doodling. She let her mind drift and pull whatever images and phrases it came across. She wrote a few lines that might become something, eventually, and let her mind drift some more. Distracted by her reveries, she didn't notice the shape in the corner of her vision until it started moving toward her, coming around the edge of her house. It was a big redheaded man with broad shoulders and a bushy red beard. Dressed in blue jeans, a white T-shirt, and tan work boots, the man looked like a lumberjack who'd wandered into the Denver suburbs by accident. The man grinned when he saw Nova and stopped a few feet away.

"Hey there, Nova."

Nova sat up in her chair and clipped her pen to the notebook. She felt a buzzing sensation in her chest that felt both good and bad.

"Colton."

The man's grin turned into a full smile. It really was Colton. Colton Morgan.

"Oh my God," Nova said. "You look so grown up."

Colton laughed, and Nova felt another round of buzzing in her chest. She remembered that laugh. She remembered sitting around a bonfire drinking beer and hearing that laugh.

She set aside her notebook and stood up. She felt like hugging Colton and running into her house to hide at the same time. Just his physical presence brought back what had happened on Claw Heart Mountain. Isaac, bleeding out on the floor of the freezer. Landon, falling off the chairlift and plunging to his death. The terrible cave, which she still visited almost every night in her dreams. Colton Morgan seemed as out of place in Nova's sunny backyard as a grizzly bear, or the Wraith itself.

"I didn't mean to trespass, but nobody answered your doorbell, so I thought I'd see if anyone was in the backyard."

Nova nodded, still trying to process.

"How'd you find my address?"

"Mackenna gave it to me. I guess she kept her old cell phone number when she got a new phone. She said you guys haven't really talked much lately."

Nova nodded. "We haven't. It was so weird when we got home. Weird and sad, you know? It was just easier to avoid her and

Wyatt. Less painful. I see them on campus sometimes and we just nod at each other."

Colton frowned and looked at his shoes. His beard made him look thirty. He also looked sadder than when they'd first met two years ago, as if he'd learned some hard truths about the world.

"At least you guys didn't go to jail," Colton said. "I was worried about that."

Nova picked up her thermos of iced tea, unscrewed its cap, and took a drink. "Yeah. Mackenna's dad got us a good lawyer and we ended up with community service. They never found the money and could never prove we kept it. You know, since we didn't."

"They never found the Wraith or its cave either," Colton said, looking up from his shoes. "You should see all the idiots that visit the mountain looking for it now. They sell Wraith T-shirts and coffee mugs at Al's Griddle. Everyone treats me like I'm this big celebrity because I was attacked by it. I'm thinking about moving to Montana or Idaho, just so I don't have to deal with all the bullshit."

Nova took another drink of iced tea and looked up at the sky. It was so blue today.

"Do you think it's still alive?"

Colton nodded. "Yeah. But I think it's hibernating now. I think it hibernates for long stretches of time and that's how it avoids getting noticed."

"Huh. That would make sense, I guess."

A lawnmower started up in the distance. During the summer, somebody always seemed to be mowing a lawn in Nova's neighborhood. As if there was a rotating schedule to make sure you could always hear a lawnmower droning.

"Mackenna said you're crushing it at college?"

Nova grinned.

"I've won a couple of poetry contests. Nothing major."

"That's awesome, Nova. Really awesome." Colton reached into his back pocket and pulled out an envelope. "Here, I have something for you."

Nova set down her iced tea and looked at the envelope. It was white and unmarked. She took it and felt its weight in her hand.

"That's a key to a storage locker near here. The address and unit information are inside the envelope."

Nova tapped the envelope against her palm. She could feel the key shift inside it.

"What—"

"There's five million dollars inside the locker. Cash."

Nova stared at Colton.

"I took the money," Colton said, still looking serious. "It was me."

Nova kept staring, the world going muffled around her.

"When we were all partying at the Overlook, you told me about finding the money and how you guys hid it in the Cave of Wonders. You were pretty drunk. I'm guessing you've never been the best at keeping secrets."

Nova blinked, the only response she could muster.

"You can do whatever you want with your half of the money," Colton continued. "I'm keeping the other half. I figure I deserve it. You guys never told me about it, even after the Russian dude almost shot us all. You got me involved without giving me a choice. I figure I earned some hazard pay."

The droning lawnmower cut off in the distance. Nova took a deep breath.

"Wow. I mean . . . Jesus. I can't believe you . . . This is insane."

"I know. Just don't do anything too obvious with the money for a few more years. The DEA might still be watching you. Keep your cash purchases and deposits under ten thousand bucks or they might notice. Be careful."

Colton turned his back to her, and Nova realized he was going to leave. He was going to lumber back into the mountains and disappear, just like the Wraith, leaving her alone to figure out what to do next.

"Why?" Nova called out, taking a step forward. "Why are you giving me half, Colton? You could have just kept all of it and nobody would've known."

Colton turned back around and looked directly at her, his eyes clear and warm. He was older and sadder now, but maybe deeper too.

"Because you stayed with me, Nova. Although the Wraith could have come back. You stayed the whole night."

————

Nova sat back down after Colton left her backyard. She didn't return to her poetry notebook or drink more iced tea. She simply sat looking at the envelope Colton had given her, held it with both hands, the paper pinched between her fingers. She could feel the weight of the key inside and felt it pull at her through the paper. It called to her like a question, and the way she'd answer could end up defining the rest of her life.

Nova closed her eyes, searching for gradations in the darkness.

Acknowledgments

I WOULD LIKE TO THANK ALL THE GOOD SOULS WHO HELP KEEP me on track (more or less). Thank you to my wife, Jen, for always listening, always caring, always loving. Thank you to Sweet Pea, the cat, for all the laughs and purr times. Thank you to Mike Mensink and Steve Norman, both for serving as co-best men at my wedding and being good, upstanding men to the point of annoyance. Thank you to the Inglorious Batters, one hell of a terrible softball team. Thank you to Jonathan Lyons and Roberto Grande. Thank you to Jen Koontz, the best supervisor anyone could ask for. Thank you to Joyce Jorgenson for watching over my aging father like a mighty Valkyrie—no one has ever earned a book dedication more than you have.

Big, big thanks to my agent and good friend Dawn Frederick at Red Sofa Literary. Dawn naturally goes above and beyond in everything she does, which is amazing, and she is also generous with her concert tickets. Thanks for selling this book, Dawnstar!

Thank you to everyone at CamCat Books, including intrepid publisher Sue Arroyo, book designer Maryann Appel for creating such a killer cover, and, of course, my editor Helga Schier, who not only whipped this novel into shape, but taught me to be a better writer with each suggested cut and idea (though I might die of old age before I fully understand when to use "like" and when to use "as if").

Finally, thank you, dear reader, for coming along on this particular ride up the mountain. May you always find your way through even the darkest wood.

About the Author

DAVID OPPEGAARD IS THE AUTHOR OF *CLAW HEART MOUNTAIN*, *The Town Built on Sorrow*, *The Firebug of Balrog County*, *The Suicide Collectors*, *And the Hills Opened Up*, and *Wormwood, Nevada*. He is also the author of the novella *Breakneck Cove*. David's work is a blend of horror, literary fiction, science fiction, and dark fantasy. He writes both adult and young adult fiction. He has been named a finalist for a Bram Stoker Award and a Minnesota Book Award.

David grew up in the small town of Lake Crystal, Minnesota, and wrote his first novel at the age of fifteen. He holds an MFA in Writing from Hamline University and a BA in English from St. Olaf College. He has worked as an optician, a receptionist, a standardized test scorer, a farmhand, an editorial assistant, a trash picker, a library assistant, a bookstore employee, as adjunct faculty at Hamline University, and as a child minder on a British cruise ship.

He currently works at the University of Minnesota and lives in St. Paul with his wife and their ravenous cat.

Website:
www.davidoppegaard.com

Twitter:
@DavidOppegaard

TikTok:
authordavidoppegaard

If you liked
David Oppegaard's
Claw Heart Mountain,
you'll like
Morgan Shamy's
The Dollmaker.

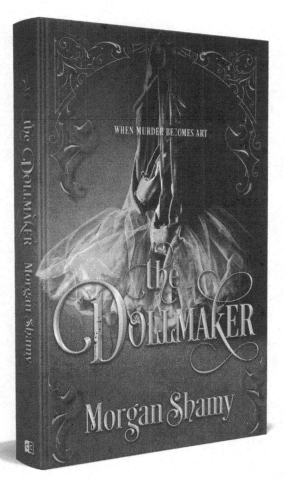

STANDING ON AIR

Newport, Rhode Island, 1920

F ingertips stretched at length, gliding through the air, smooth against the heavy beat of the music. Necks stretched long and slender, and feet pattered on the floor, pointe shoes clicking. Thin-ly muscled legs and tiny waist. The girls in the old studio wove in and out of each other, jumping in time with the music. Shadows shifted over their white tutus and pink silk tights, their bodies re-flected in the large mirror that hung on one side of the room.

Dawn Hildegard tilted her head sideways, expelling a con-stricted breath. She stood off to the side, her loose gray dress drab in the room. She was a goose surrounded by swans. She fiddled with the silk scarf around her neck and analyzed the girls more closely, checking for injuries.

She zeroed in on the ballerina in the center of the room, curls pinned tightly into her golden bun. Early-morning sunlight filtered in through the tall windows in the corner, highlighting the soft bones of her face, her lashes long and dark. Color dotted the ballerina's cheeks from exertion, but she seemed to float through the room, dancing as if it were effortless.

Rose Waterford was the prima in the company; no one touched her grace and extension.

Even though the other girls in the company looked unearthly with their slender frames and porcelain skin, Rose exceeded them all. The *Newport Gazette* had called her "poetry on air" after her performance in *Giselle* last season.

Dawn studied Rose more closely. She was favoring her right leg, a slight limp as she moved from position to position. Her feet must have been bothering her again.

The ballet master, Caldwell, paced at the front of the class, tapping a wooden stick, yelling at the girls to stay in time with the music. His jaw was cut strong along the sides of his face, his dark hair a curly mop on his head. His open white shirt exposed his chest, sweat running down his bare skin.

"Stop, stop." Caldwell waved to the pianist, and the music ceased, the deep notes hanging in the air. He faced the girls head on. "A corps de ballet needs to be *one*. Like puppets on a string, you need to all move in sync. I expect perfection, and perfect is *not* what I'm getting." A single dark brow lifted as his eyes slid to Rose. "Except for you, Ms. Waterford."

Pink flushed Rose's cheeks, but she kept her head level. The girls around her shifted their weight, some sneaking a glance at her.

"That's enough for now." Caldwell motioned for the girls to leave, his New York accent coming through. He'd only been the ballet master for about a month but clearly had command over the girls. "We will resume rehearsals onstage tonight for *Coppelia*. Rose, if I could have a word?"

The room seemed to exhale at once, and the girls departed, grabbing their hand towels from the barres. They brushed past Dawn, their thin muscles flexing as they walked, chatter drifting behind them. Dawn shifted out of the way, letting them by. She peeked at herself in the dusty mirror in front of her. She hated the way her eyes resembled two black bruises, like she hadn't slept in a week. Her dark hair hung in strings over her face, where the other girls kept their curls pinned tightly to their heads. The color of her stained dress matched her demeanor, muted against the morning light.

She wasn't surprised she was sleep deprived. Being Dr. Miller's apprentice was an endless job, often calling her to visit patients' homes in the dead of night. She had shown up on the Browns' doorstep just after midnight to aid in Mrs. Brown's labor—twins— one of which was breeched. The blood and screams still swirled inside her head, and she shivered.

Of course she was lucky to have the position at all, as it was rare for a female to have such an apprenticeship. But the title ate through her core, sitting heavy in her stomach.

It wasn't enough to be an apprentice. She wanted her *own* practice. She wanted freedom to heal, not just be the moral support. She closed her eyes for a moment, trying to breathe, before peeking them open.

She would get what she wanted.

Caldwell and Rose spoke quietly for a moment, Rose with her feet turned out and Caldwell with his sweaty hair hanging over his forehead. He rubbed his chest as he spoke, a small smile on his lips. Dawn overheard words like *exquisite* and *perfection*, but Rose only nodded in response, conveying her thanks. Caldwell lifted up a hand and brushed her cheek, and Rose's dark lashes fluttered down, stark against her pale skin. Dawn's mouth twisted downward at the corners, her brows creasing.

Caldwell's gaze flicked to Dawn in the corner, and he lowered his hand, clearing his throat.

"I'll see you tonight, Ms. Waterford."

Rose backed away as Caldwell exited the room, and as her eyes caught Dawn's, a smile lit her face.

"Dawn!" She rushed over and took her hands. "I'm so relieved you're here. I'm in so much pain." She drew Dawn over to a chair on the side of the room, planting herself down, and Dawn slung her medical pouch from her shoulder.

"Is it the feet again?" she asked.

Rose nodded, unlacing one pointe shoe. She slipped off the shoe and wiggled her stockinged toes. Dawn bent down and picked up her foot, analyzing it.

"It's swollen, that's for certain," she said. She pressed into the ball of her foot. "Soaking it with salts would be best. I can give you turmeric for the pain." She dug through her pouch. "Here." She handed Rose the herbs sealed in a small glass container.

Rose gripped the container and held it to her chest. "You're a lifesaver. I don't know what I'd do without you."

"Anything for my best friend." She smiled back, but it felt forced. Dawn took in the shadows beneath Rose's eyes. She hadn't noticed them earlier. Rose's engagement was wearing on her. "Are you all right?"

Rose bit her pink lips, the color matching her cheeks. "Any day could be my last day," she whispered. "Dancing. Performing. All of it. I don't want to give it up, Dawn." Moisture gathered in her eyes, but she blinked it away.

Dawn set her satchel down and took Rose's hands. They were unusually cold. "Then don't. You don't have to marry Chester. Don't let a man get in the way of what you want to do."

Rose shook her head, squeezing her eyes closed tight. More tears gathered in the corners.

MORE SPINE-TINGLING BOOKS FROM CAMCAT PUBLISHING

CamCat
Books

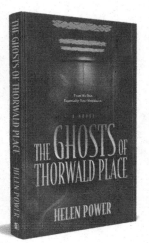

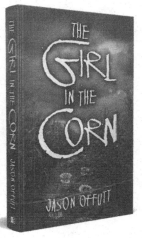

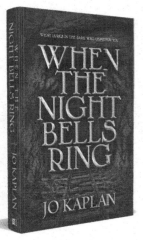

Available now, wherever books are sold.

CamCat
Books

VISIT US ONLINE FOR MORE BOOKS TO LIVE IN:
CAMCATBOOKS.COM

SIGN UP FOR CAMCAT'S FICTION NEWSLETTER FOR
COVER REVEALS, EBOOK DEALS, AND MORE EXCLUSIVE CONTENT.

CamCatBooks   @CamCatBooks   @CamCat_Books   @CamCatBooks